Robert Burns, Robert Herdman, Robert Paterson

Poems and Songs

Robert Burns, Robert Herdman, Robert Paterson

Poems and Songs

ISBN/EAN: 9783337465797

Printed in Europe, USA, Canada, Australia, Japan

Cover: Foto ©Andreas Hilbeck / pixelio.de

More available books at **www.hansebooks.com**

THE "EDINA" EDITION.

POEMS & SONGS

BY

ROBERT BURNS

WITH ORIGINAL ILLUSTRATIONS

BY

R. HERDMAN, R.S.A.   GOURLAY STEELL, R.S.A.

WALLER H. PATON, R.S.A.   D. O. HILL, R.S.A.

SAMUEL BOUGH, A.R.S.A.   JOHN M'WHIRTER, A.R.S.A.

AND OTHER EMINENT SCOTTISH ARTISTS.

ENGRAVED BY R. PATERSON.

WILLIAM P. NIMMO

LONDON, 14 KING WILLIAM STREET, STRAND
AND EDINBURGH

MDCCCLXXV

Printed by R. & R. CLARK, *Edinburgh.*

NOTE.

THE Publisher of the "EDINA" Edition of BURNS' POEMS AND SONGS
sends it forth in the hope that it may not be found unworthy of association by its title with the record of the brilliant days spent by the Poet
in the Scottish capital. The intense enjoyment and manly gratitude
with which his reception as a guest, and the recognition of his genius by
the rank and wit and beauty of Edinburgh, filled the mind and heart
of Burns, find no better witness than the lofty and withal loving strain in
which he sang the praise of "Edina, Scotia's darling seat." The Poet
might well be proud of the welcome thé city gave him; the city may
well be proud of the graceful acknowledgment of the Poet—far more
lasting than its occasion, lasting as Edina's own "rough, rude fortress."
If the designation of this volume may, in some measure, serve to keep
alive and warm the memory of the association between Burns and the
city where first he tasted the sweets of fame, the Publisher trusts that
the volume itself will not be deemed to prove the designation either in-
appropriate or presumptuous. The graphic and the typographic arts
of the Scottish capital have united in the endeavour to give not only
elegance, but also sterling value, to the book; and, as the resources ot
Edinburgh alone have been relied on for its production, so upon
Edinburgh alone will be reflected the credit of such public favour and
success as may deservedly fall to the lot of the "EDINA BURNS."

CONTENTS.

SONGS.

LIST OF ILLUSTRATIONS.

Engraved by R. Paterson.

POEMS

WINTER.

A DIRGE.

THE wintry west extends his blast,
    And hail and rain does blaw;
Or, the stormy north sends driving forth
    The blinding sleet and snaw:

B

While tumbling brown, the burn comes down,
    And roars frae bank to brae;
And bird and beast in covert rest,
    And pass the heartless day.

"The sweeping blast, the sky o'ercast,"
    The joyless winter-day,
Let others fear, to me more dear
    Than all the pride of May:
The tempest's howl, it soothes my soul,
    My griefs it seems to join;
The leafless trees my fancy please,
    Their fate resembles mine!

Thou Power Supreme, whose mighty scheme
    These woes of mine fulfil,
Here, firm, I rest, they must be best,
    Because they are Thy will!
Then all I want (oh, do Thou grant
    This one request of mine!)
Since to enjoy Thou dost deny,
    Assist me to resign.

TO A MOUSE,

ON TURNING HER UP IN HER NEST WITH THE PLOUGH,
NOVEMBER 1785.

WEE, sleekit, cow'rin', tim'rous beastie,
Oh, what a panic's in thy breastie!
Thou needna start awa sae hasty,
           Wi' bickering brattle!
I wad be laith to rin an' chase thee,
           Wi' murd'ring pattle!

I'm truly sorry man's dominion
Has broken nature's social union,

An' justifies that ill opinion
          Which makes thee startle
At me, thy poor earth-born companion,
          An' fellow-mortal !

I doubt na, whiles, but thou may thieve ;
What then ? poor beastie, thou maun live !
A daimen-icker in a thrave
          's a sma' request :
I'll get a blessin' wi' the lave,
          And never miss't !

Thy wee bit housie, too, in ruin !
Its silly wa's the win's are strewin' !
An' naething, now, to big a new ane
          O' foggage green !
An' bleak December's winds ensuin',
          Baith snell and keen !

Thou saw the fields laid bare an' waste,
An' weary winter comin' fast,
An' cozie here, beneath the blast,
          Thou thought to dwell,
Till, crash ! the cruel coulter past
          Out thro' thy cell.

That wee bit heap o' leaves and stibble
Has cost thee mony a weary nibble !
Now thou's turn'd out, for a' thy trouble,
          But house or hald,
To thole the winter's sleety dribble,
          An' cranreuch cauld !

But, Mousie, thou art no thy lane,
In proving foresight may be vain :
The best-laid schemes o' mice an' men
          Gang aft a-gley,
And lea'e us nought but grief an' pain
          For promised joy.

Still thou art blest, compared wi' me !
The present only toucheth thee :
But, och ! I backward cast my e'e,
          On prospects drear !
An' forward, tho' I canna see,
          I guess and fear.

LIBERTY: A Fragment.

Thee, Caledonia, thy wild heaths among,
Thee, famed for martial deed and sacred song,
  To thee I turn with swimming eyes ;
Where is that soul of freedom fled ?
Immingled with the mighty dead !
  Beneath the hallow'd turf where Wallace lies !
Hear it not, Wallace, in thy bed of death !
  Ye babbling winds, in silence sweep ;
  Disturb not ye the hero's sleep,
Nor give the coward secret breath.
  Is this the power in freedom's war,
  That wont to bid the battle rage ?
Behold that eye which shot immortal hate,
  Crushing the despot's proudest bearing,
That arm which, nerved with thundering fate,
  Braved usurpation's boldest daring !
One quench'd in darkness, like the sinking star,
And one the palsied arm of tottering, powerless age.

          .   .   .   .   .   .

His royal visage seam'd with many a scar,
That Caledonian rear'd his martial form,
Who led the tyrant-quelling war,
Where Bannockburn's ensanguined flood
Swell'd with mingling hostile blood,
Soon Edward's myriads struck with deep dismay,
And Scotia's troop of brothers win their way.
(Oh, glorious deed to bay a tyrant's band !
Oh, heavenly joy to free our native land !)
While high their mighty chief pour'd on the doubling storm.

THE COTTER'S SATURDAY NIGHT.[1]

My loved, my honour'd, much-respected friend,
No mercenary bard his homage pays;

With honest pride, I scorn each selfish end :
    My dearest meed, a friend's esteem and praise :
To you I sing, in simple Scottish lays,
    The lowly train in life's sequester'd scene ;
The native feelings strong, the guileless ways ;
    What Aiken in a cottage would have been ;
Ah ! tho' his worth unknown, far happier there, I ween !

November chill blaws loud wi' angry sugh ;
    The short'ning winter-day is near a close ;
The miry beasts retreating frae the pleugh ;
    The black'ning trains o' craws to their repose ;
The toil-worn cotter frae his labour goes,
    This night his weekly moil is at an end,
Collects his spades, his mattocks, and his hoes,
    Hoping the morn in ease and rest to spend,
And, weary, o'er the moor his course does hameward bend.

At length his lonely cot appears in view,
    Beneath the shelter of an aged tree ;
Th' expectant wee-things, toddlin', stacher thro'
    To meet their dad, wi' flichterin' noise an' glee.
His wee bit ingle, blinkin' bonnily,
    His clean hearthstane, his thrifty wifie's smile,
The lispin' infant prattling on his knee,
    Does a' his weary carking cares beguile,
An' makes him quite forget his labour an' his toil.

Belyve, the elder bairns come drappin' in,
    At service out, among the farmers roun' :
Some ca' the pleugh, some herd, some tentie rin
    A canny errand to a neibor town :
Their eldest hope, their Jenny, woman grown,
    In youthfu' bloom, love sparklin' in her ee,
Comes hame, perhaps to show a braw new gown,
    Or deposit her sair-won penny-fee,
To help her parents dear, if they in hardship be.

Wi' joy unfeign'd, brothers and sisters meet,
    An' each for other's weelfare kindly spiers :

The social hours, swift-wing'd, unnotic'd, fleet;
    Each tells the uncos that he sees or hears;
The parents, partial, eye their hopeful years;
    Anticipation forward points the view.
The mother, wi' her needle an' her shears,
    Gars auld claes look amaist as weel's the new;—
The father mixes a' wi' admonition due.

Their master's an' their mistress's command,
    The younkers a' are warned to obey;
An' mind their labours wi' an eydent hand,
    An' ne'er, tho' out o' sight, to jauk or play;
"An' O! be sure to fear the Lord alway!
    And mind your duty, duly, morn and night!
Lest in temptation's path ye gang astray,
    Implore His counsel an' assisting might:
They never sought in vain, that sought the Lord aright!"

But, hark! a rap comes gently to the door;
    Jenny, wha kens the meaning o' the same,
Tells how a neibor lad cam o'er the moor,
    To do some errands, and convoy her hame.
The wily mother sees the conscious flame
    Sparkle in Jenny's ee, and flush her cheek,
Wi' heart-struck anxious care, inquires his name,
    While Jenny hafflins is afraid to speak;
Weel pleas'd the mother hears it's nae wild, worthless rake.

Wi' kindly welcome, Jenny brings him ben;
    A strappin' youth; he taks the mother's eye;
Blithe Jenny sees the visit's no ill-ta'en;
    The father cracks of horses, pleughs, and kye.
The youngster's artless heart o'erflows wi' joy,
    But blate an' laithfu, scarce can weel behave;
The mother, wi' a woman's wiles, can spy
    What makes the youth sae bashfu' an' sae grave,
Weel pleased to think her bairn's respected like the lave.

O happy love ! where love like this is found !
　　O heart-felt raptures !—bliss beyond compare !
I've paced much this weary, mortal round,
　　And sage experience bids me this declare—
" If Heaven a draught of heav'nly pleasure spare,
　　One cordial in this melancholy vale,
'Tis when a youthful, loving, modest pair,
　　In other's arms, breathe out the tender tale,
Beneath the milk-white thorn that scents the ev'ning gale."

Is there in human form, that bears a heart—
　　A wretch ! a villain ! lost to love and truth !
That can, with studied, sly, ensnaring art,
　　Betray sweet Jenny's unsuspecting youth ?
Curse on his perjur'd arts ! dissembling smooth !
　　Are honour, virtue, conscience, all exiled ?
Is there no pity, no relenting ruth,
　　Points to the parents fondling o'er their child ?
Then paints the ruin'd maid, and their distraction wild !

But now the supper crowns their simple board,
　　The halesome parritch, chief of Scotia's food :
The soupe their only hawkie does afford,
　　That 'yont the hallan snugly chows her coou :
The dame brings forth, in complimental mood,
　　To grace the lad, her weel-hain'd kebbuck, fell,
An' aft he's prest, an' aft he ca's it guid ;
　　The frugal wifie, garrulous, will tell,
How 'twas a towmond auld, sin' lint was i' the bell.

The cheerfu' supper done, wi' serious face,
　　They, round the ingle, form a circle wide ;
The sire turns o'er, wi' patriarchal grace,
　　The big ha' bible, ance his father's pride ;
His bonnet rev'rently is laid aside,
　　His lyart haffets wearing thin an' bare ;
Those strains that once did sweet in Zion glide,
　　He wales a portion with judicious care ;
And " Let us worship God !" he says, with solemn air.

They chant their artless notes in simple guise ;
　　They tune their hearts, by far the noblest aim :
Perhaps " Dundee's " wild-warbling measures rise,
　　Or plaintive " Martyrs," worthy of the name ;
Or noble " Elgin " beets the heav'nward flame,
　　The sweetest far of Scotia's holy lays :
Compar'd with these, Italian trills are tame ;
　　The tickl'd ear no heart-felt raptures raise ;
Nae unison hae they with our Creator's praise.

　　The priest-like father reads the sacred page,
　　　　How Abram was the friend of GOD on high ;
Or, Moses bade eternal warfare wage
　　With Amalek's ungracious progeny :
Or how the royal bard did groaning lie
　　Beneath the stroke of Heaven's avenging ire :
Or Job's pathetic plaint, and wailing cry ;
　　Or rapt Isaiah's wild, seraphic fire ;
Or other holy seers that tune the sacred lyre.

　　Perhaps the Christian volume is the theme,
　　　　How guiltless blood for guilty man was shed ;
How HE, who bore in Heav'n the second name,
　　Had not on earth whereon to lay His head :
How His first followers and servants sped,
　　The precepts sage they wrote to many a land :
How he, who lone in Patmos banished,
　　Saw in the sun a mighty angel stand ;
And heard great Bab'lon's doom pronounc'd by Heav'n's command.

　　Then kneeling down, to HEAVEN'S ETERNAL KING !
　　　　The saint, the father, and the husband prays :
Hope " springs exulting on triumphant wing,"
　　That thus they all shall meet in future days :
There ever bask in uncreated rays,
　　No more to sigh or shed the bitter tear,
Together hymning their Creator's praise,
　　In such society, yet still more dear ;
While circling time moves round in an eternal sphere.

c

Compar'd with this, how poor Religion's pride,
  In all the pomp of method, and of art,
When men display to congregations wide,
  Devotion's ev'ry grace, except the heart!
The Pow'r, incens'd, the pageant will desert,
  The pompous strain, the sacerdotal stole:
But, haply, in some cottage far apart,
  May hear, well pleas'd, the language of the soul;
And in His book of life the inmates poor enrol.

Then homeward all take off their sev'ral way;
  The youngling cottagers retire to rest:
The parent-pair their secret homage pay,
  And proffer up to Heav'n the warm request,
That HE, who stills the raven's clam'rous nest,
  And decks the lily fair in flow'ry pride,
Would, in the way His wisdom sees the best,
  For them and for their little ones provide;
But, chiefly, in their hearts with grace divine preside.

From scenes like these old Scotia's grandeur springs
  That makes her lov'd at home, rever'd abroad:
Princes and lords are but the breath of kings,
  "An honest man's the noblest work of GOD;"
And certes, in fair virtue's heav'nly road,
  The cottage leaves the palace far behind.
What is a lordling's pomp? a cumbrous load,
  Disguising oft the wretch of human kind,
Studied in arts of hell, in wickedness refin'd!

O Scotia! my dear, my native soil!
  For whom my warmest wish to Heaven is sent!
Long may thy hardy sons of rustic toil
  Be blest with health, and peace, and sweet content!
And, oh! may Heaven their simple lives prevent
  From luxury's contagion, weak and vile!
Then, howe'er crowns and coronets be rent,
  A virtuous populace may rise the while,
And stand a wall of fire around their much-lov'd isle.

O Thou ! who pour'd the patriotic tide
　　That stream'd through Wallace's undaunted heart :
Who dar'd to, nobly, stem tyrannic pride,
　　Or nobly die, the second glorious part,
(The patriot's God, peculiarly Thou art,
　　His friend, inspirer, guardian, and reward !)
O never, never, Scotia's realm desert ;
　　But still the patriot, and the patriot-bard,
In bright succession raise, her ornament and guard !

TO A MOUNTAIN DAISY,

ON TURNING ONE DOWN WITH THE PLOUGH IN APRIL 1786.

WEE, modest, crimson-tipped flow'r,
Thou's met me in an evil hour ;
For I maun crush amang the stoure
　　　　Thy slender stem :
To spare thee now is past my pow'r,
　　　　Thou bonnie gem.

Alas ! it's no thy neebor sweet,
The bonnie lark, companion meet,
Bending thee 'mang the dewy weet,
        Wi' speckl'd breast,
When upward-springing, blythe to greet,
        The purpling east.

Cauld blew the bitter-biting north
Upon thy early, humble, birth ;
Yet cheerfully thou glinted forth
        Amid the storm,
Scarce rear'd above the parent earth
        Thy tender form.

The flaunting flow'rs our gardens yield,
High shelt'ring woods and wa's maun shield ;
But thou, beneath the random bield
        O' clod or stane,
Adorns the histie stibble-field,
        Unseen, alane.

There, in thy scanty mantle clad,
Thy snawie bosom sun-ward spread,
Thou lifts thy unassuming head
        In humble guise ;
But now the "*share*" uptears thy bed,
        And low thou lies !

Such is the fate of artless maid,
Sweet flow'ret of the rural shade !
By love's simplicity betray'd,
        And guileless trust,
Till she, like thee, all soil'd, is laid
        Low i' the dust.

Such is the fate of simple bard,
On life's rough ocean luckless starr'd !

Unskilful he to note the card
        Of prudent lore,
Till billows rage, and gales blow hard,
        And whelm him o'er!

Such fate to suffering worth is giv'n,
Who long with wants and woes has striv'n,
By human pride or cunning driv'n
        To mis'ry's brink,
Till, wrench'd of ev'ry stay but Heav'n,
        He, ruin'd, sink!

Ev'n thou who mourn'st the Daisy's fate,
That fate is thine—no distant date;
Stern Ruin's ploughshare drives, elate,
        Full on thy bloom,'
Till, crush'd beneath the furrow's weight,
        Shall be thy doom!

TO A HAGGIS.

Fair fa' your honest, sonsie face,
Great chieftain o' the puddin'-race!
Aboon them a' ye tak your place,
        Painch, tripe, or thairm:
Weel are ye wordy of a grace
        As lang's my arm.

The groaning trencher there ye fill,
Your hurdies like a distant hill,
Your pin wad help to mend a mill
        In time o' need,
While thro' your pores the dews distil
        Like amber bead.

His knife see rustic labour dight,
An' cut you up wi' ready slight,

Trenching your gushing entrails bright
   Like ony ditch;
And then, O what a glorious sight,
   Warm-reekin', rich!

Then horn for horn they stretch an' strive,
Deil tak the hinmost, on they drive,
Till a' their weel-swall'd kytes belyve
   Are bent like drums;
Then auld guidman, maist like to rive,
   Bethankit hums.

Is there that owre his French ragoût,
Or olio that wad staw a sow,
Or fricassee wad mak' her spew
   Wi' perfect scunner,
Looks down wi' sneering, scornfu' view
   On sic a dinner?

Poor devil! see him owre his trash,
As feckless as a wither'd rash,
His spindle-shank a guid whip-lash,
   His nieve a nit;
Thro' bloody flood or field to dash,
   O how unfit!

But mark the rustic, haggis-fed,
The trembling earth resounds his tread,
Clap in his walie nieve a blade,
   He'll mak it whissle;
An' legs, an' arms, an' heads will sned,
   Like taps o' thrissle.

Ye pow'rs wha mak mankind your care,
And dish them out their bill o' fare,
Auld Scotland wants nae skinking ware
   That jaups in luggies;
But, if ye wish her gratefu' pray'r,
   Gie her a Haggis!

DESPONDENCY.

AN ODE.

OPPRESS'D with grief, oppress'd with care,
A burden more than I can bear,
  I set me down and sigh:
O life! thou art a galling load,
Along a rough, a weary road,
  To wretches such as I!
Dim, backward, as I cast my view,
  What sick'ning scenes appear!
What sorrows yet may pierce me thro'
  Too justly I may fear!
    Still caring, despairing,
      Must be my bitter doom;
    My woes here shall close ne'er,
      But with the closing tomb!

Happy, ye sons of busy life,
Who, equal to the bustling strife,
  No other view regard!
Ev'n when the wished end's denied,
Yet while the busy means are ply'd,
  They bring their own reward:
Whilst I, a hope-abandoned wight,
  Unfitted with an aim,
Meet ev'ry sad returning night
  And joyless morn the same;
    You, bustling, and justling,
      Forget each grief and pain;
    I, listless, yet restless,
      Find every prospect vain.

How blest the solitary's lot,
Who, all-forgetting, all-forgot,
  Within his humble cell,
The cavern wild with tangling roots,
Sits o'er his newly-gather'd fruits,
  Beside his crystal well!

Or, haply, to his evening thought,
　By unfrequented stream,
The ways of men are distant brought,
　A faint collected dream ;
　　While praising, and raising
　　　His thoughts to heav'n on high,
　　As, wand'ring, meand'ring,
　　　He views the solemn sky.

Than I, no lonely hermit plac'd
Where never human footstep trac'd,
　Less fit to play the part ;
The lucky moment to improve.
And just to stop, and just to move,
　With self-respecting art :
But, ah ! those pleasures, loves, and joys,
　Which I too keenly taste,
The solitary can despise,
　Can want, and yet be blest !
　　He needs not, he heeds not,
　　　Or human love or hate,
　　Whilst I here must cry here
　　　At perfidy ingrate !

Oh ! enviable, early days,
When dancing thoughtless pleasure's maze,
　To care, to guilt unknown !
How ill exchang'd for riper times,
To feel the follies, or the crimes,
　Of others, or my own !
Ye tiny elves that guiltless sport,
　Like linnets in the bush,
Ye little know the ills ye court,
　When manhood is your wish !
　　The losses, the crosses,
　　　That active man engage !
　　The fears all, the tears all,
　　　Of dim declining age !

TAM O' SHANTER,[2]

A TALE.

"Of brownyis and of bogilis full is this buke."—GAWIN DOUGLAS.

WHEN chapman billies leave the street,
An' drouthy neibors, neibors meet,

D

As market-days are wearin' late,
An' folk begin to tak the gate ;
While we sit bousin' at the nappy,
An' gettin' fou an' unco happy,
We think na on the lang Scots miles,
The mosses, waters, slaps, an' stiles,
That lie between us an' our hame,
Whare sits our sulky sullen dame,
Gath'rin' her brows like gath'rin' storm,
Nursin' her wrath to keep it warm.

This truth fand honest Tam o' Shanter,
As he frae Ayr ae night did canter,
(Auld Ayr, wham ne'er a town surpasses
For honest men an' bonny lasses).

O Tam ! hadst thou but been sae wise,
As ta'en thy ain wife Kate's advice !
She tauld thee weel thou wast a skellum,
A bletherin', blusterin', drucken blellum ;
That frae November till October,
Ae market-day thou wasna sober ;
That ilka melder, wi' the miller,
Thou sat as lang as thou hadst siller ;
That ev'ry naig was ca'd a shoe on,
The smith and thee gat roarin' fou on ;
That at the L——d's house, ev'n on Sunday,
Thou drank wi' Kirkton Jean till Monday.
She prophesy'd that, late or soon,
Thou wad be found deep drown'd in Doon !
Or catch'd wi' warlocks i' the mirk,
By Alloway's auld haunted kirk.

Ah, gentle dames ! it gars me greet,
To think how mony counsels sweet,
How mony lengthen'd, sage advices,
The husband frae the wife despises !

But to our tale :—Ae market-night,
Tam had got planted unco right ;

Fast by an ingle, bleezin' finely,
Wi' reamin' swats, that drank divinely ;
An' at his elbow, Souter Johnny,
His ancient, trusty, drouthy crony ;
Tam lo'ed him like a vera brither ;
They had been fou for weeks thegither !
The night drave on wi' sangs an' clatter ;
An' aye the ale was growing better :
The landlady and Tam grew gracious ;
Wi' favours secret, sweet, and precious ;
The Souter tauld his queerest stories ;
The landlord's laugh was ready chorus :
The storm without might rair and rustle—
Tam didna mind the storm a whistle.

Care, mad to see a man sae happy,
E'en drown'd himsel amang the nappy !
As bees flee hame wi' lades o' treasure,
The minutes wing'd their way wi' pleasure :
Kings may be blest, but Tam was glorious,
O'er a' the ills o' life victorious !

But pleasures are like poppies spread,
You seize the flow'r, its bloom is shed !
Or like the snowfall in the river,
A moment white—then melts for ever ;
Or like the borealis race,
That flit ere you can point their place ;
Or like the rainbow's lovely form,
Evanishing amid the storm.
Nae man can tether time or tide ;
The hour approaches Tam maun ride ;
That hour, o' night's black arch the keystane,
That dreary hour he mounts his beast in ;
And sic a night he taks the road in
As ne'er poor sinner was abroad in.

The wind blew as 'twad blawn its last ;
The rattling show'rs rose on the blast ;

The speedy gleams the darkness swallow'd ;
Loud, deep, and lang, the thunder bellow'd :
That night, a child might understand,
The deil had business on his hand.

Weel mounted on his grey mare Meg,
A better never lifted leg,
Tam skelpit on through dub an' mire,
Despising wind, an' rain, an' fire ;
Whiles holding fast his guid blue bonnet ;
Whiles crooning o'er some auld Scots sonnet ;
Whiles glow'ring round wi' prudent cares,
Lest bogles catch him unawares ;
Kirk-Alloway was drawing nigh,
Whare ghaists an' houlets nightly cry.—
By this time he was cross the ford,
Whare in the snaw the chapman smoor'd ;
An' past the birks an' meikle stane
Whare drucken Charlie brak's neck-bane ;
An' thro' the whins, and by the cairn,
Whare hunters fand the murder'd bairn ;
An' near the thorn, aboon the well,
Whare Mungo's mither hang'd hersel.—
Before him Doon pours a' his floods ;
The doublin' storm roars thro' the woods ;
The lightnings flash frae pole to pole ;
Near and more near the thunders roll ;
When glimmerin' thro' the groanin' trees,
Kirk-Alloway seem'd in a bleeze ;
Thro' ilka bore the beams were glancin',
An' loud resounded mirth an' dancin'.—

Inspirin' bold John Barleycorn :
What dangers thou canst mak us scorn !
Wi' tippenny, we fear nae evil ;
Wi' usquabae, we'll face the Devil !—
The swats sae ream'd in Tammie's noddle,
Fair play, he car'd na deils a boddle.

But Maggie stood right sair astonish'd,
Till, by the heel an' hand admonish'd,
She ventur'd forward on the light;
And, wow! Tam saw an unco sight!
Warlocks and witches in a dance;
Nae cotillon brent-new frae France,
But hornpipes, jigs, strathspeys, and reels,
Put life and mettle i' their heels:
At winnock-bunker i' the east,
There sat auld Nick, in shape o' beast;
A towzie tyke, black, grim, and large,
To gie them music was his charge;
He screw'd the pipes, and gart them skirl,
Till roof and rafters a' did dirl.—
Coffins stood round, like open presses,
That shaw'd the dead in their last dresses;
And by some dev'lish cantrip slight
Each in its cauld hand held a light,—
By which heroic Tam was able
To note upon the haly table,
A murderer's banes in gibbet airns;
Twa span-lang, wee, unchristen'd bairns;
A thief, new-cutted frae a rape,
Wi' his last gasp his gab did gape;
Five tomahawks, wi' bluid red-rusted;
Five scimitars, wi' murder crusted;
A garter, which a babe had strangled;
A knife, a father's throat had mangled,
Whom his ain son o' life bereft,
The grey hairs yet stack to the heft:
Wi' mair o' horrible and awfu',
Which ev'n to name wad be unlawfu'.

As Tammie glowr'd, amaz'd and curious,
The mirth and fun grew fast and furious:
The piper loud and louder blew,
The dancers quick and quicker flew;
They reel'd, they set, they cross'd, they cleekit,
'Till ilka carlin swat and reekit,

And coost her duddies to the wark,
And linket at it in her sark.

Now Tam ! O Tam ! had thae been queans,
A' plump an' strappin' i' their teens ;
Their sarks, instead o' creeshie flannen,
Been snaw-white seventeen-hunder linen !
Thir breeks o' mine, my only pair,
That ance were plush, o' guid blue hair,
I wad hae gien them aff my hurdies,
For ae blink o' the bonnie burdies !

But wither'd beldams, auld and droll,
Rigwoodie hags, wad spean a foal,
Lowpin' and flingin' on a cummock,
I wonder didna turn thy stomach.

But Tam kenn'd what was what fu' brawlie,
" There was ae winsome wench and walie,"
That night enlisted in the core,
(Lang after kenn'd on Carrick shore ;
For mony a beast to dead she shot,
And perish'd mony a bonnie boat,
And shook baith meikle corn and bear.
And kept the country-side in fear.)
Her cutty-sark, o' Paisley harn,
That, while a lassie, she had worn,
In longitude though sorely scanty,
It was her best, and she was vauntie.—

Ah ! little kenn'd thy reverend Grannie,
That sark she coft for her wee Nannie,
Wi' twa pund Scots ('twas a' her riches),
Wad ever grac'd a dance o' witches !

But here my muse her wing maun cour ;
Sic flights are far beyond her pow'r ;

To sing how Nannie lap and flang,
(A souple jade she was, and strang,)
And how Tam stood, like ane bewitch'd,
And thought his very e'en enrich'd;
Ev'n Satan glowr'd, and fidg'd fu' fain,
And hotch'd and blew wi' might and main:
'Till first ae caper, syne anither,
Tam tint his reason a' thegither,
And roars out, "Weel done, Cutty-sark!"
And in an instant a' was dark;
And scarcely had he Maggie rallied,
When out the hellish legion sallied.

As bees bizz out wi' angry fyke,
When plunderin' herds assail their byke,
As open pussy's mortal foes,
When, pop! she starts before their nose;
As eager runs the market-crowd,
When "Catch the thief!" resounds aloud;
So Maggie runs, the witches follow,
Wi' mony an eldritch screech and hollow.

Ah, Tam! ah, Tam! thou'lt get thy fairin'!
In hell they'll roast thee like a herrin'!
In vain thy Kate awaits thy comin'!
Kate soon will be a woefu' woman!
Now, do thy speedy utmost, Meg,
And win the keystane o' the brig;
There at them thou thy tail may toss,
A running stream they darena cross;
But ere the keystane she could make,
The fient a tail she had to shake!
For Nannie, far before the rest,
Hard upon noble Maggie prest,
And flew at Tam wi' furious ettle;
But little wist she Maggie's mettle—
Ae spring brought off her master hale,
But left behind her ain grey tail:

The carlin claught her by the rump,
And left poor Maggie scarce a stump.

Now, wha this tale o' truth shall read,
Ilk man and mother's son, take heed :
Whane'er to drink you are inclined,
Or cutty-sarks run i' your mind,
Think ! ye may buy the joys owre dear—
Remember Tam o' Shanter's mare.

ON THE BIRTH OF A POSTHUMOUS CHILD.

SWEET flow'ret, pledge o' meikle love,
   And ward o' mony a pray'r,
What heart o' stane would thou na move,
   Sae helpless, sweet, and fair !

November hirples o'er the lea,
   Chill on thy lovely form ;
And gane, alas ! the shelt'ring tree
   Should shield thee frae the storm.

May He who gives the rain to pour,
   And wings the blast to blaw,
Protect thee frae the driving show'r,
   The bitter frost and snaw !

May He, the friend of woe and want,
   Who heals life's various stounds,
Protect and guard the mother-plant,
   And heal her cruel wounds !

But late she flourish'd, rooted fast,
   Fair on the summer-morn :
Now feebly bends she in the blast,
   Unshelter'd and forlorn.

Blest be thy bloom, thou lovely gem,
Unscath'd by ruffian hand!
And from thee many a parent stem
Arise to deck our land!

ON SCARING SOME WATER-FOWL IN LOCH TURIT,

A WILD SCENE AMONG THE HILLS OF OCHTERTYRE.

Why, ye tenants of the lake,
For me your wat'ry haunts forsake?
Tell me fellow-creatures, why
At my presence thus you fly?
Why disturb your social joys,
Parent, filial, kindred ties?—
Common friend to you and me,
Nature's gifts to all are free:

Peaceful keep your dimpling wave,
Busy feed, or wanton lave ;
Or, beneath the sheltering rock,
Bide the surging billow's shock.

Conscious, blushing for our race,
Soon, too soon, your fears I trace.
Man, your proud usurping foe,
Would be lord of all below :
Plumes himself in freedom's pride,
Tyrant stern to all beside.
The eagle, from the cliffy brow,
Marking you his prey below,
In his breast no pity dwells,
Strong necessity compels :
But man, to whom alone is giv'n
A ray direct from pitying heav'n,
Glories in his heart humane—
And creatures for his pleasure slain.
In these savage, liquid plains,
Only known to wand'ring swains,
Where the mossy riv'let strays,
Far from human haunts and ways ;
All on nature you depend,
And life's poor season peaceful spend.
Or, if man's superior might
Dare invade your native right,
On the lofty ether borne,
Man with all his powers you scorn ;
Swiftly seek, on clanging wings,
Other lakes and other springs ;
And the foe you cannot brave
Scorn at least to be his slave.

LAMENT FOR JAMES, EARL OF GLENCAIRN.

THE wind blew hollow frae the hills,
    By fits the sun's departing beam
Look'd on the fading yellow woods
    That wav'd o'er Lugar's winding stream :
Beneath a craigy steep, a bard,
    Laden with years and meikle pain,
In loud lament bewail'd his lord,
    Whom death had all untimely ta'en.

He lean'd him to an ancient aik,
    Whose trunk was mould'ring down with years ;
His locks were bleached white with time,
    His hoary cheek was wet wi' tears ;
And as he touch'd his trembling harp,
    And as he tun'd his doleful sang,
The winds, lamenting thro' their caves,
    To echo bore the notes alang :—

" Ye scatter'd birds that faintly sing
    The reliques of the vernal quire !
Ye woods that shed on a' the winds
    The honours of the aged year !
A few short months and glad and gay,
    Again ye'll charm the ear and ee ;
But nocht in all revolving time
    Can gladness bring again to me.

" I am a bending aged tree,
    That long has stood the wind and rain ;
But now has come a cruel blast,
    And my last hold of earth is gane :
Nae leaf o' mine shall greet the spring,
    Nae simmer sun exalt my bloom ;
But I maun lie before the storm,
    And ithers plant them in my room.

" I've seen sae mony changefu' years,
  On earth I am a stranger grown ;
I wander in the ways of men,
  Alike unknowing and unknown :
Unheard, unpitied, unreliev'd,
  I bear alane my lade o' care,
For silent, low, on beds of dust,
  Lie a' that would my sorrows share.

" And last (the sum of a' my griefs !)
  My noble master lies in clay ;
The flow'r among our barons bold,
  His country's pride—his country's stay !
In weary being now I pine,
  For a' the life of life is dead,
And hope has left my aged ken,
  On forward wing for ever fled.

" Awake thy last sad voice, my harp !
  The voice of woe and wild despair ;
Awake ! resound thy latest lay—
  Then sleep in silence evermair !
And thou my last best only friend,
  That fillest an untimely tomb,
Accept this tribute from the bard
  Thou brought from Fortune's mirkest gloom.

" In poverty's low barren vale
  Thick mists, obscure, involv'd me round ;
Though oft I turn'd the wistful eye,
  Nae ray of fame was to be found ;
Thou found'st me, like the morning sun,
  That melts the fogs in limpid air ;
The friendless bard and rustic song
  Became alike thy fostering care.

" Oh ! why has worth so short a date,
  While villains ripen grey with time ?
Must thou, the noble, gen'rous, great,
  Fall in bold manhood's hardy prime !

Why did I live to see that day?
  A day to me so full of woe !—
Oh ! had I met the mortal shaft
Which laid my benefactor low !

"The bridegroom may forget the bride
  Was made his wedded wife yestreen :
The monarch may forget the crown
  That on his head an hour has been ;
The mother may forget the child
  That smiles sae sweetly on her knee ;
But I'll remember thee, Glencairn,
  And a' that thou hast done for me !"

SONNET

ON HEARING A THRUSH SING IN A MORNING WALK ; WRITTEN
JAN. 25, 1793, THE BIRTHDAY OF THE AUTHOR.

SING on, sweet thrush, upon the leafless bough ;
  Sing on, sweet bird, I listen to thy strain :
  See, aged Winter, 'mid his surly reign,
At thy blithe carol clears his furrow'd brow.

So in lone Poverty's dominion drear,
  Sits meek Content with light unanxious heart,
  Welcomes the rapid moments, bids them part,
Nor asks if they bring aught to hope or fear.

I thank thee, Author of this opening day !
  Thou whose bright sun now gilds the orient skies !
  Riches denied, thy boon was purer joys,
What wealth could never give nor take away !

Yet come, thou child of poverty and care ;
The mite high Heav'n bestow'd, that mite with
  thee I'll share.

TO MISS CRUIKSHANKS.

BEAUTEOUS rosebud, young and gay,
Blooming in thy early May,
Never may'st thou, lovely flow'r,
Chilly shrink in sleety show'r !
Never Boreas' hoary path,
Never Eurus' pois'nous breath,
Never baleful stellar lights,
Taint thee with untimely blights !
Never, never reptile thief
Riot on thy virgin leaf!
Nor even Sol too fiercely view
Thy bosom blushing still with dew !

May'st thou long, sweet crimson gem,
Richly deck thy native stem :
Till some ev'ning, sober, calm,
Dropping dews, and breathing balm,
While all around the woodland rings,
And ev'ry bird thy requiem sings ;
Thou, amid the dirgeful sound,
Shed thy dying honours round,
And resign to parent earth
The loveliest form she e'er gave birth.

LINES WRITTEN ON A BANK NOTE.

WAE worth thy power, thou cursed leaf !
Fell source o' a' my woe and grief !
For lack o' thee I've lost my lass !
For lack o' thee I scrimp my glass.
I see the children of affliction
Unaided, thro' thy curs'd restriction.
I've seen the oppressor's cruel smile,
Amid his hapless victim's spoil,
And, for thy potence, vainly wish'd
To crush the villain in the dust.
For lack o' thee, I leave this much-lov'd shore,
Never, perhaps, to greet auld Scotland more.

ADDRESS TO THE TOOTHACHE.

WRITTEN WHEN THE AUTHOR WAS GRIEVOUSLY TORMENTED BY
THAT DISORDER.

My curse upon thy venom'd stang,
That shoots my tortur'd gums alang;
And thro' my lugs gies mony a twang,
      Wi' gnawing vengeance;
Tearing my nerves wi' bitter pang,
      Like racking engines!

When fevers burn, or ague freezes,
Rheumatics gnaw, or cholic squeezes ;
Our neighbour's sympathy may ease us,
                    Wi' pitying moan ;
But thee—thou hell o' a' diseases,
                    Aye mocks our groan !

Adown my beard the slavers trickle !
I kick the wee stools o'er the mickle,
As round the fire the giglets keckle,
                    To see me loup ;
While, raving mad, I wish a heckle *
                    Were in their doup.

O' a' the num'rous human dools,
Ill har'sts, daft bargains, cutty-stools,
Or worthy friends rak'd i' the mools,
                    Sad sight to see !
The tricks o' knaves, or fash o' fools,
                    Thou bear'st the gree.

Where'er that place be priests ca' hell,
Whence a' the tones o' mis'ry yell,
And ranked plagues their numbers tell,
                    In dreadfu' raw,
Thou, Toothache, surely bear'st the bell
                    Amang them a' !

O thou grim mischief-making chiel,
That gars the notes o' discord squeel,
Till daft mankind aft dance a reel
                    In gore a shoe thick,
Gie a' the faes o' Scotland's weal
                    A towmond's toothache !

* A frame in which are stuck, sharp ends uppermost, from fifty to a hundred steel
pikes, through which the hemp is drawn to straighten it for manufacturing purposes.

VERSES

ON AN EVENING VIEW OF THE RUINS OF LINCLUDEN ABBEY.

YE holy walls, that, still sublime,
Resist the crumbling touch of time;
How strongly still your form displays
The piety of ancient days!
As through your ruins, hoar and grey,—
Ruins, yet beauteous in decay,—
The silver moonbeams trembling play:
The form of ages long gone by
Crowd thick on fancy's wond'ring eye,
And wake the soul to musings high.
Ev'n now, as lost in thought profound,
I view the solemn scene around,
And, pensive, gaze with wistful eyes,
The past returns, the present flies;
Again the dome, in pristine pride,
Lifts high its roof, and arches wide,
That, knit with curious tracery,
Each Gothic ornament display.
The high-arch'd windows, painted fair,
Show, many a saint and martyr there.
As on their slender forms I'd gaze,
Methinks they brighten to a blaze!
With noiseless step and taper bright,
What are yon forms that meet my sight?
Slowly they move, while every eye
Is heav'nward rais'd in ecstasy.
'Tis the fair, spotless, vestal train,
That seek in pray'r the midnight fane.
And, hark! what more than mortal sound
Of music breathes the pile around?
'Tis the soft chanted choral song,
Whose tones the echoing aisles prolong;
Till, thence return'd, they softly stray
O'er Cluden's wave, with fond delay;

Now on the rising gale swell high,
And now in fainting murmurs die;
The boatmen on Nith's gentle stream,
That glistens in the pale moonbeam,
Suspend their dashing oars to hear
The holy anthem, loud and clear;
Each worldly thought awhile forbear,
And mutter forth a half-form'd prayer.
But, as I gaze, the vision fails,
Like frost-work touch'd by southern gales;
The altar sinks, the tapers fade,
And all the splendid scene's decay'd;
In window fair the painted pane
No longer glows with holy stain,
But, through the broken glass, the gale
Blows chilly from the misty vale;
The bird of eve flits sullen by,
Her home, these aisles and arches high!
The choral hymn that erst so clear
Broke softly sweet on fancy's ear,
Is drown'd amid the mournful scream,
That breaks the magic of my dream!
Rous'd by the sound, I start and see
The ruin'd sad reality!

THOUGH FICKLE FORTUNE HAS DECEIVED ME.

THOUGH fickle fortune has deceived me,
  She promis'd fair and perform'd but ill;
Of mistress, friends, and wealth bereav'd me,
  Yet I bear a heart shall support me still.

I'll act with prudence as far's I'm able,
  But, if success I must never find,
Then come misfortune, I bid thee welcome,
  I'll meet thee with an undaunted mind.

LAMENT of MARY QUEEN of SCOTS,

ON THE APPROACH OF SPRING.

Now Nature hangs her mantle green
   On every blooming tree,
And spreads her sheets o' daisies white
   Out o'er the grassy lea :
Now Phœbus cheers the crystal streams,
   And glads the azure skies ;
But nought can glad the weary wight
   That fast in durance lies.

Now lav'rocks wake the merry morn,
   Aloft on dewy wing ;
The merle, in his noontide bow'r,
   Makes woodland echoes ring ;

The mavis wild, wi' mony a note,
　Sing drowsy day to rest:
In love and freedom they rejoice,
　Wi' care nor thrall opprest.

Now blooms the lily by the bank,
　The primrose down the brae;
The hawthorn's budding in the glen,
　And milk-white is the slae;
The meanest hind in fair Scotland
　May rove their sweets amang;
But I, the Queen of a' Scotland,
　Maun lie in prison strang!

I was the queen o' bonny France,
　Where happy I hae been;
Fu' lightly rase I in the morn,
　As blithe lay down at een:
And I'm the sov'reign of Scotland,
　And mony a traitor there;
Yet here I lie in foreign bands,
　And never-ending care.

But as for thee, thou false woman!—
　My sister and my fae,
Grim Vengeance yet shall whet a sword
　That thro' thy soul shall gae!
The weeping blood in woman's breast
　Was never known to thee;
Nor the balm that draps on wounds of woe
　Frae woman's pitying e'e.

My son! My son! may kinder stars
　Upon thy fortune shine!
And may those pleasures gild thy reign,
　That ne'er wad blink on mine!
God keep thee frae thy mother's faes,
　Or turn their hearts to thee:
And where thou meet'st thy mother's friend,
　Remember him for me!

Oh! soon to me may summer suns
  Nae mair light up the morn!
Nae mair, to me, the autumn winds
  Wave o'er the yellow corn!
And in the narrow house o' death
  Let winter round me rave;
And the next flowers that deck the spring
  Bloom on my peaceful grave!

THE TWA DOGS.[4]

A TALE.

'TWAS in that place o' Scotland's isle,
That bears the name o' auld King Coil,

Upon a bonny day in June,
When wearing thro' the afternoon,
Twa dogs, that werena thrang at hame,
Forgather'd ance upon a time.

The first I'll name, they ca'd him Cæsar,
Was keepit for his honour's pleasure ;
His hair, his size, his mouth, his lugs,
Show'd he was nane o' Scotland's dogs ;
But whalpit some place far abroad,
Where sailors gang to fish for cod.

His locked, letter'd, braw brass collar
Show'd him the gentleman and scholar ;
But tho' he was o' high degree,
The fient a pride—nae pride had he ;
But wad hae spent an hour caressin',
Even wi' a tinkler-gypsy's messan.
At kirk or market, mill or smiddie,
Nae tawted tyke, though e'er sae duddie,
But he wad stan't, as glad to see him,
And stroan't on stanes and hillocks wi' him.

The tither was a ploughman's collie,
A rhyming, ranting, raving billie,
Wha for his friend and comrade had him,
And in his freaks had Luath ca'd him,
After some dog in Highland sang,*
Was made lang syne—Lord knows how lang.

He was a gash and faithfu' tyke,
As ever lap a sheugh or dyke.
His honest, sonsie, baws'nt face,
Aye gat him friends in ilka place.
His breast was white, his touzie back
Weel clad wi' coat o' glossy black ;

---

* Cuchullin's dog in Ossian's "Fingal."

His gaucie tail, wi' upward curl,
Hung o'er his hurdies wi' a swirl.

Nae doubt but they were fain o' ither,
An' unco pack and thick thegither;
Wi' social nose whyles snuff'd and snowkit,
Whyles mice and moudieworts they howkit;
Whyles scour'd awa in lang excursion,
And worried ither in diversion;
Until wi' daffin' weary grown,
Upon a knowe they sat them down,
And there began a lang digression
About the lords o' the creation.

CÆSAR.

I've aften wonder'd, honest Luath,
What sort o' life poor dogs like you have;
An' when the gentry's life I saw,
What way poor bodies lived ava.

Our laird gets in his racked rents,
His coals, his kain, and a' his stents;
He rises when he likes himsel;
His flunkies answer at the bell;
He ca's his coach, he ca's his horse;
He draws a bonny silken purse
As lang's my tail, where through the steeks,
The yellow-letter'd Geordie keeks.

Frae morn tae e'en it's nought but toiling,
At baking, roasting, frying, boiling;
And tho' the gentry first are stechin,
Yet ev'n the ha' folk fill their pechan
Wi' sauce, ragouts, and siclike trashtrie,
That's little short o' downright wastrie.
Our whipper-in, wee, blastit wonner,
Poor worthless elf, it eats a dinner

Better than ony tenant man
His honour has in a' the lan';
And what poor cot-folk pit their painch in,
I own it's past my comprehension.

LUATH.

Trowth, Cæsar, whyles they're fasht eneugh ;
A cottar howkin' in a sheugh,
Wi' dirty stanes biggin' a dike,
Baring a quarry, and siclike ;
Himsel, a wife, he thus sustains,
A smytrie o' wee duddie weans,
And nought but his han' darg to keep
Them right and tight in thack and rape.

And when they meet wi' sair disasters,
Like loss o' health or want o' masters,
Ye maist wad think, a wee touch langer,
And they maun starve o' cauld and hunger :
But, how it comes, I never kenn'd yet,
They're maistly wonderfu' contented :
And buirdly chiels, and clever hizzies,
Are bred in sic a way as this is.

CÆSAR.

But then, to see how ye're negleckit,
How huff'd, and cuff'd, and disrespeckit !
Lord, man, our gentry care as little
For delvers, ditchers, and sic cattle ;
They gang as saucy by poor folk
As I wad by a stinkin' brock.
I've notic'd, on our laird's court-day,
And mony a time my heart's been wae,
Poor tenant bodies, scant o' cash,
How they maun thole a factor's snash :

He'll stamp and threaten, curse and swear,
He'll apprehend them, poind their gear ;
While they maun stan', wi' aspect humble,
And hear it a', and fear and tremble !

I see how folk live that hae riches ;
But surely poor folk maun be wretches !

LUATH.

They're no sae wretched's ane wad think ;
Tho' constantly on poortith's brink :
They're sae accustom'd wi' the sight,
The view o't gies them little fright.

Then chance and fortune are sae guided,
They're aye in less or mair provided ;
And tho' fatigued wi' close employment,
A blink o' rest's a sweet enjoyment.

The dearest comfort o' their lives,
Their grushie weans and faithfu' wives ;
The prattling things are just their pride,
That sweetens a' their fireside ;
And whiles twalpennie worth o' nappy
Can mak' the bodies unco happy ;
They lay aside their private cares,
To mind the Kirk and State affairs :
They'll talk o' patronage and priests,
Wi' kindling fury in their breasts ;
Or tell what new taxation's comin',
And ferlie at the folk in Lun'on.

As bleak-fac'd Hallowmas returns,
They get the jovial ranting kirns,
When rural life, o' ev'ry station,
Unite in common recreation ;
Love blinks, Wit slaps, and social Mirth
Forgets there's Care upo' the earth.

That merry day the year begins
They bar the door on frosty win's ;
The nappy reeks wi' mantling ream,
And sheds a heart-inspiring steam ;
The luntin pipe and sneeshin-mill
Are handed round wi' right guid will ;
The cantie auld folks crackin' crouse,
The young anes rantin' thro' the house,—
My heart has been sae fain to see them,
That I for joy hae barkit wi' them.

Still it's owre true that ye hae said,
Sic game is now owre aften play'd.
There's mony a creditable stock
O' decent, honest, fawsont folk,
Are riven out baith root and branch,
Some rascal's pride'fu' greed to quench,
Wha thinks to knit himsel the faster
In favour wi' some gentle master,
Wha aiblins, thrang a parliamentin',
For Britain's guid his saul indentin'—

CÆSAR.

Haith, lad, ye little ken about it ;
For Britain's guid ! guid faith ! I doubt it.
Say rather, gaun as Premiers lead him,
And saying Ay or No's they bid him :
At operas and plays parading,
Mortgaging, gambling, masquerading ;
Or maybe, in a frolic daft,
To Hague or Calais tak's a waft,
To mak' a tour, and tak' a whirl,
To learn *bon ton*, and see the worl'

There, at Vienna or Versailles,
He rives his father's auld entails ;

Or by Madrid he takes the route,
To thrum guitars, and fecht wi' nowte ;
Or down Italian vista startles,
Whore-hunting among groves o' myrtles,
Then bouses drumly German water,
To mak' himsel look fair and fatter,
And clear the consequential sorrows,
Love-gifts of Carnival signoras.
For Britain's guid !—for her destruction !
Wi' dissipation, feud, and faction !

LUATH.

Hech man ! dear sirs ! is that the gate,
They waste sae mony a braw estate !
Are we sae foughten and harrass'd
For gear to gang that gate at last !

O would they stay aback frae courts,
And please themselves wi' country sports,
It wad for ev'ry ane be better,
The Laird, the Tenant, and the Cotter !
For thae frank, rantin', ramblin' billies,
Fient haet o' them's ill-hearted fellows ;
Except for breakin' o' their timmer,
Or speakin' lightly o' their limmer,
Or shootin' o' a hare or moorcock,
The ne'er a bit they're ill to poor folk.

But will ye tell me, Master Cæsar,
Sure great folk's life's a life o' pleasure ?
Nae cauld nor hunger e'er can steer them,
The very thought o't needna fear them.

CÆSAR.

Lord, man, were ye but whiles where I am,
The gentles ye wad ne'er envy 'em.

Its true they needna starve nor sweat,
Thro' winter's cauld, or simmer's heat ;
They've nae sair wark to craze their banes,
And fill auld age wi' grips and granes :
But human bodies are sic fools,
For a' their colleges and schools,
That when nae real ills perplex them,
They mak' enow themsels to vex them ;
And aye the less they hae to sturt them,
In like proportion less will hurt them.

A country fellow at the pleugh,
His acres till'd, he's right eneugh ;
A country girl at her wheel,
Her dizzens done, she's unco weel :
But Gentlemen, and Ladies warst,
Wi' ev'ndown want o' wark are curst.
They loiter, lounging, lank, and lazy ;
Tho' deil haet ails them, yet uneasy ;
Their days insipid, dull, and tasteless ;
Their nights unquiet, lang, and restless ;
And e'en their sports, their balls and races,
Their gallopin' thro' public places,
There's sic parade, sic pomp, and art,
The joy can scarcely reach the heart.

The men cast out in party matches,
Then sowther a' in deep debauches ;
Ae night they're mad wi' drink and whoring,
Neist day their life is past enduring.

The ladies arm-in-arm in clusters,
As great and gracious a' as sisters ;
But hear their absent thoughts o' ither,
They're a' run deils and jads thegither.
Whiles owre the wee bit cup and platie,
They sip the scandal potion pretty :

Or lee-lang nights, wi' crabbit leuks,
Pore owre the devil's pictur'd beuks ;
Stake on a chance a farmer's stackyard,
And cheat like ony unhang'd blackguard.
There's some exception, man and woman ;
But this is Gentry's life in common.

By this, the sun was out o' sight,
And darker gloaming brought the night :
The bum-clock humm'd wi' lazy drone ;
The kye stood rowtin' i' the loan :
When up they gat and shook their lugs,
Rejoic'd they werena men, but dogs ;
And each took aff his several way,
Resolv'd to meet some ither day.

ELEGY ON CAPTAIN MATTHEW HENDERSON,'

A GENTLEMAN WHO HELD THE PATENT FOR HIS HONOURS IMMEDIATELY FROM ALMIGHTY GOD.

" Should the poor be flattered ?"—SHAKESPEARE.

But now his radiant course is run,
    For Matthew's course was bright :
His soul was like the glorious sun,
    A matchless heav'nly light !

O DEATH ! thou tyrant fell and bloody !
The meikle devil wi' a woodie
Haurl thee hame to his black smiddie,
            O'er hurcheon hides,
And like stock-fish come o'er his studdie
            Wi' thy auld sides !

He's gane ! he's gane ! he's frae us torn !
The ae best fellow e'er was born !
Thee, Matthew, Nature's sel' shall mourn
            By wood and wild,
Where, haply, Pity strays forlorn,
            Frae man exil'd !

Ye hills ! near neebors o' the starns,
That proudly cock your cresting cairns !

Ye cliffs, the haunts of sailing yearns,
        Where echo slumbers !
Come join, ye Nature's sturdiest bairns,
        My wailing numbers !

Mourn, ilka grove the cushat kens !
Ye haz'lly shaws and briery dens !
Ye burnies, wimplin' down your glens,
        Wi' toddlin' din,
Or foaming strang, wi' hasty stens,
        Frae lin to lin !

Mourn, little harebells o'er the lea ;
Ye stately foxgloves fair to see ;
Ye woodbines, hanging bonnilie
        In scented bow'rs ;
Ye roses on your thorny tree,
        The first o' flow'rs.

At dawn, when ev'ry grassy blade,
Droops with a diamond at its head,
At ev'n, when beans their fragrance shed,
        I' th' rustling gale,
Ye maukins, whiddin' thro' the glade,
        Come, join my wail.

Mourn, ye wee songsters o' the wood ;
Ye grouse that crap the heather-bud ;
Ye curlews calling thro' a clud ;
        Ye whistling plover ;
And mourn, ye whirling paitrick brood !—
        He's gane for ever.

Mourn, sooty coots, and speckled teals ;
Ye fisher herons, watching eels ;
Ye duck and drake, wi' airy wheels
        Circling the lake ;
Ye bitterns, till the quagmire reels,
        Rair for his sake.

Mourn, clam'ring craiks at close o' day,
'Mang fields o' flow'ring clover gay;
And when ye wing your annual way
      Frae our cauld shore,
'Tell thae far warlds, wha lies in clay,
      Wham we deplore.

Ye houlets, frae your ivy bow'r,
In some auld tree, or eldritch tow'r,
What time the moon, wi' silent glow'r,
      Sets up her horn,
Wail thro' the dreary midnight hour
      'Till waukrife morn!

O, rivers, forests, hills, and plains!
Oft have ye heard my canty strains:
But now, what else for me remains
      But tales of woe?
And frae my een the drapping rains
      Maun ever flow.

Mourn, spring, thou darling of the year!
Ilk cowslip cup shall kep a tear;
Thou, simmer, while each corny spear
      Shoots up its head,
Thy gay, green, flow'ry tresses shear
      For him that's dead!

Thou, autumn, wi' thy yellow hair,
In grief thy sallow mantle tear!
Thou, winter, hurling thro' the air
      The roaring blast,
Wide o'er the naked world declare,
      The worth we've lost!

Mourn him, thou sun, great source of light!
Mourn, empress of the silent night!
And you, ye twinkling stamies bright,
      My Matthew mourn!

For through your orbs he's ta'en his flight,
      Ne'er to return.

Oh, Henderson ! the man—the brother !
And art thou gone, and gone for ever?
And hast thou crost that unknown river,
      Life's dreary bound?
Like thee, where shall I find another
      The world around?

Go to your sculptur'd tombs, ye great,
In a' the tinsel trash o' state !
But by thy honest turf I'll wait,
      Thou man of worth !
And weep the ae best fellow's fate
      E'er lay in earth.

THE EPITAPH.

STOP, passenger !—my story's brief,
    And truth I shall relate, man ;
I tell nae common tale o' grief—
    For Matthew was a great man.

If thou uncommon merit hast,
    Yet spurn'd at fortune's door, man,
A look of pity hither cast—
    For Matthew was a poor man.

If thou a noble sodger art,
    That passest by this grave, man,
There moulders here a gallant heart—
    For Matthew was a brave man.

If thou 'on men, their works and ways,
    Canst throw uncommon light, man,
Here lies wha weel had won thy praise—
    For Matthew was a bright man !

If thou at friendship's sacred ca'
    Wad life itself resign, man,
Thy sympathetic tear maun fa'—
    For Matthew was a kind man !

If thou art staunch without a stain,
    Like the unchanging blue, man,
This was a kinsman o' thy ain—
    For Matthew was a true man !

If thou hast wit, an' fun, an' fire,
    An' ne'er guid wine did fear, man,
This was thy billie, dam, and sire—
    For Matthew was a queer man.

If ony whiggish whingin' sot,
    To blame poor Matthew dare, man,
May dool and sorrow be his lot !
    For Matthew was a rare man.

A WINTER NIGHT.

"Poor naked wretches, wheresoe'er you are,
    That bide the pelting of the pitiless storm !
    How shall your houseless heads, and unfed sides,
    Your loop'd and window'd raggedness defend you,
    From seasons such as these ?"—SHAKESPEARE.

WHEN biting Boreas, fell and doure,
Sharp shivers thro' the leafless bow'r ;
When Phœbus gies a short-liv'd glow'r
            Far south the lift,
Dim dark'ning thro' the flaky show'r,
            Or whirling drift :

Ae night the storm the steeples rock'd,
Poor labour sweet in sleep was lock'd,
While burns, wi' snawy wreaths up-chok'd,
    Wild-eddying swirl,
Or thro' the mining outlet bock'd,
    Down headlong hurl.

List'ning the doors and winnocks rattle,
I thought me on the ourie cattle,
Or silly sheep, wha bide this brattle
    O' winter war,
And thro' the drift, deep-lairing sprattle,
    Beneath a scaur.

Ilk happing bird, wee, helpless thing,
That, in the merry months o' spring,
Delighted me to hear thee sing,
    What comes o' thee ?
Whare wilt thou cow'r thy chittering wing,
    And close thy e'e ?

Ev'n you, on murd'ring errands toil'd,
Lone from your savage homes exil'd,
The blood-stain'd roost, and sheep-cot spoil'd,
    My heart forgets,
While pitiless the tempest wild
    Sore on you beats.

Now Phœbe, in her midnight reign,
Dark-muffled, view'd the dreary plain ;
Still crowding thoughts, a pensive train,
    Rose in my soul,
When on my ear this plaintive strain,
    Slow, solemn, stole :—

" Blow, blow, ye winds, with heavier gust !
And freeze, thou bitter-biting frost !
Descend, ye chilly, smothering snows !
Not all your rage, as now united, shows

More hard unkindness, unrelenting
Vengeful malice unrepenting,
Than heav'n-illumin'd man on brother man bestows !

See stern oppression's iron grip,
Or mad ambition's gory hand,
Sending, like blood-hounds from the slip,
Woe, want, and murder o'er a land !

Ev'n in the peaceful rural vale,
  'Truth, weeping, tells the mournful tale,
How pamper'd luxury, flatt'ry by her side,
  The parasite empoisoning her ear,
  With all the servile wretches in the rear,
Looks o'er proud property, extended wide ;
  And eyes the simple rustic hind,
    Whose toil upholds the glitt'ring show,
  A creature of another kind,
  Some coarser substance unrefin'd,
Plac'd for her lordly use, thus far, thus vile, below.
  Where, where is love's fond, tender throe,
  With lordly honour's lofty brow,
    The pow'rs you proudly own ?
  Is there, beneath love's noble name,
  Can harbour dark the selfish aim,
    To bless himself alone !
  Mark maiden innocence a prey
    To love-pretending snares,
  This boasted honour turns away,
  Shunning soft pity's rising sway,
Regardless of the tears and unavailing pray'rs !
  Perhaps, this hour, in mis'ry's squalid nest,
  She strains your infant to her joyless breast,
And with a mother's fears shrinks at the rocking blast !
  O ye ! who, sunk in beds of down,
  Feel not a want but what yourselves create,
  Think, for a moment, on his wretched fate
    Whom friends and fortune quite disown !
  Ill-satisfied keen nature's clam'rous call,
    Stretch'd on his straw he lays himself to sleep,
  While thro' the ragged roof and chinky wall,
  Chill o'er his slumbers piles the drifty heap !
  Think on the dungeon's grim confine,
  Where guilt and poor misfortune pine !
  Guilt, erring man, relenting view !
  But shall thy legal rage pursue
  The wretch, already crushed low
  By cruel fortune's undeserved blow ?

Affliction's sons are brothers in distress,
A brother to relieve, how exquisite the bliss!"

I heard nae mair, for chanticleer
Shook off the pouthery snaw,
And hail'd the morning with a cheer—
A cottage-rousing craw.

But deep this truth impress'd my mind—
Through all His works abroad,
The heart benevolent and kind
The most resembles God.

A PRAYER IN THE PROSPECT OF DEATH.

O THOU unknown, Almighty Cause
Of all my hope and fear!
In whose dread presence, ere an hour,
Perhaps I must appear!

If I have wandered in those paths
Of life I ought to shun;
As something, loudly, in my breast,
Remonstrates I have done;

Thou know'st that Thou hast form'd me
With passions wild and strong;
And list'ning to their witching voice
Has often led me wrong.

Where human weakness has come short,
Or frailty stept aside,
Do Thou, All-Good! for such Thou art,
In shades of darkness hide.

Where with intention I have err'd,
No other plea I have,
But, Thou art good; and Goodness still
Delighteth to forgive.

THE DEATH AND DYING WORDS OF POOR MAILIE,[6]

THE AUTHOR'S ONLY PET YOWE.

(An Unco Mournfu' Tale.)

As Mailie, an' her lambs thegither,
Were ae day nibbling on the tether,
Upon her cloot she coost a hitch,
An' owre she warsl'd in the ditch :
There, groaning, dying, she did lie,
When Hughoc he cam doytin by.
Wi' glowrin' e'en an' lifted han's,
Poor Hughoc like a statue stan's ;
He saw her days were near-hand ended,
But, waes my heart! he couldna mend it!
He gaped wide, but naething spak—
At length poor Mailie silence brak.

"O thou, whase lamentable face
Appears to mourn my woefu' case !
My dying words attentive hear,
An' bear them to my master dear.

"Tell him, if e'er again he keep
As muckle gear as buy a sheep,
O bid him never tie them mair
Wi' wicked strings o' hemp or hair !
But ca' them out to park or hill,
An' let them wander at their will ;
So may his flock increase, an' grow
To scores o' lambs, an' packs o' woo' !

"Tell him he was a master kin',
An' aye was guid to me an mine ;
An' now my dying charge I gie him,
My helpless lambs I trust them wi' him.

"O bid him save their harmless lives
Frae dogs, an' tods, an' butchers' knives !
But gie them guid cow-milk their fill,
Till they be fit to fend themsel ;
An' tent them duly, e'en an' morn,
Wi' teats o' hay, an' rips o' corn.

"An' may they never learn the gaets
Of ither vile, wanrestfu' pets !
To slink thro' slaps, an' reave an' steal,
At stacks o' peas or stocks o' kail.
So may they, like their great forbears,
For mony a year come thro' the shears :
So wives will gie them bits o' bread,
An' bairns greet for them when they're dead.

"My poor toop-lamb, my son an' heir,
O bid him breed him up wi' care !
An' if he live to be a beast,
To put some havins in his breast !

An' warn him, what I winna name,
To stay content wi' yowes at hame :
An' no to rin an' wear his cloots,
Like ither menseless, graceless brutes.

    " An' neist my yowie, silly thing,
Guid keep thee frae a tether string !
O, may thou ne'er forgather up
Wi' ony blastit, moorland toop,
But aye keep mind to moop an' mell
Wi' sheep o' credit like thysel' !

    " An' now, my bairns, wi' my last breath
I lea'e my blessin' wi' you baith :
An' when you think upo' your mither,
Mind to be kin' to ane anither.

    " Now, honest Hughoc, dinna fail
To tell my master a' my tale ;
An' bid him burn this cursed tether,
An', for thy pains, thou's get my blether."

This said, poor Mailie turn'd her head,
And clos'd her een amang the dead.

The Elegy.

LAMENT in rhyme, lament in prose,
Wi' saut tears trickling down your nose ;
Our bardie's fate is at a close,
        Past a' remead ;
The last sad cape-stane of his woes ;
        Poor Mailie's dead !

It's no the loss o' warl's gear,
That could sae bitter draw the tear,
Or mak our bardie, dowie, wear
        The mourning weed :

He's lost a friend and neibor dear
      In Mailie dead.

Thro' a' the toon she trotted by him ;
A lang half-mile she could descry him ;
Wi' kindly bleat, when she did spy him,
      She ran wi' speed :
A friend mair faithfu' ne'er cam nigh him
      Than Mailie dead.

I wat she was a sheep o' sense,
An' could behave hersel' wi' mense :
I'll say't, she never brak a fence,
      Thro' thievish greed.
Our bardie, lanely, keeps the spence*
      Sin' Mailie's dead.

Or, if he wanders up the howe,
Her living image in her yowe
Comes bleating to him, owre the knowe.
      For bits o' bread ;
An' down the briny pearls rowe
      For Mailie dead.

She was nae get o' moorland tips,
Wi' tawted ket an' hairy hips ;
For her forbears were brought in ships
      Frae yont the Tweed :
A bonnier fleesh ne'er cross'd the clips
      Than Mailie dead.

Wae worth the man wha first did shape
That vile, wanchancie thing—a rape !
It maks guid fellows girn an' gape,
      Wi' chokin' dread ;
An' Robin's bonnet wave wi' crape,
      For Mailie dead.

* Shuts himself up in the parlour with his sorrow.

Oh, a' ye bards on bonny Doon !
An' wha on Ayr your chanters tune !
Come, join the melancholious croon
        O' Robin's reed !
His heart will never get aboon
        His Mailie dead.

MACPHERSON'S FAREWELL.'

FAREWELL, ye dungeons dark and strong,
  The wretch's destinie !
Macpherson's time will not be long
  On yonder gallows-tree.

Sae rantingly, sae wantonly,
　　Sae dauntingly gaed he ;
He play'd a spring, and danc'd it round,
　　Below the gallows-tree.

Oh ! what is death but parting breath ?—
　　On mony a bloody plain
I've dar'd his face, and in this place
　　I scorn him yet again !

Untie these bands from off my hands,
　　And bring to me my sword !
And there's no a man in all Scotland
　　But I'll brave him at a word.

I've liv'd a life of sturt and strife ;
　　I die by treacherie :
It burns my heart I must depart
　　And not avenged be.

Now farewell light—thou sunshine bright,
　　And all beneath the sky !
May coward shame distain his name,
　　The wretch that dares not die !

EPISTLE TO DAVIE,

A BROTHER POET.

WHILE winds frae off Ben Lomond blaw,
And bar the doors wi' driving snaw,
　　And hing us owre the ingle,
I set me down to pass the time,
And spin a verse or twa o' rhyme,
　　In hamely westlin jingle.
While frosty winds blaw in the drift,
　　Ben to the chimla lug,
I grudge a wee the great folks' gift,
　　That live sae bien and snug :

I tent less, and want less
　　Their roomy fireside ;
But hanker and canker
　　To see their cursed pride.

It's hardly in a body's pow'r
To keep, at times, frae being sour,
　To see how things are shar'd ;
How best o' chiels are whiles in want,
While coofs on countless thousands rant,
　And ken na how to wair't ;
But, Davie, lad, ne'er fash your head,
　Tho' we hae little gear,
We're fit to win our daily bread,
　As lang's we're hale and fier :
　　" Mair spier na, nor fear na,"
　　　Auld age ne'er mind a feg,
　　The last o't, the warst o't,
　　　Is only but to beg.

To lie in kilns and barns at e'en,
When banes are craz'd, and blood is thin,
　Is, doubtless, great distress !
Yet then content could make us blest ;
. Ev'n then, sometimes, we'd snatch a taste
　Of truest happiness.
The honest heart that's free frae a'
　Intended fraud or guile,
However fortune kick the ba',
　Has aye some cause to smile.
　　And mind still, you'll find still,
　　　A comfort this nae sma' ;
　　Nae mair then, we'll care then,
　　　Nae farther can we fa'.

What tho', like commoners of air,
We wander out we know not where,
　But either house or hall ?

Yet Nature's charms, the hills and woods,
The sweeping vales, and foaming floods,
  Are free alike to all.
In days when daisies deck the ground,
  And blackbirds whistle clear,
With honest joy our hearts will bound
  To see the coming year :
    On braes when we please, then,
      We'll sit and sowth a tune :
    Syne rhyme till't, we'll time till't,
      And sing't when we hae done.

It's no in titles nor in rank ;
It's no in wealth like Lon'on bank,
  To purchase peace and rest :
It's no in makin' muckle mair ;
It's no in books ; it's no in lear ;
  To make us truly blest ;
If happiness hae not her seat
  And centre in the breast,
We may be wise, or rich, or great,
  But never can be blest :
    Nae treasures, nor pleasures,
      Could make us happy lang :
    The heart aye's the part aye
      That makes us right or wrang.

Think ye, that sic as you and I,
Wha drudge and drive thro' wet and dry
  Wi' never-ceasing toil ;
Think ye, are we less blest than they
Wha scarcely tent us in their way,
  As hardly worth their while ?
Alas ! how aft in haughty mood,
  God's creatures they oppress !
Or else, neglecting a' that's guid,
  They riot in excess !
    Baith careless and fearless
      Of either heav'n or hell !

  Esteeming and deeming,
   It a' an idle tale!

Then let us cheerfu' acquiesce ;
Nor make our scanty pleasures less,
 By pining at our state ;
And, even should misfortunes come,
I, here wha sit, hae met wi' some,
 An's thankfu' for them yet.
They gie the wit of age to youth ;
 They let us ken oursel' ;
They make us see the naked truth,
 The real guid and ill.
  Tho' losses and crosses
   Be lessons right severe,
  There's wit there, ye'll get there,
   Ye'll find nae other where.

But tent me, Davie, ace o' hearts !
(To say aught else wad wrang the cartes,
 And flatt'ry I detest,)
This life has joys for you and I ;
And joys that riches ne'er could buy :
 And joys the very best.
There's a' the pleasures o' the heart,
 The lover and the frien' ;
Ye hae your Meg, your dearest part,
 And I my darling Jean !
  It warms me, it charms me,
   To mention but her name :
  It heats me, it beets me,
   And sets me a' on flame !

O, all ye pow'rs who rule above !
O Thou, whose very self art love !
 Thou know'st my words sincere !
The life-blood streaming thro' my heart,
Or my more dear immortal part,
 Is not more fondly dear !

When heart-corroding care and grief
  Deprive my soul of rest,
Her dear idea brings relief
  And solace to my breast,
    Thou being, All-seeing,
      O hear my fervent pray'r !
    Still take her, and make her
      Thy most peculiar care !

All hail ! ye tender feelings dear !
The smile of love, the friendly tear,
  The sympathetic glow !
Long since, this world's thorny ways
Had number'd out my weary days,
  Had it not been for you !
Fate still has blest me with a friend,
  In every care and ill ;
And oft a more endearing band,
  A tie more tender still.
    It lightens, it brightens
      The tenebrific scene,
    To meet with, and greet with,
      My Davie or my Jean !

O how that name inspires my style !
The words come skelpin, rank and file,
  Amaist before I ken !
The ready measure rins as fine
As Phœbus and the famous Nine
  Were glow'rin' owre my pen.
My spaviet Pegasus will limp,
  'Till ance he's fairly het ;
And then he'll hilch, and stilt, and jimp,
  And rin an unco fit :
    But lest then, the beast then,
      Should rue this hasty ride,
    I'll light now, and dight now
      His sweaty, wizen'd hide.

TO THE OWL.

Sᴀᴅ bird of night, what sorrow calls thee forth
To vent thy plaints thus in the midnight hour?

K

Is it some blast that gathers in the north,
   Threat'ning to nip the verdure of thy bow'r ?

Is it, sad owl, that Autumn strips the shade,
   And leaves thee here, unshelter'd and forlorn ?
Or fear that Winter will thy nest invade ?
   Or friendless melancholy bids thee mourn ?

Shut out, lone bird, from all the feather'd train,
   To tell thy sorrows to th' unheeding gloom ;
No friend to pity when thou dost complain,
   Grief all thy thought, and solitude thy home.

Sing on, sad mourner ! I will bless thy strain,
   And pleas'd in sorrow listen to thy song :
Sing on, sad mourner ! to the night complain,
   While the lone echo wafts thy notes along.

Is beauty less, when down the glowing cheek
   Sad, piteous tears, in native sorrows fall ?
Less kind the heart when anguish bids it break ?
   Less happy he who lists to pity's call ?

Ah no, sad owl ! nor is thy voice less sweet,
   That sadness tunes it, and that grief is there ;
That spring's gay notes, unskill'd, thou canst repeat ;
   That sorrow bids thee to the gloom repair.

Nor that the treble songsters of the day
   Are quite estrang'd, sad bird of night ! from thee ;
Nor that the thrush deserts the ev'ning spray,
   When darkness calls thee from thy reverie.

From some old tow'r, thy melancholy dome,
   While the grey walls, and desert solitudes,
Return each note, responsive to the gloom
   Of ivied coverts and surrounding woods.

There hooting, I will list more pleas'd to thee
  Than ever lover to the nightingale;
Or drooping wretch, oppress'd with misery,
  Lending his ear to some condoling tale.

EPISTLE TO JOHN LAPRAIK,

AN OLD SCOTTISH BARD.

WHILE briers an' woodbines budding green,
An' paitricks scraichin' loud at e'en,
An' morning pussie whiddin' seen,
      Inspire my muse,
This freedom in an unknown frien'
      I pray excuse.

On Fasten-e'en we had a rockin',
To ca' the crack and weave our stockin';
An' there was muckle fun an' jokin',
      Ye need na doubt;
At length we had a hearty yokin'
      At sang about.

There was ae sang amang the rest,
Aboon them a' it pleas'd me best,
That some kind husband had addrest
      To some sweet wife:
It thirl'd the heart-strings thro' the breast,
      A' to the life.

I've scarce heard ought describ'd sae weel,
What gen'rous, manly bosoms feel;
Thought I, "Can this be Pope, or Steele,
      Or Beattie's wark?"
They tauld me 'twas an odd kind chiel
      About Muirkirk.

It pat me fidgin-fain to hear't,
And sae about him there I spier't,
Then a' that ken't him round declar'd
      He had ingine,
That nane excell'd it, few cam near't,
      It was sae fine.

That set him to a pint of ale,
An' either douce or merry tale,
Or rhymes an' sangs he'd made himsel',
      Or witty catches:
'Tween Inverness and Teviotdale,
      He had few matches.

Then up I gat, an' swoor an aith,
Tho' I should pawn my pleugh and graith,
Or die a cadger pownie's death,
      At some dyke-back,
A pint an' gill I'd gie them baith
      To hear your crack.

But, first and foremost, I should tell,
Amaist as soon as I could spell,
I to the crambo-jingle fell,
      Tho' rude an' rough:
Yet crooning to a body's sel',
      Does weel eneugh.

I am nae poet, in a sense,
But just a rhymer, like by chance,
An' hae to learnin' nae pretence,
      Yet, what the matter?
Whene'er my muse does on me glance,
      I jingle at her.

Your critic-folk may cock their nose,
And say, "How can you e'er propose,
You, wha ken hardly verse frae prose,
      To mak' a sang?"

But, by your leaves, my learned foes,
    Ye're maybe wrang.

What's a' your jargon o' your schools,
Your Latin names for horns an' stools ;
If honest nature made you fools,
    What sairs your grammars ?
Ye'd better ta'en up spades and shools,
    Or knappin-hammers.

A set o' dull, conceited hashes,
Confuse their brains in college classes !
They gang in stirks, and come out asses,
    Plain truth to speak ;
An' syne they think to climb Parnassus
    By dint o' Greek.

Gie me ae spark o' Nature's fire !
That's a' the learning I desire ;
Then, tho' I drudge thro' dub an' mire
    At pleugh or cart,
My muse, though hamely in attire,
    May touch the heart.

O for a spunk o' Allan's glee,
Or Fergusson's, the bauld and slee,
Or bright Lapraik's, my friend to be,
    If I can hit it !
That would be lear enough for me,
    If I could get it !

Now, sir, if ye hae friends enow,
Tho' real friends, I b'lieve, are few,
Yet, if your catalogue be fu',
    I'se no insist,
But gif ye want ae friend that's true—
    I'm on your list.

I winna blaw about mysel';
As ill I like my fauts to tell;
But friends an' folk that wish me well,
         They sometimes roose me;
Tho' I maun own, as mony still
         As far abuse me.

There's ae wee faut they whiles lay to me,
I like the lasses—Gude forgie me!
For mony a plack they wheedle frae me,
         At dance or fair;
Maybe some ither thing they gie me
         They weel can spare.

But Mauchline race, or Mauchline fair,
I should be proud to meet you there;
We'se gie ae night's discharge to care,
         If we forgather,
An' hae a swap o' rhymin'-ware
         Wi' ane anither.

The four-gill chap, we'se gar him clatter,
An' kirsen him wi' reekin' water;
Syne we'll sit doun an' tak our whitter,
         To cheer our heart;
An' faith, we'se be acquainted better
         Before we part.

[There's naething like the honest nappy!
Whar'll ye e'er see men sae happy,
Or women sonsie, saft, an' sappy,
         'Tween morn and morn,
As them wha like to taste the drappy
         In glass or horn!

I've seen me daez't upon a time,
I scarce could wink, or see a styme;
Just ae half-mutchkin does me prime,
         Aught less is little,

Then back I rattle on the rhyme,
      As gleg's a whittle !]

Awa, ye selfish war'ly race,
Wha think that havins, sense, an' grace,
Ev'n love an' friendship, should give place
      To catch-the-plack !
I dinna like to see your face,
      Nor hear your crack.

But ye whom social pleasure charms,
Whose hearts the tide of kindness warms
Who hold your being on the terms,
      " Each aid the others,"
Come to my bowl, come to my arms,
      My friends, my brothers.

But, to conclude my long epistle,
As my auld pen's worn to the grissle ;
Twa lines frae you wad gar me fissle,
      Who am, most fervent,
While I can either sing, or whissle,
      Your friend and servant.

THE HUMBLE PETITION OF BRUAR WATER

TO THE NOBLE DUKE OF ATHOLE.

My Lord, I know your noble ear
    Woe ne'er assails in vain ;
Embolden'd thus, I beg you'll hear
    Your humble slave complain,
How saucy Phœbus' scorching beams,
    In flaming summer pride,
Dry-with'ring, waste my foamy streams,
    And drink my crystal tide.

The lightly-jumpin', glowrin' trouts,
    That thro' my waters play,
If, in their random, wanton spouts,
    They near the margin stray ;
If, hapless chance ! they linger lang,
    I'm scorching up so shallow,
They're left, the whit'ning stanes amang,
    In gasping death to wallow.

Last day I grat wi' spite and teen,
    As Poet Burns came by,
That, to a bard, I should be seen
    Wi' half my channel dry :
A panegyric rhyme, I ween,
    Even as I was he shor'd me ;
But had I in my glory been,
    He, kneeling, wad ador'd me.

Here, foaming down the shelvy rocks,
    In twisting strength I rin ;
There, high my boiling torrent smokes,
    Wild-roaring o'er a linn :
Enjoying large each spring and well,
    As nature gave them me,
I am, altho' I say't mysel',
    Worth gaun a mile to see.

Would then my noblest master please
    To grant my highest wishes,
He'll shade my banks wi' tow'ring trees,
    And bonnie spreading bushes.
Delighted doubly then, my Lord,
    You'll wander on my banks,
And listen mony a grateful bird
    Return you tuneful thanks.

The sober lav'rock, warbling wild,
    Shall to the skies aspire ;
The gowdspink, music's gayest child,
    Shall sweetly join the choir :

The blackbird strong, the lintwhite clear,
The mavis mild and mellow;
The robin pensive autumn cheer,
In all her locks of yellow.

L

This, too, a covert shall insure,
    To shield them from the storms ;
And coward maukins sleep secure
    Low in their grassy forms :
The shepherd here shall make his seat,
    To weave his crown of flow'rs ;
Or find a shelt'ring safe retreat,
    From prone descending show'rs.

And here, by sweet endearing stealth,
    Shall meet the loving pair,
Despising worlds, with all their wealth,
    As empty idle care.
The flow'rs shall vie in all their charms
    The hour of heav'n to grace,
And birks extend their fragrant arms
    To screen the dear embrace.

Here haply, too, at vernal dawn,
    Some musing bard may stray,
And eye the smoking, dewy lawn,
    And misty mountain grey ;
Or, by the reaper's nightly beam,
    Mild chequ'ring thro' the trees,
Rave to my darkly-dashing stream,
    Hoarse swelling on the breeze.

Let lofty firs, and ashes cool,
    My lowly banks o'erspread,
And view, deep-bending in the pool,
    Their shadows' wat'ry bed !
Let fragrant birks in woodbines drest
    My craggy cliffs adorn ;
And, for the little songster's nest,
    The close-embow'ring thorn.

So may old Scotia's darling hope,
    Your little angel band,
Spring, like their fathers, up to prop
    Their honour'd native land !

So may, thro' Albion's farthest ken,
To social-flowing glasses,
The grace be—"Athole's honest men,
And Athole's bonny lasses!"

A PRAYER,

LEFT BY THE AUTHOR AT A REVEREND FRIEND'S
HOUSE IN THE ROOM WHERE HE SLEPT.

O THOU dread Pow'r, who reign'st above!
I know Thou wilt me hear,
When, for this scene of peace and love,
I make my prayer sincere.

The hoary sire—the mortal stroke,
Long, long, be pleased to spare
To bless his filial little flock,
And show what good men are.

She, who her lovely offspring eyes
With tender hopes and fears,
O, bless her with a mother's joys,
But spare a mother's tears!

Their hope—their stay—their darling youth,
In manhood's dawning blush—
Bless him, thou GOD of love and truth,
Up to a parent's wish!

The beauteous, seraph sister-band,
With earnest tears I pray,
Thou know'st the snares on ev'ry hand—
Guide Thou their steps alway!

When soon or late they reach that coast,
O'er life's rough ocean driv'n,
May they rejoice, no wand'rer lost,
A family in Heav'n!

HALLOWEEN.[8]

THE following poem will, by many readers, be well enough understood; but for the sake of those who are unacquainted with the manners and traditions of the country.where the scene is cast, notes are given at the end of the volume, which explain the principal charms and spells of that night, so big with prophecy to the peasantry in the west of Scotland. The passion of prying into futurity makes a striking part of the history of human nature in its rude state, in all ages and nations; and it may be some entertainment to a philosophic mind, if any such should honour the author with a perusal, to see the remains of it among the more unenlightened in our own.

> "Yes! let the rich deride, the proud disdain,
>   The simple pleasures of the lowly train:
>   To me more dear, congenial to my heart,
>   One native charm, than all the gloss of art."
>   GOLDSMITH.

UPON that night, when fairies light
  On Cassilis Downans[a] dance,
Or owre the lays, in splendid blaze,
  On sprightly coursers prance;
Or for Colean, the route is ta'en,
  Beneath the moon's pale beams;
There, up the cove,[b] to stray an' rove,
  Amang the rocks and streams
              To sport that night.

Amang the bonnie winding banks
  Where Doon rins, wimplin', clear,
Where Bruce[c] ance rul'd the martial ranks,
  An' shook his Carrick spear,
Some merry, friendly, countra-folks,
  Together did convene,
To burn their nits, an' pou their stocks,
  An' haud their Halloween
              Fu' blythe that night.

The lasses feat, an' cleanly neat,
  Mair braw than when they're fine;
Their faces blythe, fu' sweetly kythe,
  Hearts leal, an' warm, an' kin':
The lads sae trig, wi' wooer-babs,
  Weel knotted on their garten,
Some unco blate, an' some wi' gabs,
  Gar lasses hearts gang startin'
              Whiles fast at night.

Then, first and foremost, thro' the kail,
  Their stocks^d maun a' be sought ance ;
They steek their een, an' graip an' wale,
  For muckle anes an' straught anes.
Poor hav'rel Will fell aff the drift,
  An' wander'd thro' the bow-kail,
An' pou't, for want o' better shift,
  A runt was like a sow-tail,
                    Sae bow't that night.

Then, straught or crooked, yird or nane,
  They roar an' cry a' throu'ther ;
The vera wee-things, todlin', rin,
  Wi' stocks out-owre their shouther ;
An' gif the custoc's sweet or sour,
  Wi' joctelegs they taste them ;
Syne coziely, aboon the door,
  Wi' cannie care, they've placed them,
                    To lie that night.

The lasses staw frae 'mang them a'
  To pou their stalks o' corn :
But Rab slips out, an' jinks about,
  Behint the muckle thorn :
He grippit Nelly hard an' fast ;
  Loud skirl'd a' the lasses ;
But her tap-pickle maist was lost,
  When kuittlin' in the fause-house
                    Wi' him that night.

The auld guidwife's weel-hoorded nits
  Are round an' round divided,
An' mony lads' an' lasses' fates
  Are there that night decided :
Some kindle, couthie, side by side,
  An' burn thegither trimly ;
Some start awa' wi saucy pride,
  An' jump out-owre the chimlie
                    Fu' high that night.

Jean slips in twa wi' tentie e'e ;
    Wha 'twas she wadna tell ;
But this is Jock, an' this is me,
    She says in to hersel' :
He bleez'd owre her, an' she owre him,
    As they wad never mair part ;
'Till, fuff ! he started up the lum,
    An' Jean had e'en a sair heart
                To see't that night.

Poor Willie, wi' his bow-kail runt,
    Was brunt wi' primsie Mallie ;
An' Mallie, nae doubt, took the drunt,
    To be compar'd to Willie ;
Mall's nit lap out wi' pridefu' fling,
    An' her ain fit it brunt it ;
While Willie lap, an' swoor by jing,
    'Twas just the way he wanted
                To be that night.

Nell had the fause-house in her min',
    She pits hersel' an' Rob in ;
In loving bleeze they sweetly join,
    Till white in ase they're sobbin' ;
Nell's heart was dancin' at the view,
    She whisper'd Rob to leuk for't :
Rob, stowlins, prie'd her bonnie mou',
    Fu' cozie in the neuk for't,
                Unseen that night.

But Merran sat behint their backs,
    Her thoughts on Andrew Bell ;
She lea'es them gashin' at their cracks,
    An' slips out by hersel' :
She thro' the yard the nearest taks,
    An' to the kiln she goes then,
An' darklins graipit for the bauks,
    An' in the blue-clue* throws then,
              Right fear't that night.

An' aye she win't, an' aye she swat,
  I wat she made nae jaukin',
'Till something held within the pat,
  Guid Lord ! but she was quakin' !
But whether 'twas the deil himsel',
  Or whether 'twas a bauk-en',
Or whether it was Andrew Bell,
  She didna wait on talkin'
              To spier that night.

Wee Jenny to her grannie says,
  "Will ye go wi' me, grannie ?
I'll eat the apple at the glass,'
  I gat frae Uncle Johnnie : "
She fuff't her pipe wi' sic a lunt,
  In wrath she was sae vap'rin',
She notic't na' an aizle brunt
  Her braw new worset apron
              Out thro' that night.

"Ye little skelpie-limmer's face !
  How daur you try sic sportin',
As seek the foul thief ony place,
  For him to spae your fortune ?
Nae doubt but ye may get a sight !
  Great cause ye hae to fear it ;
For mony a ane has gotten a fright,
  An' liv'd an' di'd deleerit
              On sic a night.

'Ae hairst afore the Sherramoor,—
  I mind't as weel's yestreen,
I was a gilpey then, I'm sure
  I wasna past fyfteen ;
The simmer had been cauld an' wat,
  An' stuff was unco green ;
An' aye a rantin' kirn we gat,
  An' just on Halloween
              It fell that night.

" Our stibble-rig was Rab M'Graen,
  A clever, sturdy fallow :
He's sin' gat Eppie Sim wi' wean,
  That liv'd in Achmacalla :

He gat hemp-seed, * I mind it weel,
  An' he made unco light o't ;
But mony a day was by himsel',
  He was sae sairly frighted
        That very night."

Then up gat fechtin' Jamie Fleck,
  An' he swoor by his conscience,
That he could saw hemp-seed a peck;
  For it was a' but nonsense.
The auld guidman raught down the pock,
  An' out a handfu' gied him;
Syne bad him slip frae 'mang the folk,
  Some time when nae ane see'd him,
          An' try't that night.

He marches thro' amang the stacks,
  Tho' he was something sturtin';
The graip he for a harrow taks,
  An' haurls at his curpin;
An' ev'ry now an' then he says,
  "Hemp seed, I saw thee,
An' her that is to be my lass,
  Come after me, an' draw thee
          As fast this night."

He whistled up Lord Lennox' march,
  To keep his courage cheerie;
Altho' his hair began to arch,
  He was sae fley'd an' eerie;
Till presently he hears a squeak,
  An' then a grane an' gruntle;
He by his shouther gae a keek,
  An' tumbl'd wi' a wintle
          Out-owre that night.

He roar'd a horrid murder-shout,
  In dreadfu' desperation!
An' young an' auld came rinnin' out
  An' hear the sad narration:
He swoor 'twas hilchin Jean M'Craw,
  Or crouchie Merran Humphie,
Till, stop! she trotted thro' them a';
  An' wha was it but grumphie
          Asteer that night!

Meg fain wad to the barn hae gane,
    To win three wechts o' naething ;'
But for to meet the deil her lane,
    She pat but little faith in :
She gies the herd a pickle nits,
    An' twa red-cheekit apples,
To watch, while for the barn she sets,
    In hopes to see Tam Kipples
                That very night.

She turns the key wi' cannie thraw,
    An' owre the threshold ventures ;
But first on Sawnie gies a ca',
    Syne bauldly in she enters :
A ratton rattled up the wa',
    An' she cried, Lord, preserve her !
An' ran thro' midden-hole an' a',
    An' pray'd wi' zeal an' fervour,
                Fu' fast that night.

They hoy't out Will, wi' sair advice ;
    They hecht him some fine braw ane ;
It chanc'd the stack he faddom'd thrice,"
    Was timmer-propt for thrawin' ;
He tacks a swirlie, auld moss-oak,
    For some black, grousome carlin ;
An' loot a winz, an' drew a stroke,
    Till skin in blypes cam haurlin'
                Aff's nieves that night.

A wanton widow Leezie was,
    As canty as a kittlin ;
But, och ! that night, amang the shaws,
    She got a fearfu' settlin' !
She thro' the whins, an' by the cairn,
    An' owre the hill gaed scrievin',
Whare three lairds' lands met at a burn,"
    To dip her left sark-sleeve in,
                Was bent that night.

Whiles owre a linn the burnie plays,
    As thro' the glen it wimpl't;
Whiles round a rocky scaur it strays;
    Whiles in a wiel it dimpl't;

Whiles glitter'd to the nightly rays,
   Wi' bickering, dancing dazzle ;
Whiles cookit underneath the braes,
   Below the spreading hazel,
             Unseen that night.

Amang the brachens, on the brae,
   Between her an' the moon,
The deil, or else an outler quey,
   Gat up an' gie a croon :
Poor Leezie's heart maist lap the hool !
   Near lav'rock-height she jumpit ;
But mist a fit, an' in the pool
   Out-owre the lugs she plumpit,
             Wi' a plunge that night.

In order, on the clean hearth-stane,
   The luggies three ° are ranged,
And ev'ry time great care is ta'en
   To see them duly changed :
Auld Uncle John, wha wedlock's joys
   Sin' Mar's-year did desire,
Because he gat the toom dish thrice,
   He heav'd them on the fire
             In wrath that night.

Wi' merry sangs, an' friendly cracks,
   I wat they didna weary ;
An' unco' tales, an' funny jokes,
   Their sports were cheap and cheery ;
Till butter'd so'ns,° wi' fragrant lunt,
   Set a' their gabs a-steerin' ;
Syne, wi' a social glass o' strunt,
   They parted aff careerin'
             Fu' blythe that night.

TAM SAMSON'S ELEGY.[1]

" An honest man's the noblest work of God."—POPE.

HAS auld Kilmarnock seen the deil?
Or great M'Kinlay thrawn his heel?
Or Robinson again grown weel,
    To preach an' read?
" Na, waur than a' !" cries ilka chiel,
    Tam Samson's dead !

Kilmarnock lang may grunt an' grane,
An' sigh, an' sob, an' greet her lane,
An' cleed her bairns, man, wife, and wean,
    In mourning weed ;
To death she's dearly paid the kane—
    Tam Samson's dead !

The brethren o' the mystic level
May hing their head in waefu' bevel,
While by their nose the tears will revel,
    Like ony bead ;
Death's gi'en the lodge an unco devel—
    Tam Samson's dead !

When winter muffles up his cloak,
And binds the mire up like a rock ;
When to the lochs the curlers flock,
    Wi' gleesome speed,
Wha will they station at the cock ?—
    Tam Samson's dead !

He was the king o' a' the core,
To guard, or draw, or wick a bore ;
Or up the rink like Jehu roar
    In time o' need ;
But now he lags on death's hog-score,—
    Tam Samson's dead !

Now safe the stately sawmont sail,
And trouts be-dropp'd wi' crimson hail,
And eels weel kenn'd for souple tail,
    And geds for greed,
Since dark in death's fish-creel we wail
    Tam Samson dead !

Rejoice, ye birring paitricks a' ;
Ye cootie moorcocks, crousely craw ;
Ye maukins, cock your fuds fu' braw,
    Withouten dread ;
Your mortal fae is now awa',—
    Tam Samson's dead !

That waefu' morn be ever mourn'd
Saw him in shootin' graith adorn'd,
While pointers round impatient burn'd,
    Frae couples freed ;
But, och ! he gaed an' ne'er returned !
    Tam Samson's dead !

In vain auld age his body batters ;
In vain the gout his ankles fetters ;
In vain the burns cam' doun like waters,
    An acre braid !
Now ev'ry auld wife, greetin', clatters,
    Tam Samson's dead !

Owre mony a weary hag he limpit,
An' aye the tither shot he thumpit,
Till coward death behind him jumpit,
    Wi' deadly feide ;
Now he proclaims, wi' tout o' trumpet,
    Tam Samson's dead !

When at his heart he felt the dagger,
He reel'd his wonted bottle-swagger,
But yet he drew the mortal trigger
    Wi' weel-aim'd heed ;

"L—d, five!" he cry'd, an' owre did stagger—
      Tam Samson's dead!

Ilk hoary hunter mourn'd a brither;
Ilk sportsman youth bemoan'd a father;
Yon auld grey stane, among the heather,
      Marks out his head,
Whare Burns has wrote, in rhyming blether,
      Tam Samson's dead!

There low he lies, in lasting rest;
Perhaps upon his mould'ring breast
Some spitefu' muirfowl bigs her nest,
      To hatch an' breed;
Alas! nae mair he'll them molest!
      Tam Samson's dead!

When August winds the heather wave,
And sportsmen wander by yon grave,
Three volleys let his mem'ry crave
      O' pouther an' lead,
'Till Echo answer, frae her cave,
      Tam Samson's dead!

Heav'n rest his saul, whare'er he be!
Is th' wish o' mony mae than me;
He had twa fauts, or may be three,
      Yet what remead?
Ae social, honest man want we;
      Tam Samson's dead!

EPITAPH.

Tam Samson's weel-worn clay here lies
  Ye canting zealots spare him!
If honest worth in heaven rise,
  Ye'll mend or ye win near him.

PER CONTRA.

Go, Fame, an' canter like a filly,
Thro' a' the streets an' neuks o' Killie,
Tell ev'ry social, honest billie
        To cease his grievin',
For yet, unskaith'd by death's gleg gullie,
        Tam Samson's livin'.

MAN WAS MADE TO MOURN.

A DIRGE.

When chill November's surly blast
Made fields and forests bare,
One ev'ning, as I wander'd forth
Along the banks of Ayr,

I spy'd a man whose aged step
  Seem'd weary, worn with care ;
His face was furrow'd o'er with years,
  And hoary was his hair.

" Young stranger, whither wand'rest thou ? "
  Began the rev'rend sage ;
" Does thirst of wealth thy step constrain,
  Or youthful pleasure's rage ?
Or haply, prest with cares and woes,
  Too soon thou hast began
To wander forth, with me, to mourn
  The miseries of man.

" The sun that overhangs yon moors,
  Out spreading far and wide,
Where hundreds labour to support
  A haughty lordling's pride ;
I've seen yon weary winter sun
  Twice forty times return,
And ev'ry time has added proofs
  That man was made to mourn.

" O man ! while in thy early years,
  How prodigal of time !
Misspending all thy precious hours,
  Thy glorious youthful prime !
Alternate follies take the sway ;
  Licentious passions burn :
Which tenfold force gives nature's law,
  That man was made to mourn.

" Look not alone on youthful prime,
  Or manhood's active might :
Man then is useful to his kind,
  Supported is his right :
But see him on the edge of life,
  With cares and sorrows worn ;
Then age and want—O ill-match'd pair !—
  Show man was made to mourn.

N

"A few seem favourites of fate,
    In pleasure's lap carest ;
  Yet, think not all the rich and great
    Are likewise truly blest.
  But, oh ! what crowds in ev'ry land
    Are wretched and forlorn !
  Thro' weary life this lesson learn—
    That man was made to mourn.

" Many and sharp the num'rous ills
    Inwoven with our frame !
  More pointed still we make ourselves,
    Regret, remorse, and shame !
  And man, whose heav'n-erected face
    The smiles of love adorn,
  Man's inhumanity to man
    Makes countless thousands mourn !

"See yonder poor, o'er labour'd wight,
    So abject, mean, and vile,
  Who begs a brother of the earth
    To give him leave to toil ;
  And see his lordly fellow-worm
    The poor petition spurn,
  Unmindful, tho' a weeping wife
    And helpless offspring mourn.

" If I'm design'd yon lordling's slave—
    By Nature's law design'd—
  Why was an independent wish
    E'er planted in my mind ?
  If not, why am I subject to
    His cruelty, or scorn ?
  Or why has man the will and pow'r
    To make his fellow mourn ?

" Yet, let not this too much, my son,
    Disturb thy youthful breast ;
  This partial view of human-kind
    Is surely not the last !

The poor, oppressed, honest man,
    Had never, sure, been born,
Had there not been some recompense
    To comfort those that mourn !

"O Death ! the poor man's dearest friend—
    The kindest and the best !
Welcome the hour my aged limbs
    Are laid with thee at rest !
The great, the wealthy, fear thy blow,
    From pomp and pleasure torn ;
But, oh ! a blest relief to those
    That weary-laden mourn !"

REMORSE : A FRAGMENT.

OF all the numerous ills that hurt our peace,
That press the soul, or wring the mind with anguish,
Beyond comparison, the worst are those
That to our folly or our guilt we owe.
In every other circumstance, the mind
Has this to say—"It was no deed of mine ;"
But when, to all the evil of misfortune,
This sting is added—"Blame thy foolish self,"
Or, worser far, the pangs of keen remorse—
The torturing, gnawing consciousness of guilt—
Of guilt, perhaps, where we've involved others,
The young, the innocent, who fondly loved us,
Nay, more—that very love their cause of ruin !
Oh, burning hell ! in all thy store of torments,
There's not a keener lash !
Lives there a man so firm, who, while his heart
Feels all the bitter horrors of his crime,
Can reason down its agonising throbs ;
And, after proper purpose of amendment,
Can firmly force his jarring thoughts to peace ?
Oh, happy, happy, enviable man !
Oh, glorious magnanimity of soul !

LINES WRITTEN IN FRIARS-CARSE HERMITAGE,

ON THE BANKS OF NITH.

Thou whom chance may hither lead,
Be thou clad in russet weed,
Be thou deckt in silken stole,
'Grave these maxims on thy soul :

Life is but a day at most,
Sprung from night, in darkness lost ;
Day, how rapid in its flight—
Day, how few must see the night ;
Hope not sunshine every hour,
Fear not clouds will always lour.

Happiness is but a name,
Make content and ease thy aim :
Ambition is a meteor gleam ;
Fame an idle restless dream :
Pleasures, insects on the wing
Round Peace, the tend'rest flower of Spring !
Those that sip the dew alone,
Make the butterflies thy own ;
Those that would the bloom devour,
Crush the locusts—save the flower.
For the future be prepar'd,
Guard whatever thou canst guard ;
But thy utmost duly done,
Welcome what thou canst not shun.
Follies past give thou to air,
Make their consequence thy care :
Keep the name of man in mind,
And dishonour not thy kind.
Reverence, with lowly heart,
Him whose wond'rous work thou art ;
Keep His goodness still in view,
Thy Trust—and thy Example, too.

Stranger, go ! Heaven be thy guide ;
Quoth the Beadsman on Nithside.

THE AULD FARMER'S NEW-YEAR MORNING SALUTATION TO HIS AULD MARE MAGGIE,

ON GIVING HER THE ACCUSTOMED RIP OF CORN TO HANSEL IN THE NEW YEAR.

A GUID New Year I wish thee, Maggie!
Hae, there's a rip to thy auld baggie :

Tho' thou's howe-backit, now, an' knaggie,
          I've seen the day
Thou could hae gaen like ony staggie
          Out-owre the lay.

Tho' now thou's dowie, stiff, and crazy, .
An' thy auld hide's as white's a daisy,
I've seen thee dappl't, sleek, an' glazie,
          A bonny grey :
He should been tight that daur't to raize thee,
          Ance in a day.

Thou ance was i' the foremost rank,
A filly buirdly, steeve, an' swank,
An' set weel doun a shapely shank,
          As e'er tread yird ;
An' could hae flown out-owre a stank
          Like ony bird.

It's now some nine-and-twenty year,
Sin' thou was my guid father's meere :
He gied me thee, o' tocher clear,
          An' fifty mark ;
Tho' it was sma', 'twas weel-won gear,
          An' thou was stark.

When first I gaed to woo my Jenny,
Ye then was trottin' wi' your minnie :
Tho' ye was trickie, slee, an' funnie,
          Ye ne'er was donsie ;
But hamely, tawie, quiet, an' cannie,
          An' unco sonsie.

That day ye pranc'd wi' muckle pride,
When ye bure hame my bonny bride :
An' sweet an' gracefu' she did ride,
          Wi' maiden air !
Kyle-Stewart I could hae bragged wide
          For sic a pair.

Tho' now ye dow but hoyte an' hoble,
An' wintle like a saumont-coble,
That day ye was a jinker noble,
                    For heels an' win' !
An' ran them till they a' did wauble,
                    Far, far behin' !

When thou an' I were young an' skeigh,
An' stable-meals at fairs were dreigh,
How thou would prance, an' snore, an' skreigh,
                    An' tak the road !
Town's bodies ran, and stood abeigh,
                    An' ca't thee mad.

When thou was corn't, an' I was mellow,
We took the road aye like a swallow :
At Brooses thou had ne'er a fellow,
                    For pith an' speed ;
But every tail thou pay't them hollow,
                    Whare'er thou gaed.

The sma' droop-rumpl't hunter cattle
Might aiblins waur't thee for a brattle ;
But sax Scotch miles thou try't their mettle,
                    An' gar't them whaizle :
Nae whip nor spur, but just a wattle
                    O' saugh or hazel.

Thou was a noble fittie-lan',
As e'er in tug or tow was drawn !
Aft thee an' I, in aught hours gaun,
                    In guid March weather,
Hae turn'd sax rood beside our han',
                    For days thegither.

Thou never braindg't an' fech't, an' fliskit,
But thy auld tail thou wad hae whiskit,

An' spread abreed thy weel-fill'd brisket,
                    Wi' pith an' pow'r,
'Till spritty knowes wad rair't and risket,
                    An' slypet owre.

When frosts lay lang, an' snaws were deep,
An' threaten'd labour back to keep,
I gied thy cog a wee bit heap
                    Aboon the timmer;
I kenn'd my Maggie wadna sleep
                    For that, or simmer.

In cart or car thou never reestit;
The steyest brae thou wad hae fac'd it;
Thou never lap, an' stent', an' breastit,
                    Then stood to blaw;
But just thy step a wee thing hastit,
                    Thou snoov't awa.

My pleugh is now thy bairn-time a';
Four gallant brutes as e'er did draw;
Forbye sax mae, I've sell't awa',
                    That thou hast nurst:
They drew me thretteen pund an' twa,
                    The vera warst.

Mony a sair daurk we twa hae wrought,
An' wi' the weary warl' fought!
An' mony an anxious day, I thought
                    We wad be beat!
Yet here to crazy age we're brought,
                    Wi' something yet.

An' thinkna, my auld trusty servan',
That now perhaps thou's less deservin',
An' thy auld days may end in starvin',
                    For my last fou,
A heapit stimpart, I'll reserve ane
                    Laid by for you.

We've worn to crazy years thegither ;
We'll toyte about wi' ane anither ;
Wi' tentie care I'll flit thy tether
         To some hain'd rig,
Whare ye may nobly rax your leather,
         Wi' sma' fatigue.

STANZAS IN THE PROSPECT OF DEATH.

Why am I loth to leave this earthly scene ?
  Have I so found it full of pleasing charms ?
Some drops of joy with draughts of ill between :
  Some gleams of sunshine 'mid renewing storms.
Is it departing pangs my soul alarms ?
  Or death's unlovely, dreary, dark abode ?
For guilt, for guilt, my terrors are in arms :
  I tremble to approach an angry God,
And justly smart beneath His sin-avenging rod.

Fain would I say, " Forgive my foul offence ! "
  Fain promise never more to disobey ;
But should my Author health again dispense,
  Again I might desert fair virtue's way :
Again in folly's path might go astray ;
  Again exalt the brute and sink the man ;
Then how should I for Heav'nly mercy pray,
  Who act so counter Heav'nly mercy's plan ?
Who sin so oft have mourn'd, yet to temptation ran ?

O Thou great Governor of all below !
  If I may dare a lifted eye to Thee,
Thy nod can make the tempest cease to blow,
  Or still the tumult of the raging sea :
With that controuling pow'r assist ev'n me,
  Those headlong furious passions to confine ,
For all unfit I feel my pow'rs to be,
  To rule their torrent in th' allowed line ;
O, aid me with Thy help, Omnipotence Divine !

LINES WRITTEN WITH A PENCIL

OVER THE CHIMNEY-PIECE IN THE PARLOUR OF THE INN AT KENMORE, TAYMOUTH.

ADMIRING Nature in her wildest grace,
These northern scenes with weary feet I trace;
O'er many a winding dale and painful steep,
Th' abodes of covey'd grouse and timid sheep,
My savage journey, curious, I pursue,
'Till fam'd Breadalbane opens to my view.—
The meeting cliffs each deep-sunk glen divides,
The woods, wild scatter'd, clothe their ample sides;
Th' outstretching lake, embosomed 'mong the hills,
The eye with wonder and amazement fills;
The Tay, meand'ring sweet in infant pride,
The palace, rising on its verdant side;
The lawns, wood-fring'd in Nature's native taste;
The hillocks, dropt in Nature's careless haste;
The arches, striding o'er the new-born stream;
The village, glitt'ring in the noon-tide beam—

    *   *   *   *

Poetic ardours in my bosom swell,
Lone wand'ring by the hermit's mossy cell:
The sweeping theatre of hanging woods;
Th' incessant roar of headlong tumbling floods—

    *   *   *   *

Here Poesy might wake her heav'n-taught lyre,
And look through Nature with creative fire;
Here, to the wrongs of Fate half-reconcil'd,
Misfortune's lighten'd steps might wander wild;
And Disappointment, in these lonely bounds,
Find balm to soothe her bitter, rankling wounds:
Here heart-struck Grief might heav'n-ward stretch her scan,
And injur'd Worth forget and pardon man.

    *   *   *   *

THE VISION.[10]

DUAN FIRST.

The sun had clos'd the winter day,
The curlers quat their roaring play,

An' hunger'd maukin ta'en her way,
          To kailyards green,
While faithless snaws ilk step betray
          Whare she has been.

The thresher's weary flingin'-tree
The lee-lang day had tired me ;
An' when the day had closed his e'e,
          Far i' the west,
Ben' i' the spence, right pensivelie,
          I gaed to rest.

There, lanely, by the ingle cheek,
I sat and ey'd the spewing reek,
That fill'd, wi' hoast-provoking smeek,
          The auld clay biggin':
An' heard the restless rattons squeak
          About the riggin'.

All in this mottie, misty clime,
I backward mus'd on wasted time,
How I had spent my youthfu' prime,
          An' done naething,
But stringin' blethers up in rhyme,
          For fools to sing.

Had I to guid advice but harkit,
I might, by this, hae led a market,
Or strutted in a bank an' clerkit
          My cash account :
While here, half-mad, half-fed, half-sarkit,
          Is a' th' amount.

I started, mutt'ring, Blockhead : coof !
An' heav'd on high my waukit loof,
To swear by a' yon starry roof,
          Or some rash aith,
That I, henceforth, would be rhyme-proof,
          Till my last breath—

When, click ! the string the sneck did draw ;
An', jee ! the door gaed to the wa' ;
An' by my ingle-lowe I saw,
   Now bleezin' bright,
A tight, outlandish hizzie, braw,
   Come full in sight.

Ye needna doubt, I held my whisht ;
The infant aith, half-form'd, was crusht ;
I glow'r'd as eerie's I'd been dusht
   In some wild glen ;
When sweet, like modest worth, she blusht,
   An' stepped ben.

Green, slender, leaf-clad holly-boughs
Were twisted, gracefu', round her brows,
I took her for some Scottish Muse,
   By that same token :
An' come to stop those reckless vows,
   Would soon been broken.

A "hare-brain'd, sentimental trace"
Was strongly marked in her face ;
A wildly-witty, rustic grace
   Shone full upon her ;
Her eye, ev'n turned on empty space,
   Beam'd keen with honour.

Down flow'd her robe, a tartan sheen,
'Till half a leg was scrimply seen ;
And such a leg ! my bonny Jean
   Could only peer it ;
Sae straught, sae taper, tight, and clean,
   Nane else came near it.

Her mantle large, of greenish hue,
My gazing wonder chiefly drew ;
Deep lights and shades, bold-mingling, threw
   A lustre grand ;

And seem'd, to my astonish'd view,
      A well-known land.

Here, rivers in the sea were lost,;
There, mountains to the skies were tost :
Here, tumbling billows mark'd the coast
      With surging foam ;
There, distant shone Art's lofty boast,
      The lordly dome.

Here, Doon pour'd down his far-fetch'd floods ;
There, well-fed Irwine stately thuds :
Auld hermit Ayr staw through his woods,
      On to the shore ;
And many a lesser torrent scuds,
      With seeming roar.

Low, in a sandy valley spread,
An ancient borough[a] rear'd her head :
Still, as in Scottish story read,
      She boasts a race
To ev'ry nobler virtue bred,
      And polish'd grace.

By stately tow'r or palace fair,
Or ruins pendent in the air,
Bold stems of heroes, here and there,
      I could discern ;
Some seem'd to muse, some seem'd to dare,
      With features stern.

My heart did glowing transport feel,
To see a race[b] heroic wheel,
And brandish round the deep-dy'd steel
      In sturdy blows ;
While back-recoiling seem'd to reel
      Their Southron foes.

His country's saviour,[c] mark him well !
Bold Richardton's[d] heroic swell ;

The chief on Sark' who glorious fell,
      In high command ;
And he whom ruthless fates expel
      His native land.

There, where a sceptr'd Pictish shade
Stalk'd round his ashes lowly laid,
I mark'd a martial race, portray'd
      In colours strong ;
Bold, soldier-featur'd, undismay'd
      They strode along.

Thro' many a wild romantic grove,
Near many a hermit-fancied cove,
(Fit haunts for friendship or for love),
      In musing mood,
An aged judge, I saw him rove,
      Dispensing good.

With deep-struck reverential awe
The learned sire and son I saw,
To Nature's God and Nature's law
      They gave their lore,
This, all its source and end to draw ;
      That, to adore.

Brydone's brave ward' I well could spy,
Beneath old Scotia's smiling eye :
Who call'd on Fame, low standing by,
      To hand him on,
Where many a patriot name on high
      And hero shone.

DUAN SECOND.

WITH musing-deep, astonish'd stare,
I view'd the heav'nly seeming fair ;
A whisp'ring throb did witness bear
      Of kindred sweet,

When with an elder sister's air
        She did me greet.

"All hail! my own inspired bard!
In me thy native Muse regard;
Nor longer mourn thy fate is hard,
        Thus poorly low! ·
I come to give thee such reward
        As we bestow.

"Know, the great genius of this land
Has many a light, aërial band,
Who, all beneath his high command,
        Harmoniously,
As arts or arms they understand,
        Their labours ply.

"They Scotia's race among them share:
Some fire the soldier on to dare:
Some rouse the patriot up to bare
        Corruption's heart:
Some teach the bard, a darling care,
        The tuneful art.

"'Mong swelling floods of reeking gore,
They, ardent, kindling spirits, pour;
Or, 'mid the venal senate's roar,
        They, sightless, stand,
To mend the honest patriot-lore,
        And grace the hand.

"And when the bard, or hoary sage,
Charm or instruct the future age,
They bind the wild, poetic rage
        In energy,
Or point the inconclusive page
        Full on the eye.

"Hence Fullarton, the brave and young;
Hence Dempster's zeal-inspired tongue;

Hence sweet harmonious Beattie sung
        His Minstrel lays;
Or tore, with noble ardour stung,
        The sceptic's bays.

" 'To lower orders are assign'd
The humbler ranks of humankind,
The rustic bard, the lab'ring hind,
        The artizan;
All choose, as various they're inclin'd,
        The various man.

" When yellow waves the heavy grain,
The threat'ning storm some, strongly, rein;
Some teach to meliorate the plain,
        With tillage skill;
And some instruct the shepherd-train,
        Blythe o'er the hill.

" Some hint the lover's harmless wile;
Some grace the maiden's artless smile;
Some soothe the lab'rer's weary toil,
        For humble gains,
And make his cottage-scenes beguile
        His cares and pains.

" Some, bounded to a district-space,
Explore at large man's infant race,
To mark the embryotic trace
        Of rustic bard:
And careful note each op'ning grace,
        A guide and guard.

" Of these am I—Coila my name,
And this district as mine I claim,
Where once the Campbells, chiefs of fame,
        Held ruling pow'r;
I mark'd thy embryo tuneful flame,
        Thy natal hour.

P

" With future hope, I oft would gaze,
  Fond, on thy little early ways,
  Thy rudely-caroll'd, chiming phrase,
                    In uncouth rhymes,
  Fir'd at the simple, artless lays
                    Of other times.

" I saw thee seek the sounding shore,
  Delighted with the dashing roar ;
  Or when the north his fleecy store
                    Drove thro' the sky,
  I saw grim nature's visage hoar
                    Struck thy young eye.

" Or when the deep green-mantl'd earth
  Warm cherish'd every flow'ret's birth,
  And joy and music pouring forth
                    In ev'ry grove,
  I saw thee eye the general mirth
                    With boundless love.

" When ripen'd fields, and azure skies,
  Call'd forth the reaper's rustling noise,
  I saw thee leave their ev'ning joys,
                    And lonely stalk,
  To vent thy bosom's swelling rise
                    In pensive walk.

" When youthful love, warm-blushing, strong,
  Keen-shivering shot thy nerves along,
  Those accents, grateful to thy tongue,
                    Th' adored Name,
  I taught thee how to pour in song,
                    To soothe thy flame.

" I saw thy pulse's maddening play,
  Wild, send thee pleasure's devious way,
  Misled by Fancy's meteor-ray,
                    By passion driven ;

But yet the light that led astray
          Was light from Heaven.

" I taught thy manners-painting strains,
  The loves, the ways of simple swains,
  Till now, o'er all my wide domains
          Thy fame extends ;
  And some, the pride of Coila's plains,
          Become thy friends.

" Thou canst not learn, nor can I show,
  To paint with Thomson's landscape glow ;
  Or wake the bosom-melting throe,
          With Shenstone's art ;
  Or pour, with Gray, the moving flow
          Warm on the heart.

" Yet all beneath the unrivall'd rose,
  The lowly daisy sweetly blows ;
  Tho' large the forest's monarch throws
          His army shade,
  Yet green the juicy hawthorn grows
          Adown the glade.

" Then never murmur nor repine ;
  Strive in thy humble sphere to shine :
  And, trust me, not Potosi's mine,
          Nor kings' regard,
  Can give a bliss o'ermatching thine—
          A rustic bard.

" To give my counsels all in one,
  Thy tuneful flame still careful fan ;
  Preserve the dignity of man,
          With soul erect ;
  And trust, the universal plan
          Will all protect

"And wear thou this,"—she solemn said,
And bound the holly round my head :
The polish'd leaves, and berries red,
   Did rustling play ;
And, like a passing thought, she fled
   In light away.

ODE TO RUIN.

ALL hail ! inexorable lord !
At whose destruction-breathing word,
 The mightiest empires fall !
Thy cruel, woe-delighted train,
The ministers of grief and pain,
 A sullen welcome, all !
With stern-resolv'd, despairing eye,
 I see each aimed dart ;
For one has cut my dearest tie,
 And quivers in my heart.
  Then low'ring and pouring,
   The storm no more I dread ;
  Tho' thick'ning and black'ning
   Round my devoted head.

And thou grim pow'r, by life abhorr'd,
While life a pleasure can afford,
 Oh ! hear a wretch's prayer !
No more I shrink appall'd, afraid ;
I court, I beg, thy friendly aid
 To close this scene of care !
When shall my soul, in silent peace,
 Resign life's joyless day ;
My weary heart its throbbings cease,
 Cold mould'ring in the clay ?
  No fear more, no tear more,
   To stain my lifeless face ;
  Enclasped, and grasped
   Within thy cold embrace !

THE BRIGS OF AYR.

A POEM.

INSCRIBED TO JOHN BALLANTYNE, ESQ., AYR.

THE simple Bard, rough at the rustic plough,
Learning his tuneful trade from ev'ry bough ;
The chanting linnet, or the mellow thrush,
Hailing the setting sun, sweet, in the green-thorn bush ;
The soaring lark, the perching red-breast shrill,
Or deep-ton'd plovers, grey, wild-whistling o'er the hill ;
Shall he, nurst in the peasant's lowly shed,
To hardy independence bravely bred,

By early poverty to hardship steel'd,
And train'd to arms in stern misfortune's field—
Shall he be guilty of their hireling crimes,
The servile, mercenary Swiss of rhymes?
Or labour hard the panegyric close,
With all the venal soul of dedicating prose?
No! tho' his artless strains he rudely sings,
And throws his hand uncouthly o'er the strings,
He glows with all the spirit of the Bard,
Fame, honest fame, his great, his dear reward!
Still, if some patron's gen'rous care he trace,
Skill'd in the secret, to bestow with grace;
When Ballantyne befriends his humble name,
And hands the rustic stranger up to fame,
With heart-felt throes his grateful bosom swells,
The god-like bliss, to give, alone excels.

'Twas when the stacks get on their winter-hap,
An' thack an' rape secure the toil-won crap;
Potato-bings are snugged up frae skaith
O' coming Winter's biting, frosty breath;
The bees, rejoicing o'er their summer-toils,
Unnumber'd buds, an' flow'rs' delicious spoils,
Seal'd up with frugal care in massive waxen piles,
Are doom'd by man, that tyrant o'er the weak,
The death o' devils, smoor'd wi' brimstone reek:
The thund'ring guns are heard on ev'ry side,
The wounded coveys, reeling, scatter wide;
The feather'd field-mates, bound by Nature's tie,
Sires, mothers, children, in one carnage lie:
(What warm, poetic heart, but inly bleeds,
And execrates man's savage, ruthless deeds!)
Nae mair the flow'r in field or meadow springs,
Nae mair the grove with airy concert rings,
Except, perhaps, the robin's whistling glee,
Proud o' the height o' some bit half-lang tree:
The hoary morns precede the sunny days,
Mild, calm, serene, wide spreads the noon-tide blaze,
While thick the gossamer waves wanton in the rays.

'Twas in that season, when a simple bard,
Unknown and poor, simplicity's reward,
Ae night, within the ancient burgh of Ayr,
By whim inspir'd, or haply press'd wi' care,
He left his bed, and took his wayward route,
And down by Simpson's wheel'd the left about :
(Whether impell'd by all-directing Fate,
To witness what I after shall narrate ;
[Or penitential pangs for former sins,
Led him to rove by quondam Merran Dins ;]
Or whether, rapt in meditation high,
He wander'd out, he knew not where nor why)
The drowsy Dungeon clock had number'd two,
And Wallace tow'r had sworn the fact was true :
The tide-swoll'n Firth, wi' sullen sounding roar,
Through the still night dash'd hoarse along the shore.
All else was hush'd as Nature's closed e'e :
The silent moon shone high o'er tow'r and tree :
The chilly frost, beneath the silver beam,
Crept, gently-crusting, o'er the glittering stream.—

When, lo ! on either hand the list'ning Bard,
The clanging sugh of whistling wings he heard ;
Two dusky forms dart thro' the midnight air,
Swift as the gos drives on the wheeling hare ;
Ane on th' Auld Brig his airy shape uprears,
The ither flutters o'er the rising piers :
Our warlock Rhymer instantly descry'd
The sprites that owre the Brigs of Ayr preside.
(That Bards are second-sighted is nae joke,
And ken the lingo of the sp'ritual folk ;
Fays, Spunkies, Kelpies, a', they can explain them,
And ev'n the vera deils they brawly ken them.)
Auld Brig appear'd o' ancient Pictish race,
The very wrinkles Gothic in his face :
He seem'd as he wi' Time had warstl'd lang,
Yet, teughly doure, he bade an unco bang.
New Brig was buskit in a braw new coat,
That he, at Lon'on, frae ane Adams, got ;

In's hand five taper staves as smooth's a bead,
Wi' virls and whirlygigums at the head.
The Goth was stalking round with anxious search,
Spying the time-worn flaws in every arch ;—
It chanc'd his new-come neebor took his e'e,
And e'en a vex'd and angry heart had he !
Wi' thieveless sneer to see his modish mien,
He, down the water, gies him this guid e'en :—

AULD BRIG.

I doubt na', frien', ye'll think ye're nae sheepshank,
Ance ye were streekit owre frae bank to bank !
But gin ye be a brig as auld as me,
Tho' faith, that date I doubt ye'll never see ;
There'll be, if that day come, I'll wad a boddle,
Some fewer whigmeleeries in your noddle.

NEW BRIG.

Auld Vandal, ye but show your little mense,
Just much about it wi' your scanty sense ;
Will your poor narrow foot-path of a street,
Where twa wheel-barrows tremble when they meet—
Your ruin'd, formless bulk o' stane an' lime,
Compare wi' bonnie brigs o' modern time ?
There's men o' taste would tak the Ducat-stream,
Tho' they should cast the very sark and swim,
Ere they would grate their feelings wi' the view
O' sic an ugly Gothic hulk as you.

AULD BRIG.

Conceited gowk ! puff'd up wi' windy pride !—
This mony a year I've stood the flood an' tide ;
And tho' wi' crazy eild I'm sair forfairn,
I'll be a brig, when ye're a shapeless cairn !
As yet ye little ken about the matter,
But twa-three winters will inform ye better.

When heavy, dark, continued, a'-day rains,
Wi' deep'ning deluges o'erflow the plains;
When from the hills where springs the brawling Coil,
Or stately Lugar's mossy fountains boil,
Or where the Greenock winds his moorland course,
Or haunted Garpal draws his feeble source,
Arous'd by blust'ring winds an' spotting thowes,
In mony a torrent down his snaw-broo rowes;
While crashing ice, borne on the roaring speat,
Sweeps dams, an' mills, an' brigs, a' to the gate;
And from Glenbuck, down to the Ratton-key,
Auld Ayr is just one lengthen'd tumbling sea—
Then down ye'll hurl, deil nor ye never rise!
And dash the gumlie jaups up to the pouring skies.
A lesson sadly teaching to your cost,
That Architecture's noble art is lost!

NEW BRIG.

Fine Architecture, trowth, I needs must say o't!
The Lord be thankit that we've tint the gate o't!
Gaunt, ghastly, ghaist-alluring edifices,
Hanging with threat'ning jut, like precipices;
O'er-arching, mouldy, gloom-inspiring coves,
Supporting roofs fantastic, stony groves;
Windows and doors, in nameless sculpture drest,
With order, symmetry, or taste unblest;
Forms like some bedlam Statuary's dream,
The craz'd creations of misguided whim;
Forms might be worshipp'd on the bended knee,
And still the second dread command be free,
Their likeness is not found on earth, in air, or sea.
Mansions that would disgrace the building taste
Of any mason reptile, bird, or beast;
Fit only for a doited monkish race,
Or frosty maids forsworn the dear embrace;
Or cuifs of later times wha held the notion
That sullen gloom was sterling true devotion;
Fancies that our guid Brugh denies protection!
And soon may they expire, unblest with resurrection!

AULD BRIG.

O ye, my dear remember'd ancient yealings,
Were ye but here to share my wounded feelings !
Ye worthy Proveses, and mony a Bailie,
Wha in the paths o' righteousness did toil aye !
Ye dainty Deacons and ye douce Conveeners,
To whom our moderns are but causey-cleaners!
Ye godly Councils wha hae blest this town ;
Ye godly brethren o' the sacred gown,
Wha meekly gie your hurdies to the smiters;
And (what would now be strange) ye godly Writers ;
A' ye douce folk I've borne aboon the broo,
Were ye but here, what would ye say or do !
How would your spirits groan in deep vexation,
To see each melancholy alteration ;
And, agonising, curse the time and place
When ye begat the base, degen'rate race !
Nae langer Rev'rend Men, their country's glory,
In plain braid Scots hold forth a plain braid story !
Nae langer thrifty citizens an' douce,
Meet owre a pint, or in the council-house ;
But staumrel, corky-headed, graceless Gentry,
The herryment and ruin of the country ;
Men, three parts made by tailors and by barbers,
Wha waste your weel-hain'd gear on d—d new Brigs and
        Harbours !

NEW BRIG.

Now haud you there ! for faith ye've said enough,
And muckle mair than ye can mak to through,
[That's aye a string auld doyted Grey-beards harp on,
A topic for their peevishness to carp on.]
As for your Priesthood, I shall say but little,
Corbies and Clergy are a shot right kittle :
But, under favour o' your langer beard,
Abuse o' Magistrates might weel be spar'd :
To liken them to your auld-warld squad,
I must needs say, comparisons are odd.

In Ayr, wag-wits nae mair can have a handle
To mouth 'a citizen,' a term o' scandal;
Nae mair the Council waddles down the street,
In all the pomp of ignorant conceit;
[No difference but bulkiest or tallest,
With comfortable Dulness in for ballast;
Nor shoals nor currents need a Pilot's caution,
For regularly slow, they only witness motion.]
Men wha grew wise priggin' owre hops an' raisins,
Or gather'd lib'ral views in Bonds and Seisins,
If haply knowledge, on a random tramp,
Had shor'd them wi' a glimmer of his lamp,
And would to Common-sense for once betray'd them,
Plain, dull Stupidity stept kindly in to aid them.

———

What farther clishmaclaver might been said,
What bloody wars, if Sprites had blood to shed,
No man can tell; but all before their sight,
A fairy train appear'd in order bright:
Adown the glitt'ring stream they featly danc'd;
Bright to the moon their various dresses glanc'd:
They footed o'er the wat'ry glass so neat,
The infant ice scarce bent beneath their feet;
While arts of minstrelsy among them rung,
And soul-ennobling Bards heroic ditties sung.—
O had M'Lauchlan, thairm-inspiring Sage,
Been there to hear this heav'nly band engage,
When thro' his dear strathspeys they bore with Highland rage;
Or when they struck old Scotia's melting airs,
The lover's raptur'd joys or bleeding cares;
How would his Highland lug been nobler fir'd,
And ev'n his matchless hand with finer touch inspir'd!
No guess could tell what instrument appear'd,
But all the soul of Music's self was heard;
Harmonious concert rung in ev'ry part,
While simple melody pour'd moving on the heart.

The genius of the stream in front appears,
A venerable Chief advanc'd in years;

His hoary head with water-lilies crown'd,
His manly leg with garter-tangle bound.
Next came the loveliest pair in all the ring,
Sweet Female Beauty hand in hand with Spring ;
Then, crown'd with flow'ry hay, came Rural Joy,
And Summer, with his fervid-beaming eye :
All-cheering Plenty, with her flowing horn,
Led yellow Autumn, wreath'd with nodding corn ;
Then Winter's time-bleach'd locks did hoary show,
By Hospitality with cloudless brow.
Next follow'd Courage, with his martial stride,
From where the Feal wild-woody coverts hide ;
Benevolence, with mild, benignant air,
A female form, came from the tow'rs of Stair :
Learning and Worth in equal measures trode
From simple Catrine, their long-lov'd abode :
Last white-rob'd Peace, crown'd with a hazel wreath,
To rustic Agriculture did bequeath
The broken, iron instruments of death ;
At sight of whom our Sprites forgat their kindling wrath.

JOHN BARLEYCORN.

A BALLAD.

There were three kings into the east,
    Three kings both great and high ;
An' they ha'e swore a solemn oath
    John Barleycorn should die.

They took a plough and plough'd him down,
    Put clods upon his head ;
An' they ha'e swore a solemn oath
    John Barleycorn was dead.

But the cheerful spring came kindly on,
    And show'rs began to fall ;
John Barleycorn got up again,
    And sore surpris'd them all.

The sultry suns of summer came,
  And he grew thick and strong;
His head weel arm'd wi' pointed spears,
  That no one should him wrong.

The sober autumn enter'd mild,
  When he grew wan and pale;
His bending joints and drooping head
  Show'd he began to fail.

His colour sicken'd more and more,
  He faded into age;
And then his enemies began
  To show their deadly rage.

They've ta'en a weapon, long and sharp,
  And cut him by the knee;
Then tied him fast upon a cart,
  Like a rogue for forgerie.

They laid him down upon his back,
  And cudgell'd him full sore;
They hung him up before the storm,
  And turn'd him o'er and o'er.

They filled up a darksome pit
  With water to the brim;
They heaved in John Barleycorn,
  There let him sink or swim.

They laid him out upon the floor,
  To work him farther woe:
And still, as signs of life appear'd,
  They toss'd him to and fro.

They wasted o'er a scorching flame
  The marrow of his bones;
But a miller us'd him worst of all—
  He crush'd him 'tween two stones.

And they hae ta'en his very heart's blood,
 And drank it round and round;
And still the more and more they drank,
 Their joy did more abound.

John Barleycorn was a hero bold,
 Of noble enterprise;
For if you do but taste his blood,
 'Twill make your courage rise.

'Twill make a man forget his woe;
 'Twill heighten all his joy:
'Twill make the widow's heart to sing,
 Tho' the tear were in her eye.

Then let us toast John Barleycorn,
 Each man a glass in hand;
And may his great posterity
 Ne'er fail in old Scotland!

VERSES[1]

ON SEEING A WOUNDED HARE LIMP BY ME WHICH A FELLOW
HAD JUST SHOT.

INHUMAN man! curse on thy barb'rous art,
 And blasted be thy murder-aiming eye;
 May never pity soothe thee with a sigh,
Nor ever pleasure glad thy cruel heart!

Go live, poor wanderer of the wood and field!
 The bitter little that of life remains:
 No more the thickening brakes and verdant plains
To thee shall home, or food, or pastime yield.

Seek, mangled wretch, some place of wonted rest,
 No more of rest, but now thy dying bed!
 The sheltering rushes whistling o'er thy head,
The cold earth with thy bloody bosom prest.

Oft as by winding Nith, I, musing, wait
  The sober eve, or hail the cheerful dawn ;
  I'll miss thee sporting o'er the dewy lawn,
And curse the ruffian's aim, and mourn thy hapless fate.

THE FAREWELL.

"The valiant in himself, what can he suffer?
  Or what does he regard his single woes?
  But when, alas! he multiplies himself,
. To dearer selves, to the lov'd tender fair,
  To those whose bliss, whose beings hang upon him,
  To helpless children! then, O then! he feels
  The point of misery fest'ring in his heart,
  And weakly weeps his fortune like a coward.
  Such, such am I! undone!"
                    THOMSON'S *Edward and Eleanora.*

FAREWELL, old Scotia's bleak domains,
Far dearer than the torrid plains
    Where rich ananas blow!
Farewell, a mother's blessing dear!
A brother's sigh! a sister's tear!
    My Jean's heart-rending throe!
Farewell, my Bess! tho' thou'rt bereft
    Of my parental care;
A faithful brother I have left,
    My part in him thou'lt share!
        Adieu too, to you too,
            My Smith, my bosom frien';
        When kindly you mind me,
            Oh then befriend my Jean!

What bursting anguish tears my heart'
From thee, my Jeannie, must I part!
    Thou, weeping, answ'rest, "No!"
Alas! misfortune stares my face,
And points to ruin and disgrace,
    I, for thy sake, must go!
Thee, Hamilton and Aiken dear,
    A grateful, warm adieu!
I, with a much-indebted tear,
    Shall still remember you!

All-hail then, the gale then,
    Wafts me from thee, dear shore !
It rustles, and whistles—
    I'll never see thee more !

ELEGY ON MISS BURNET OF MONBODDO.

LIFE ne'er exulted in so rich a prize
As Burnet, lovely from her native skies ;
Nor envious death so triumph'd in a blow,
As that which laid th' accomplish'd Burnet low.

Thy form and mind, sweet maid, can I forget ?
In richest ore the brightest jewel set !

In thee, high Heav'n above was truest shown,
As by his noblest work the Godhead best is known.

In vain ye flaunt in summer's pride, ye groves;
    Thou crystal streamlet with thy flow'ry shore,
Ye woodland choir that chant your idle loves,
    Ye cease to charm—Eliza is no more!

Ye heathy wastes, immix'd with reedy fens;
    Ye mossy streams, with sedge and rushes stor'd;
Ye rugged cliffs, o'erhanging dreary glens,
    To you I fly, ye with my soul accord.

Princes, whose cumb'rous pride was all their worth,
    Shall venal lays their pompous exit hail?
And thou, sweet excellence! forsake our earth,
    And not a muse in honest grief bewail?

We saw thee shine in youth and beauty's pride,
    And virtue's light, that beams beyond the spheres;
But, like the sun eclips'd at morning tide,
    Thou left'st us darkling in a world of tears.

The parent's heart that nestled fond in thee,
    That heart how sunk, a prey to grief and care;
So deckt the woodbine sweet yon aged tree;
    So from it ravish'd, leaves it bleak and bare.

EPISTLE TO A YOUNG FRIEND.

I LANG hae thought, my youthfu' friend,
    A something to have sent you,
Tho' it should serve nae other end
    Than just a kind memento;
But how the subject-theme may gang,
    Let time and chance determine;
Perhaps it may turn out a sang,
    Perhaps turn out a sermon.

Ye'll try the world fu' soon, my lad,
　And, Andrew dear, believe me,
Ye'll find mankind an unco squad,
　And muckle they may grieve ye :
For care and trouble set your thought,
　Ev'n when your end's attained ;
An' a' your views may come to nought,
　Where ev'ry nerve is strained.

I'll no say men are villains a' ;
　The real, harden'd wicked,
Wha hae nae check but human law,
　Are to a few restricked :
But, och ! mankind are unco weak,
　An' little to be trusted ;
If self the wavering balance shake,
　Its rarely right adjusted !

Yet they wha fa' in fortune's strife,
　Their fate we should na censure,
For still th' important end of life
　They equally may answer ;
A man may hae an honest heart ;
　Tho' poortith hourly stare him ;
A man may tak a neebor's part,
　Yet hae nae cash to spare him.

Ay free, aff han' your story tell,
　When wi' a bosom crony ;
But still keep something to yoursel'
　Ye scarcely tell to ony.
Conceal yoursel', as weel's ye can,
　Frae critical dissection ;
But keek thro' ev'ry other man,
　Wi' sharpen'd, sly inspection.

The sacred lowe o' weel-plac'd love,
　Luxuriantly indulge it ;
But never tempt th' illicit rove,
　Tho' naething should divulge it :

I waive the quantum o' the sin,
  The hazard of concealing ;
But, och ! it hardens a' within,
  And petrifies the feeling !

To catch dame Fortune's golden smile,
  Assiduous wait upon her ;
And gather gear by ev'ry wile
  That's justified by honour ;
Not for to hide it in a hedge,
  Nor for a train-attendant ;
But for the glorious privilege
  Of being independent.

The fear o' hell's a hangman's whip
  To haud the wretch in order ;
But where ye feel your honour grip,
  Let that aye be your border :
Its slightest touches, instant pause—
  Debar a' side pretences ;
And resolutely keep its laws,
  Uncaring consequences.

The great Creator to revere
  Must sure become the creature ;
But still the preaching cant forbear,
  And ev'n the rigid feature :
Yet ne'er with wits profane to range,
  Be complaisance extended ;
An Atheist's laugh's a poor exchange
  For Deity offended !

When ranting round in pleasure's ring,
  Religion may be blinded ;
Or if she gie a random sting,
  It may be little minded ;
But when on life we're tempest-driv'n,
  A conscience but a canker—
A correspondence fix'd wi' Heav'n
  Is sure a noble anchor !

Adieu, dear, amiable youth !
　Your heart can ne'er be wanting !
May prudence, fortitude, and truth
　Erect your brow undaunting !
In ploughman phrase, " God send you speed,"
　Still daily to grow wiser :
And may you better reck the rede
　Than ever did th' adviser !

TO THE GUIDWIFE OF WAUCHOPE HOUSE.

[MRS. SCOTT OF WAUCHOPE.]

GUIDWIFE,
I MIND it weel, in early date,
When I was beardless, young, an' blate,
　An' first could thresh the barn
Or haud a yokin' at the pleugh ;
An' tho' forfoughten sair eneugh,
　Yet unco proud to learn :
When first amang the yellow corn
　A man I reckon'd was,
An' wi' the lave ilk merry morn
　Could rank my rig and lass,
　　Still shearing, and clearing,
　　　The tither stooked raw,
　　Wi' claivers, an' haivers,
　　　Wearing the day awa.

Ev'n then, a wish (I mind its pow'r),
A wish, that to my latest hour
　Shall strongly heave my breast—
That I for poor auld Scotland's sake
Some usefu' plan or beuk could make,
　Or sing a sang at least.
The rough bur-thistle, spreading wide
　Amang the bearded bear,
I turn'd the weeding-heuk aside,
　An' spar'd the symbol dear :

No nation, no station,
    My envy e'er could raise,
A Scot still, but blot still,
    I knew nae higher praise.

But still the elements o' sang
In formless jumble, right an' wrang,
    Wild floated in my brain;
'Till on that hairst I said before,
My partner in the merry core,
    She rous'd the forming strain:
I see her yet, the sonsie quean,
    That lighted up my jingle,
Her witching smile, her pauky een
    That gart my heart-strings tingle!
        I fired, inspired,
            At every kindling keek,
        But bashing, and dashing,
            I feared aye to speak.

For you, no bred to barn and byre,
Wha sweetly tune the Scottish lyre,
    Thanks to you for your line:
The marled plaid ye kindly spare
By me should gratefully be ware;
    'T'wad please me to the Nine.
I'd be mair vauntie o' my hap,
    Douce hingin' owre my curple,
Than ony ermine ever lap,
    Or proud imperial purple.
        Fareweel then, lang heal then,
            And plenty be your fa':
        May losses and crosses
            Ne'er at your hallan ca'.

ADDRESS TO EDINBURGH.

EDINA ! Scotia's darling seat !
  All hail thy palaces and tow'rs,
Where once beneath a monarch's feet
  Sat Legislation's sov'reign pow'rs !

From marking wildly-scatter'd flow'rs,
  As on the banks of Ayr I stray'd,
And singing, lone, the ling'ring hours,
  I shelter in thy honour'd shade.

Here wealth still swells the golden tide,
  As busy Trade his labour plies !
There Architecture's noble pride
  Bids elegance and splendour rise ;
Here Justice, from her native skies,
  High wields her balance and her rod ;
There Learning, with his eagle eyes,
  Seeks Science in her coy abode.

Thy sons, Edina ! social, kind,
  With open arms the stranger hail ;
Their views enlarg'd, their lib'ral mind,
  Above the narrow, rural vale ;
Attentive still to sorrow's wail,
  Or modest merit's silent claim ;
And never may their sources fail !
  And never envy blot their name !

Thy daughters bright thy walks adorn,
  Gay as the gilded summer sky,
Sweet as the dewy milk-white thorn,
  Dear as the raptur'd thrill of joy !
Fair Burnet strikes th' adoring eye,
  Heav'n's beauties on my fancy shine ;
I see the Sire of Love on high,
  And own His work indeed divine !

There, watching high the least alarms,
  Thy rough, rude fortress gleams afar ;
Like some bold vet'ran, grey in arms,
  And mark'd with many a seamy scar :
The pond'rous wall and massy bar,
  Grim-rising o'er the rugged rock,
Have oft withstood assailing war,
  And oft repell'd th' invader's shock.

With awe-struck thought, and pitying tears,
  I view that noble, stately dome,
Where Scotia's kings of other years,
  Fam'd heroes ! had their royal home :
Alas, how chang'd the times to come !
  Their royal name low in the dust !
Their hapless race wild-wand'ring roam !
  Tho' rigid law cries out, 'Twas just.

Wild beats my heart, to trace your steps,
  Whose ancestors, in days of yore,
Thro' hostile ranks and ruin'd gaps
  Old Scotia's bloody lion bore :
Ev'n I who sing in rustic lore,
  Haply, my sires have left their shed,
And fac'd grim danger's loudest roar,
  Bold-following where your fathers led !

Edina ! Scotia's darling seat !
  All hail thy palaces and tow'rs,
Where once beneath a monarch's feet
  Sat Legislation's sov'reign pow'rs !
From marking wildly-scatter'd flow'rs,
  As on the banks of Ayr I stray'd,
And singing, lone, the ling'ring hours,
  I shelter in thy honour'd shade.

ELEGY ON THE DEATH OF ROBERT RUISSEAUX.

Now Robin lies in his last lair,
He'll gabble rhyme, nor sing nae mair,
Cauld poverty, wi' hungry stare,
            Nae mair shall fear him ;
Nor anxious fear, nor cankert care,
            E'er mair come near him.

To tell the truth, they seldom fash't him,
Except the moment that they crush't him :
For sune as chance or fate had hush't 'em,
            Tho' e'er sae short,
Then wi' a rhyme or sang he lash't 'em,
            And thought it sport.

Tho' he was bred to kintra wark,
And counted was baith wight and stark,
Yet that was never Robin's mark
            To mak a man ;
But tell him, he was learn'd and clark,
            Ye roos'd him than !

SONGS

THE BIRKS OF ABERFELDY.

Tune—*The Birks of Aberfeldy.*

Bonnie lassie, will ye go,
Will ye go, will ye go ;
Bonnie lassie, will ye go
To the birks of Aberfeldy ?

Now simmer blinks on flowery braes,
And o'er the crystal streamlet plays;
Come, let us spend the lightsome days
  In the birks of Aberfeldy.

While o'er their heads the hazels hing,
The little birdies blithely sing,
Or lightly flit on wanton wing
  In the birks of Aberfeldy.

The braes ascend like lofty wa's,
The foaming stream deep-roaring fa's,
O'erhung wi' fragrant spreading shaws,
  The birks of Aberfeldy.

The hoary cliffs are crown'd wi' flowers,
White o'er the linns the burnie pours,
And rising, weets wi' misty showers
  The birks of Aberfeldy.

Let fortune's gifts at random flee,
They ne'er shall draw a wish frae me,
Supremely blest wi' love and thee,
  In the birks of Aberfeldy.

MY NANNIE, O.

Tune—*My Nannie, O.*

Behind yon hills, where Lugar flows,
  'Mang moors and mosses many, O,
The wintry sun the day has clos'd,
  And I'll awa to Nannie, O.

The westlin wind blaws loud an' shrill;
  The night's baith mirk and rainy, O;
But I'll get my plaid, an' out I'll steal,
  An' owre the hills to Nannie, O.

My Nannie's charming, sweet, an' young;
  Nae artfu' wiles to win ye, O :
May ill befa' the flattering tongue
  That wad beguile my Nannie, O.

Her face is fair, her heart is true,
  As spotless as she's bonnie, O :
The op'ning gowan, wat wi' dew,
  Nae purer is than Nannie, O.

A country lad is my degree,
  An' few there be that ken me, O ;
But what care I how few they be?
  I'm welcome aye to Nannie, O.

My riches a's my penny-fee,
  An' I maun guide it cannie, O ;
But warl's gear ne'er troubles me,
  My thoughts are a', my Nannie, O.

Our auld guidman delights to view
  His sheep an' kye thrive bonnie, O ;
But I'm as blithe that hauds his pleugh,
  An' has nae care but Nannie, O.

Come weel, come woe, I care na by,
  I'll tak what Heav'n will sen' me, O ;
Nae ither care in life have I,
  But live, an' love my Nannie, O.

ON CESSNOCK BANKS.

Tune—If he be a butcher neat and trim.

On Cessnock banks there lives a lass,
  Could I describe her shape and mien ;
The graces of her weelfar'd face,
  And the glancin' of her sparklin' een.

She's fresher than the morning dawn
   When rising Phœbus first is seen,
When dew-drops twinkle o'er the lawn ;
   An' she's twa glancin', sparklin' een.

She's stately, like yon youthful ash,
   That grows the cowslip braes between,
An' shoots its head above each bush ;
   An' she's twa glancin', sparklin' een.

She's spotless as the flow'ring thorn,
   With flow'rs so white and leaves so green,
When purest in the dewy morn ;
   An' she's twa glancin', sparklin' een.

Her looks are like the sportive lamb,
   When flow'ry May adorns the scene,
That wontons round its bleating dam ;
   An' she's twa glancin', sparklin' een.

Her hair is like the curling mist
   That shades the mountain-side at e'en,
When flow'r-reviving rains are past ;
   An' she's twa glancin', sparklin' een.

Her forehead's like the show'ry bow,
   When shining sunbeams intervene,
An' gild the distant mountain's brow ;
   An' she's twa glancin', sparklin' een.

Her voice is like the ev'ning thrush
   That sings on Cessnock banks unseen,
While his mate sits nestling in the bush ;
   An' she's twa glancin', sparklin' een.

Her lips are like the cherries ripe
   That sunny walls from Boreas screen—
They tempt the taste and charm the sight ;
   An' she's twa glancin', sparklin' een.

Her teeth are like a flock of sheep,
   With fleeces newly washen clean,
That slowly mount the rising steep ;
   An' she's twa glancin', sparklin' een.

Her breath is like the fragrant breeze
   That gently stirs the blossom'd bean,
When Phœbus sinks behind the seas ;
   An' she's twa glancin', sparklin' een.

But it's not her air, her form, her face,
   Tho' matching beauty's fabled queen ;
But the mind that shines in ev'ry grace,
   An' chiefly in her sparklin' een.

ROBIN.

TUNE—*Daintie Davie.*

THERE was a lad was born in Kyle,
But what'n a day o' what'n a style,
I doubt it's hardly worth the while,
   To be sae nice wi' Robin.
    Robin was a rovin' boy,
      Rantin' rovin', rantin' rovin' ;
    Robin was a rovin' boy,
      Rantin' rovin' Robin !

Our monarch's hindmost year but ane
Was five-and-twenty days begun,
'Twas then a blast o' Jan'war win'
   Blew hansel in on Robin.

The gossip keekit in his loof,
Quo' she, wha lives will see the proof,
This waly boy will be nae coof—
   I think we'll ca' him Robin.

He'll hae misfortunes great and sma',
But aye a heart aboon them a';
He'll be a credit till us a',
  We'll a' be proud o' Robin.

But, sure as three times three mak nine,
I see, by ilka score and line,
This chap will dearly like our kin',
  So leeze me on thee, Robin.

Guid faith, quo' she, I doubt ye gar
The bonnie lasses lie aspar,
But twenty fauts ye may hae waur,
    So blessin's on thee, Robin !
      Robin was a rovin' boy,
        Rantin' rovin', rantin' rovin' ;
      Robin was a rovin' boy,
        Rantin' rovin' Robin !

MY JEAN.

TUNE—*The Northern Lass.*

THO' cruel fate should bid us part,
  Far as the pole and line,
Her dear idea round my heart
  Should tenderly entwine.
Tho' mountains rise, and deserts howl,
  And oceans roar between ;
Yet, dearer than my deathless soul,
  I still would love my Jean.

THE DEIL'S AWA WI' TH' EXCISEMAN.

TUNE—*The Deil cam fiddling through the Town.*

THE deil cam fiddling thro' the town,
  And danc'd awa wi' th' Exciseman,
And ilka wife cries—" Auld Mahoun,
  I wish you luck o' the prize, man !"

The deil's awa, the deil's awa,
The deil's awa wi' th' Exciseman :

He's danc'd awa, he's danc'd awa,
He's danc'd awa wi' th' Exciseman !

We'll mak our maut, we'll brew our drink,
　　We'll dance, and sing, and rejoice, man ;
And mony braw thanks to the meikle black deil,
　　That danc'd awa wi' th' Exciseman.

There's threesome reels, there's foursome reels,
　　There's hornpipes and strathspeys, man ;
But the ae best dance e'er cam to the land
　　Was—the deil's awa wi' th' Exciseman.

　　The deil's awa, the deil's awa,
　　　　The deil's awa wi' th' Exciseman :
　　He's danc'd awa, he's danc'd awa,
　　　　He's danc'd awa wi' th' Exciseman.

THE BRAES O' BALLOCHMYLE.

TUNE—*Braes o' Ballochmyle.*

THE Catrine woods were yellow seen,
　　The flowers decay'd on Catrine lea,
Nae lav'rock sang on hillock green,
　　But nature sicken'd on the e'e.
Thro' faded groves Maria sang,
　　Hersel' in beauty's bloom the while,
And aye the wild-wood echoes rang,
　　Fareweel the Braes o' Ballochmyle !

Low in your wintry beds, ye flowers,
　　Again ye'll flourish fresh and fair ;
Ye birdies dumb, in with'ring bowers,
　　Again ye'll charm the vocal air.
But here, alas ! for me nae mair
　　Shall birdie charm, or floweret smile ;
Fareweel the bonnie banks of Ayr,
　　Fareweel, fareweel ! sweet Ballochmyle !

MENIE.

AGAIN rejoicing nature sees
  Her robe assume its vernal hues,
Her leafy locks wave in the breeze,
  All freshly steep'd in morning dews

    And maun I still on Menie doat,
      And bear the scorn that's in her e'e?
    For it's jet, jet black, and it's like a hawk,
      And it winna let a body be!

In vain to me the cowslips blaw,
  In vain to me the vi'lets spring;
In vain to me, in glen or shaw,
  The mavis and the lintwhite sing.

The merry ploughboy cheers his team,
  Wi' joy the tentie seedsman stalks;
But life to me's a weary dream,
  A dream of ane that never wauks.

The wanton coot the water skims,
  Amang the reeds the ducklings cry,
The stately swan majestic swims,
  And every thing is blest but I.

The sheep-herd steeks his faulding slap,
  And owre the moorlands whistles shrill;
Wi' wild, unequal, wand'ring step,
  I meet him on the dewy hill.

And when the lark, 'tween light and dark,
  Blithe waukens by the daisy's side,
And mounts and sings on flittering wings,
  A woe-worn ghaist I hameward glide.

Come, Winter, with thine angry howl,
  And raging bend the naked tree ;
Thy gloom will soothe my cheerless soul,
  When nature all is sad like me !

    And maun I still on Menie doat,
      And bear the scorn that's in her e'e ?
    For it's jet, jet black, and it's like a hawk,
      And it winna let a body be.

THE LASS O' BALLOCHMYLE.

Tune—*Miss Forbes' Farewell to Banff.*

'Twas even—the dewy fields were green,
  On ev'ry blade the pearls hang,
The zephyrs wanton'd round the bean,
  And bore its fragrant sweets alang :
In ev'ry glen the mavis sang,
  All nature listening seem'd the while,
Except where greenwood echoes rang,
  Amang the braes o' Ballochmyle.

With careless step I onward stray'd,
  My heart rejoic'd in nature's joy,
When musing in a lonely glade,
  A maiden fair I chanc'd to spy ;
Her look was like the morning's eye,
  Her air like nature's vernal smile,
Perfection whisper'd, passing by,
  Behold the lass o' Ballochmyle !

Fair is the morn in flow'ry May,
  And sweet is night in autumn mild ;
When roving thro' the garden gay,
  Or wand'ring in the lonely wild :

But Woman, Nature's darling child!
  There all her charms she does compile ;
Ev'n there her other works are foil'd
  By the bonnie lass o' Ballochmyle.

O ! had she been a country maid,
  And I the happy country swain,
Tho' shelter'd in the lowest shed
  That ever rose on Scotland's plain :
Thro' weary winter's wind and rain,
  With joy, with rapture, I would toil ;
And nightly to my bosom strain
  The bonnie lass o' Ballochmyle.

Then pride might climb the slipp'ry steep,
  Where fame and honours lofty shine ;
And thirst of gold might tempt the deep,
  Or downward seek the Indian mine ;
Give me the cot below the pine,
  To tend the flocks, or till the soil,
And every day have joys divine
  With the bonnie lass o' Ballochmyle.

MY HANDSOME NELL.

Tune—*I am a man unmarried.*

O, once I lov'd a bonnie lass,
  Ay, and I love her still ;
And, whilst that virtue warms my breast,
  I'll love my handsome Nell.
                Fal, lal de ral, etc.

As bonnie lasses I hae seen,
  And mony full as braw ;
But for a modest, gracefu' mien,
  The like I never saw.

A bonnie lass, I will confess,
   Is pleasant to the e'e,
But without some better qualities,
   She's no a lass for me.

But Nelly's looks are blithe and sweet,
   And what is best of a'—
Her reputation is complete,
   And fair without a flaw.

She dresses aye sae clean and neat,
   Baith decent and genteel :
An' then there's something in her gait
   Gars ony dress look weel.

A gaudy dress and gentle air
   May slightly touch the heart ;
But it's innocence and modesty
   That polishes the dart.

'Tis this in Nelly pleases me,
   'Tis this enchants my soul !
For absolutely in my breast
   She reigns without control.
               Fal, lal de ral, etc.

MONTGOMERY'S PEGGY.

Tune—*Gala Water.*

ALTHO' my bed were in yon muir,
   Amang the heather, in my plaidie,
Yet happy, happy would I be,
   Had I my dear Montgomery's Peggy.

When o'er the hill beat surly storms,
   And winter nights were dark and rainy ;
I'd seek some dell, and in my arms
   I'd shelter dear Montgomery's Peggy.

Were I a baron proud and high,
   And horse and servants waiting ready,
Then a' 'twad gie o' joy to me,
   The sharin' 't wi' Montgomery's Peggy.

LASSIE WI' THE LINT-WHITE LOCKS.

TUNE—*Rothemurchie's Rant.*

Now nature cleeds the flowery lea,
   And a' is young and sweet like thee;
O wilt thou share its joy wi' me,
   And say thou'lt be my dearie, O?

Lassie wi' the lint-white locks,
   Bonnie lassie, artless lassie,
Wilt thou wi' me tent the flocks ?
   Wilt thou be my dearie, O ?

And when the welcome simmer shower
Has cheer'd ilk drooping little flower,
We'll to the breathing woodbine bower
   At sultry noon, my dearie, O.

When Cynthia lights, wi' silver ray,
The weary shearer's hameward way ;
Thro' yellow waving fields we'll stray,
   And talk o' love, my dearie, O.

And when the howling wintry blast
Disturbs my lassie's midnight rest ;
Enclasped to my faithfu' breast,
   I'll comfort thee, my dearie, O.

   Lassie wi' the lint-white locks,
      Bonnie lassie, artless lassie,
   Wilt thou wi' me tent the flocks ?
      Wilt thou be my dearie, O ?

MY FATHER WAS A FARMER.

TUNE—*The Weaver and his Shuttle, O.*

My father was a farmer
   Upon the Carrick border, O,
And carefully he bred me
   In decency and order, O ;
He bade me act a manly part,
   Tho' I had ne'er a farthing, O ;
For without an honest manly heart,
   No man was worth regarding, O.

Then out into the world
  My course I did determine, O ;
Tho' to be rich was not my wish,
  Yet to be great was charming, O :
My talents they were not the worst,
  Nor yet my education, O ;
Resolv'd was I, at least to try,
  To mend my situation, O.

In many a way, and vain essay,
  I courted fortune's favour, O ;
Some cause unseen still stept between,
  To frustrate each endeavour, O :
Sometimes by foes I was o'erpower'd ;
  Sometimes by friends forsaken, O ;
And when my hope was at the top,
  I still was worst mistaken, O.

Then sore harass'd, and tir'd at last,
  With fortune's vain delusion, O,
I dropt my schemes, like idle dreams,
  And came to this conclusion, O :
The past was bad, and the future hid ;
  Its good or ill untried, O ;
But the present hour was in my pow'r,
  And so I would enjoy it, O.

No help, nor hope, nor view had I,
  Nor person to befriend me, O ;
So I must toil, and sweat, and broil,
  And labour to sustain me, O :
To plough and sow, to reap and mow,
  My father bred me early, O ;
For one, he said, to labour bred,
  Was a match for fortune fairly, O.

Thus all obscure, unknown, and poor,
  Thro' life I'm doom'd to wander, O,
Till down my weary bones I lay,
  In everlasting slumber, O.

No view nor care, but shun whate'er
   Might breed me pain or sorrow, O :
I live to-day as well's I may,
   Regardless of to-morrow, O.

But cheerful still, I am as well,
   As a monarch in a palace, O,
Tho' fortune's frown still hunts me down,
   With all her wonted malice, O :
I make indeed my daily bread,
   But ne'er can make it farther, O ;
But, as daily bread is all I need,
   I do not much regard her, O.

When sometimes by my labour
   I earn a little money, O,
Some unforeseen misfortune
   Comes gen'rally upon me, O :
Mischance, mistake, or by neglect,
   Or my good-natur'd folly, O ;
But come what will, I've sworn it still,
   I'll ne'er be melancholy, O.

All you who follow wealth and power
   With unremitting ardour, O,
The more in this you look for bliss,
   You leave your view the farther, O :
Had you the wealth Potosi boasts,
   Or nations to adore you, O,
A cheerful honest-hearted clown
   I will prefer before you, O.

A ROSEBUD BY MY EARLY WALK.

Tune—*The Rose-bud.*

A Rose-bud by my early walk,
Adown a corn-enclosed bawk,
Sae gently bent its thorny stalk,
   All on a dewy morning.

Ere twice the shades of dawn are fled,
In a' its crimson glory spread
And drooping rich the dewy head,
    It scents the early morning.

Within the bush, her covert nest
A little linnet fondly prest,
The dew sat chilly on her breast
    Sae early in the morning.
She soon shall see her tender brood,
The pride, the pleasure o' the wood,
Amang the fresh green leaves bedew'd,
    Awake the early morning.

So thou, dear bird, young Jeany fair!
On trembling string, or vocal air,
Shall sweetly pay the tender care
    That tends thy early morning.
So thou, sweet rose-bud, young and gay,
Shall beauteous blaze upon the day,
And bless the parent's evening ray
    That watch thy early morning.

STRATHALLAN'S LAMENT.

Thickest night, o'erhang my dwelling!
    Howling tempests, o'er me rave!
Turbid torrents, wintry swelling,
    Still surround my lonely cave!

Crystal streamlets gently flowing,
    Busy haunts of base mankind,
Western breezes softly blowing,
    Suit not my distracted mind.

In the cause of right engaged,
  Wrongs injurious to redress,
Honour's war we strongly waged,
  But the heavens denied success.

[Farewell, fleeting, fickle treasure,
  'Tween Misfortune and Folly shar'd!
Farewell Peace, and farewell Pleasure!
  Farewell, flattering man's regard!]

Ruin's wheel has driven o'er us,
  Not a hope that dare attend,
The wide world is all before us—
  But a world without a friend!

I DREAM'D I LAY WHERE FLOWERS WERE SPRINGING.

I DREAM'D I lay where flowers were springing,
  Gaily in the sunny beam;
List'ning to the wild birds singing,
  By a falling, crystal stream:
Straight the sky grew black and daring;
  Thro' the woods the whirlwinds rave;
Trees with aged arms were warring,
  O'er the swelling, drumlie wave.

Such was my life's deceitful morning,
  Such the pleasures I enjoy'd;
But lang or noon, loud tempests storming,
  A' my flow'ry bliss destroy'd.
Tho' fickle fortune has deceiv'd me,
  (She promis'd fair, and perform'd but ill;)
Of mony a joy and hope bereav'd me,
  I bear a heart shall support me still.

HAD I A CAVE.

TUNE—*Robin Adair.*

HAD I a cave on some wild, distant shore,
    Where the winds howl to the waves' dashing roar;

There would I weep my woes,
There seek my lost repose,
Till grief my eyes should close,
Ne'er to wake more.

Falsest of womankind, canst thou declare
All thy fond plighted vows—fleeting as air!
To thy new lover hie,
Laugh o'er thy perjury,
Then in thy bosom try
What peace is there!

BLITHE WAS SHE.

TUNE—*Andrew and his Cutty Gun.*

BLITHE, blithe, and merry was she,
Blithe was she but and ben;
Blithe by the banks of Earn,
And blithe in Glenturit glen.

By Auchtertyre grows the aik,
On Yarrow banks the birken shaw;
But Phemie was a bonnier lass
Than braes o' Yarrow ever saw.

Her looks were like a flow'r in May,
Her smile was like a simmer morn;
She tripped by the banks of Earn,
As light's a bird upon a thorn.

Her bonnie face it was as meek
As ony lamb upon a lea;
The evening sun was ne'er sae sweet,
As was the blink o' Phemie's e'e.

The Highland hills I've wander'd wide,
And o'er the Lowlands I hae been;
But Phemie was the blithest lass
That ever trod the dewy green.

Blithe, blithe, and merry was she,
  Blithe was she but and ben ;
Blithe by the banks of Earn,
  And blithe in Glenturit glen.

PEGGY.

Tune—*I had a Horse, I had nae mair.*

Now westlin winds and slaught'ring guns
  Bring autumn's pleasant weather ;
The moorcock springs, on whirring wings,
  Amang the blooming heather :
Now waving grain, wide o'er the plain,
  Delights the weary farmer ;
And the moon shines bright, when I rove at night,
  To muse upon my charmer.

The partridge loves the fruitful fells ;
  The plover loves the mountains ;
The woodcock haunts the lonely dells ;
  The soaring hern the fountains :
Thro' lofty groves the cushat roves,
  The path of man, to shun it ;
The hazel bush o'erhangs the thrush,
  The spreading thorn the linnet.

Thus ev'ry kind their pleasure find,
  The savage and the tender ;
Some social join, and leagues combine ;
  Some solitary wander :
Avaunt, away ! the cruel sway,
  Tyrannic man's dominion ;
The sportsman's joy, the murd'ring cry,
  The flutt'ring, gory pinion !

But Peggy, dear, the ev'ning's clear,
  Thick flies the skimming swallow ;

The sky is blue, the fields in view,
  All fading-green and yellow :
Come, let us stray our gladsome way,
  And view the charms of nature ;
The rustling corn, the fruited thorn,
  And ev'ry happy creature.

We'll gently walk, and sweetly talk,
  Till the silent moon shine clearly ;
I'll grasp thy waist, and, fondly prest,
  Swear how I love thee dearly :
Not vernal show'rs to budding flow'rs,
  Not autumn to the farmer,
So dear can be, as thou to me,
  My fair, my lovely charmer !

MARY !

TUNE—*Blue Bonnets.*

POWERS celestial ! whose protection
  Ever guards the virtuous fair,
While in distant climes I wander,
  Let my Mary be your care ;
Let her form sae fair and faultless,
  Fair and faultless as your own,
Let my Mary's kindred spirit
  Draw your choicest influence down.

Make the gales you waft around her
  Soft and peaceful as her breast ;
Breathing in the breeze that fans her,
  Soothe her bosom into rest :
Guardian Angels ! O protect her,
  When in distant lands I roam ;
To realms unknown while fate exiles me,
  Make her bosom still my home !

WHAT CAN A YOUNG LASSIE DO?

Tune—*What can a young lassie do wi' an auld man?*

WHAT can a young lassie, what shall a young lassie,
What can a young lassie do wi' an auld man?
Bad luck on the pennie that tempted my minnie
To sell her poor Jenny for siller an' lan'!
Bad luck on the pennie, etc.

He's always compleenin' frae mornin' to e'enin',
   He hosts and he hirples the weary day lang ;
He's doyl't and he's dozin', his bluid it is frozen,
   O, dreary's the night wi' a crazy auld man !
      He's doylt and he's dozin', etc.

He hums and he hankers, he frets and he cankers,
   I never can please him, do a' that I can ;
He's peevish and jealous of a' the young fellows :
   O, dool on the day I met wi' an auld man !
      He's peevish and jealous, etc.

My auld auntie Katie upon me taks pity,
   I'll do my endeavour to follow her plan !
I'll cross him, and wrack him, until I heart-break him,
   And then his auld brass will buy me a new pan.
      I'll cross him, and wrack him, etc.

THE HIGHLAND LASSIE.

TUNE.—*The Deuk's dang o'er my Daddy !*

NAE gentle dames, tho' e'er sae fair,
Shall ever be my muse's care :
Their titles a' are empty show ;
Gie me my Highland Lassie, O,

      Within the glen sae bushy, O,
      Aboon the plains sae rushy, O,
      I set me down wi' right good will,
      To sing my Highland Lassie, O.

Oh, were yon hills and valleys mine,
Yon palace and yon gardens fine !
The world then the love should know
I bear my Highland Lassie, O.

But fickle fortune frowns on me,
And I maun cross the raging sea !
But while my crimson currents flow,
I'll love my Highland Lassie, O.

Altho' through foreign climes I range,
I know her heart will never change,
For her bosom burns with honour's glow,
My faithful Highland Lassie, O,

For her I'll dare the billow's roar,
For her I'll trace the distant shore,
That Indian wealth may lustre throw
Around my Highland Lassie, O,

She has my heart, she has my hand,
My sacred truth and honour's band!
'Till the mortal stroke shall lay me low,
I'm thine, my Highland Lassie, O!

    Fareweel the glen sae bushy, O!
    Fareweel the plain sae rushy, O!
    To other lands I now must go,
    To sing my Highland Lassie, O!

ELIZA.

Tune—*Gilderoy.*

From thee, Eliza, I must go,
  And from my native shore;
The cruel Fates between us throw
  A boundless ocean's roar:
But boundless oceans, roaring wide,
  Between my love and me,
They never, never can divide
  My heart and soul from thee!

Farewell, farewell, Eliza dear,
  The maid that I adore!
A boding voice is in mine ear,
  We meet to part no more!
The latest throb that leaves my heart,
  While death stands victor by,
That throb, Eliza, is thy part,
  And thine that latest sigh!

THE FAREWELL TO THE BRETHREN OF ST. JAMES'S LODGE, TARBOLTON.

TUNE—*Good night, and joy be wi' you a' !*

ADIEU ! a heart-warm, fond adieu !
  Dear brothers of the mystic tie !
Ye favour'd, ye enlighten'd few,
  Companions of my social joy !
Tho' I to foreign lands must hie,
  Pursuing Fortune's slidd'ry ba',
With melting heart, and brimful eye,
  I'll mind you still, tho' far awa'.

Oft have I met your social band,
  And spent the cheerful, festive night;
Oft, honour'd with supreme command,
  Presided o'er the sons of light :
And, by that hieroglyphic bright,
  Which none but craftsmen ever saw !
Strong mem'ry on my heart shall write
  Those happy scenes when far awa' !

May freedom, harmony, and love,
  Unite you in the grand design,
Beneath th' Omniscient eye above,
  The glorious Architect Divine !
That you may keep th' unerring line,
  Still rising by the plummet's law,
Till order bright completely shine,
  Shall be my pray'r when far awa'.

And you, farewell ! whose merits claim,
  Justly, that highest badge to wear !
Heav'n bless your honour'd, noble name,
  To masonry and Scotia dear !
A last request permit me here,
  When yearly ye assemble a',
One round—I ask it with a tear,
  To him, the Bard that's far awa'.

DUNCAN GRAY.

Duncan Gray cam' here to woo,
　　Ha, ha, the wooing o't,
On blithe yule night when we were fou,
　　Ha, ha, the wooing o't.
Maggie coost her head fu' high,
Look'd asklent and unco skiegh,
Gart poor Duncan stand abiegh;
　　Ha, ha, the wooing o't.

Duncan fleech'd, and Duncan pray'd,
　　Ha, ha, the wooing o't;
Meg was deaf as Ailsa Craig,
　　Ha, ha, the wooing o't.

Duncan sigh'd baith out and in,
Grat his een baith bleer't and blin',
Spak' o' lowpin' ower a linn;
    Ha, ha, the wooing o't.

Time and chance are but a tide;
    Ha, ha, the wooing o't;
Slighted love is sair to bide;
    Ha, ha, the wooing o't.
Shall I, like a fool, quoth he,
For a haughty hizzie die?
She may gae to—France for me!
    Ha, ha, the wooing o't.

How it comes let doctors tell;
    Ha, ha, the wooing o't;
Meg grew sick—as he grew hale;
    Ha, ha, the wooing o't.
Something in her bosom wrings,
For relief a sigh she brings;
And O, her een, they spak sic things!
    Ha, ha, the wooing o't.

Duncan was a lad o' grace;
    Ha, ha, the wooing o't.
Maggie's was a piteous case;
    Ha, ha, the wooing o't.
Duncan couldna be her death,
Swelling pity smoor'd his wrath;
Now they're crouse and canty baith;
    Ha, ha, the wooing o't.

SONG,

IN THE CHARACTER OF A RUINED FARMER.

TUNE—*Go from my window, love, do.*

THE sun he has sunk in the west,
All creatures retired to rest,

While here I sit all sore beset
  With sorrow, grief, and woe ;
And it's O, fickle Fortune, O !

The prosperous man is asleep,
Nor hears how the whirlwinds sweep ;
But Misery and I must watch
  The surly tempest blow :
And it's O, fickle Fortune, O !

There lies the dear partner of my breast,
Her cares for a moment at rest ;
Must I see thee, my youthful pride,
  Thus brought so very low !
And it's O, fickle Fortune, O !

There lie my sweet babies in her arms,
No anxious ffear their little heart alarms ;
But for their sake my heart doth ache,
  With many a bitter throe :
And it's O, fickle Fortune, O !

I once was by Fortune carest,
I once could relieve the distrest :
Now, life's poor support hardly earn'd,
  My fate will scarce bestow :
And it's O, fickle Fortune, O !

No comfort, no comfort I have !
How welcome to me were the grave !
But then my wife and children dear,
  O whether would they go ?
And it's O, fickle Fortune, O !

O whither, O whither shall I turn !
All friendless, forsaken, forlorn !
For in this world rest or peace
  I never more shall know !
And it's O, fickle Fortune, O !

Y

YOUNG PEGGY.

TUNE—*Last time I cam o'er the Muir.*

Young Peggy blooms our bonniest lass,
  Her blush is like the morning,
The rosy dawn, the springing grass,
  With pearly gems adorning :
Her eyes outshine the radiant beams
  That gild the passing shower,
And glitter o'er the crystal streams,
  And cheer each fresh'ning flower.

Her lips, more than the cherries bright,
  A richer dye has grac'd them ;
They charm th' admiring gazer's sight,
  And sweetly tempt to taste them ;
Her smile is, like the evening, mild,
  When feather'd tribes are courting,
And little lambkins wanton wild,
  In playful bands disporting.

Were Fortune lovely Peggy's foe,
  Such sweetness would relent her ;
As blooming Spring unbends the brow
  Of surly, savage Winter.
Detraction's eye no aim can gain,
  Her winning powers to lessen ;
And spiteful Envy grins in vain,
  The poison'd tooth to fasten.

Ye powers of Honour, Love, and Truth,
  From every ill defend her ;
Inspire the highly-favour'd youth
  The destinies intend her ;
Still fan the sweet connubial flame,
  Responsive in each bosom ;
And bless the dear parental name
  With many a filial blossom.

GREEN GROW THE RASHES, O!

A FRAGMENT.

TUNE.—*Green grow the Rashes.*

GREEN grow the rashes, O !
  Green grow the rashes, O !
The sweetest hours that e'er I spend,
  Are spent amang the lasses, O.

There's nought but care on ev'ry han',
  In ev'ry hour that passes, O :
What signifies the life o' man,
  An' 'twere na for the lasses, O ?

The warl'ly race may riches chase,
  An' riches still may fly them, O ;
An' tho' at last they catch them fast,
  Their hearts can ne'er enjoy them, O.

But gie me a canny hour at e'en,
  My arms about my dearie, O :
An' warl'ly cares, an warl'ly men,
  May a' gae tapsalteerie, O.

For you sae douce, ye sneer at this,
  Ye're nought but senseless asses, O :
The wisest man the warl' e'er saw,
  He dearly lov'd the lasses, O.

Auld Nature swears the lovely dears
  Her noblest work she classes, O :
Her 'prentice han' she tried on man,
  An' then she made the lasses, O.

  Green grow the rashes, O !
    Green grow the rashes, O !
  The sweetest hours that e'er I spend
    Are spent amang the lasses, O.

MY PEGGY'S FACE.

TUNE—*My Peggy's Face.*

My Peggy's face, my Peggy's form,
The frost of hermit age might warm ;
My Peggy's worth, my Peggy's mind,
Might charm the first of human kind.
I love my Peggy's angel air,
Her face so truly, heav'nly fair,
Her native grace so void of art,
But I adore my Peggy's heart.

The lily's hue, the rose's dye,
The kindling lustre of an eye ;
Who but owns their magic sway !
Who but knows they all decay !
The tender thrill, the pitying tear,
The gen'rous purpose, nobly dear,
The gentle look, that rage disarms—
These are all immortal charms.

STAY, MY CHARMER.

TUNE—*An Gille dubh ciar dhubh.*

Stay, my charmer, can you leave me ?
Cruel, cruel to deceive me !
Well you know how much you grieve me
  Cruel charmer, can you go ?
  Cruel charmer, can you go ?

By my love so ill requited ;
By the faith you fondly plighted ;
By the pangs of lovers slighted ;
  Do not, do not leave me so !
  Do not, do not leave me so !

THE RIGS O' BARLEY.

TUNE—*Corn Rigs are Bonnie.*

IT was upon a Lammas night,
   When corn rigs are bonnie,
Beneath the moon's unclouded light,
   I held awa to Annie :
The time flew by, wi' tentless heed,
   'Till 'tween the late and early,
Wi' sma' persuasion she agreed
   To see me thro' the barley.

The sky was blue, the wind was still,
   The moon was shining clearly ;
I set her down, wi' right good will,
   Amang the rigs o' barley :

I ken't her heart was a' my ain;
  I lov'd her most sincerely:
I kiss'd her owre and owre again,
  Amang the rigs o' barley.

I lock'd her in my fond embrace!
  Her heart was beating rarely:
My blessings on that happy place,
  Amang the rigs o' barley!
But by the moon and stars so bright,
  That shone that hour so clearly!
She aye shall bliss that happy night,
  Amang the rigs o' barley.

I hae been blithe wi' comrades dear;
  I hae been merry drinkin'!
I hae been joyfu' gath'rin' gear;
  I hae been happy thinkin':
But a' the pleasures e'er I saw,
  Tho' three times doubl'd fairly,
That happy night was worth them a',
  Amang the rigs o' barley.

CHORUS.

Corn rigs, an' barley rigs,
  An' corn rigs are bonnie:
I'll ne'er forget that happy night,
  Amang the rigs wi' Annie.

THE CURE FOR ALL CARE.

TUNE—*Prepare, my dear Brethren, to the tavern let's fly.*

No churchman am I for to rail and to write,
No statesman nor soldier to plot or to fight,
No sly man of business contriving a snare—
For a big-belly'd bottle's the whole of my care.

The peer I don't envy, I give him his bow;
I scorn not the peasant, tho' ever so low;
But a club of good fellows, like those that are here,
And a bottle like this, are my glory and care.

Here passes the squire on his brother—his horse;
There centum per centum, the cit with his purse;
But see you the crown, how it waves in the air!
There a big-belly'd bottle still eases my care.

The wife of my bosom, alas! she did die;
For sweet consolation to church I did fly;
I found that old Solomon proved it fair,
That a big-belly'd bottle's a cure for all care.

I once was persuaded a venture to make;
A letter inform'd me that all was to wreck;—
But the pursy old landlord just waddl'd up stairs,
With a glorious bottle that ended my cares.

"Life's cares they are comforts,"—a maxim laid down
By the bard, what d'ye call him, that wore the black gown;
And faith, I agree with th' old prig to a hair;
For a big-belly'd bottle's a heav'n of a care.

THERE WAS A LASS.

Tune—*Duncan Davison.*

THERE was a lass, they ca'd her Meg,
   And she held o'er the moors to spin;
There was a lad that follow'd her,
   They ca'd him Duncan Davison.
The moor was driegh, and Meg was skiegh,
   Her favour Duncan couldna win;
For wi' the rock she wad him knock,
   And aye she shook the temper-pin.

As o'er the moor they lightly foor,
  A burn was clear, a glen was green,
Upon the banks they cas'd their shanks,
  And aye she set the wheel between :
But Duncan swore a haly aith,
  That Meg should be a bride the morn,
Then Meg took up her spinnin' graith,
  And flang them a' out o'er the burn.

We'll big a house—a wee, wee house,
  And we will live like king and queen,
Sae blithe and merry we will be
  When ye set by the wheel at e'en.
A man may drink and no be drunk ;
  A man may fight and no be slain ;
A man may kiss a bonnie lass,
  And aye be welcome back again.

LUCKLESS FORTUNE.

O RAGING fortune's withering blast
  Has laid my leaf full low, O !
O raging fortune's withering blast
  Has laid my leaf full low, O !

My stem was fair, my bud was green,
  My blossom sweet did blow, O ;
The dew fell fresh, the sun rose mild,
  And made my branches grow, O.

But luckless fortune's northern storms
  Laid a' my blossoms low, O ;
But luckless fortune's northern storms
  Laid a' my blossoms low, O.

OF A' THE AIRTS THE WIND CAN BLAW.

Tune—*Miss Admiral Gordon's Strathspey.*

Of a' the airts the wind can blaw,
   I dearly like the west,
For there the bonnie lassie lives,
   The lassie I lo'e best :
There wild woods grow, and rivers row,
   And mony a hill between ;
But day and night my fancy's flight
   Is ever wi' my Jean.

I see her in the dewy flowers,
   I see her sweet and fair :
I hear her in the tunefu' birds,
   I hear her charm the air :
There's not a bonnie flower that springs
   By fountain, shaw, or green,
There's not a bonnie bird that sings,
   But minds me o' my Jean.

Upon the banks o' flowing Clyde
   The lassies busk them braw ;
But when their best they hae put on,
   My Jeannie dings them a' :
In hamely weeds she far exceeds
   The fairest o' the town ;
Baith sage and gay confess it sae,
   Tho' drest in russet gown.

The gamesome lamb, that sucks its dam,
   Mair harmless canna be ;
She has nae faut (if sic ye ca't),
   Except her love for me ;
The sparkling dew, o' clearest hue,
   Is like her shining een :
In shape and air nane can compare
   Wi' my sweet lovely Jean.

O blaw ye westlin winds, blaw saft
    Amang the leafy trees,
Wi' balmy gale, frae hill and dale
    Bring hame the laden bees;
And bring the lassie back to me
    That's aye sae neat and clean;
Ae smile o' her wad banish care,
    Sae charming is my Jean.

What sighs and vows amang the knowes
    Hae passed atween us twa!
How fond to meet, how wae to part,
    That night she gaed awa!
The powers aboon can only ken,
    To whom the heart is seen,
That nane can be sae dear to me
    As my sweet lovely Jean!

THE CHEVALIER'S LAMENT.

Tune—*Captain O'Kean.*

THE small birds rejoice in the green leaves returning,
    The murmuring streamlet winds clear thro' the vale;
The hawthorn trees blow, in the dew of the morning,
    And wild scatter'd cowslips bedeck the green dale:
But what can give pleasure, or what can seem fair,
While the lingering moments are number'd by care?
    No flow'rs gaily springing, nor birds sweetly singing,
Can soothe the sad bosom of joyless despair.

The deed that I dared, could it merit their malice,
    A king, and a father, to place on his throne?
His right are these hills, and his right are these valleys,
    Where the wild beasts find shelter, but I can find none:
But 'tis not my sufferings thus wretched,—forlorn,
My brave gallant friends! 'tis your ruin I mourn;
    Your deeds prov'd so loyal in hot-bloody trial—
Alas! can I make you no sweeter return?

ON THE SEAS AND FAR AWAY.

How can my poor heart be glad,
When absent from my sailor lad?

How can I the thought forego?
He's on the seas to meet the foe.
Let me wander, let me rove,
Still my heart is with my love :
Nightly dreams, and thoughts by day,
Are with him that's far away.

 On the seas and far away,
 On stormy seas and far away;
 Nightly dreams, and thoughts by day,
 Are aye with him that's far away.

When in summer noon I faint,
As weary flocks around me pant,
Haply in this scorching sun
My sailor's thund'ring at his gun :
Bullets, spare my only joy !
Bullets, spare my darling boy !
Fate do with me what you may—
Spare but him that's far away.

At the starless midnight hour,
When winter rules with boundless power ;
As the storms the forest tear,
And thunders rend the howling air,
Listening to the doubling roar,
Surging on the rocky shore,
All I can—I weep and pray,
For his weal that's far away.

Peace, thy olive wand extend,
And bid wild war his ravage end,
Man with brother man to meet,
And as a brother kindly greet :
Then may heaven with prosp'rous gales
Fill my sailor's welcome sails,
To my arms their charge convey—
My dear lad that's far away.

BONNIE PEGGY ALISON.

Tune—*Braes o' Balquhidder.*

I'll kiss thee yet, yet,
　An' I'll kiss thee o'er again ;
An' I'll kiss thee yet, yet,
　My bonnie Peggy Alison !

Ilk care and fear, when thou art near,
　I ever mair defy them, O ;
Young kings upon their hansel throne
　Are nae sae blest as I am, O !

When in my arms, wi' a' thy charms,
　I clasp my countless treasure, O,
I seek nae mair o' heaven to share,
　Then sic a moment's pleasure, O !

And by thy een, sae bonnie blue,
　I swear I'm thine for ever, O !—
And on thy lips I seal my vow,
　And break it shall I never, O !

　　I'll kiss thee yet, yet,
　　　An' I'll kiss thee o'er again ;
　　An' I'll kiss thee yet, yet,
　　　My bonnie Peggy Alison !

O, WERE I ON PARNASSUS' HILL.

Tune—*My love is lost to me.*

O, were I on Parnassus' hill !
Or had of Helicon my fill ;
That I might catch poetic skill
　To sing how dear I love thee.
But Nith maun be my muse's well,
My muse maun be thy bonnie sel' ;
On Corsincon I'll glow'r and spell,
　And write how dear I love thee.

Then come, sweet muse, inspire my lay !
For a' the lee-lang simmer's day
I coudna sing, I coudna say,
   How much, how dear, I love thee.
I see thee dancing o'er the green,
Thy waist sae jimp, thy limbs sae clean,
Thy tempting lips, thy roguish een—
   By heaven and earth I love thee !

By night, by day, a-field, at hame,
The thoughts o' thee my breast inflame ;
And aye I muse and sing thy name—
   I only live to love thee.
Tho' I were doom'd to wander on
Beyond the sea, beyond the sun,
Till my last weary sand was run ;
   Till then—and then I'd love thee.

THE JOYFUL WIDOWER.

Tune—*Maggy Lauder.*

I married with a scolding wife,
   The fourteenth of November;
She made me weary of my life,
   By one unruly member.
Long did I bear the heavy yoke,
   And many griefs attended ;
But, to my comfort be it spoke,
   Now, now her life is ended.

We liv'd full one-and-twenty years,
   A man and wife together ;
At length from me her course she steer'd,
   And gone I know not whither :
Would I could guess, I do profess,
   I speak, and do not flatter,
Of all the women in the world,
   I never could come at her.

Her body is bestowed well,
  A handsome grave does hide her;
But sure her soul is not in hell,
  The deil could ne'er abide her.
I rather think she is aloft,
  And imitating thunder;
For why,—methinks I hear her voice
  Tearing the clouds asunder.

THE POOR AND HONEST SODGER.

AIR—*The Mill, Mill, O !*

WHEN wild war's deadly blast was blawn,
  And gentle peace returning,
Wi' mony a sweet babe fatherless,
  And mony a widow mourning;

I left the lines and tented field,
　Where lang I'd been a lodger,
My humble knapsack a' my wealth,
　A poor and honest sodger.

A leal, light heart was in my breast,
　My hand unstain'd wi' plunder,
And for fair Scotia, hame again,
　I cheery on did wander.
I thought upon the banks o' Coil,
　I thought upon my Nancy,
I thought upon the witching smile
　That caught my youthful fancy.

At length I reach'd the bonnie glen
　Where early life I sported ;
I pass'd the mill, and trysting thorn,
　Where Nancy aft I courted :
Wha spied I but my ain dear maid,
　Down by her mother's dwelling !
And turn'd me round to hide the flood
　That in my een was swelling.

Wi' alter'd voice, quoth I, Sweet lass,
　Sweet as yon hawthorn's blossom,
O ! happy, happy may he be,
　That's dearest to thy bosom !
My purse is light, I've far to gang,
　And fain would be thy lodger ;
I've serv'd my king and country lang—
　Take pity on a sodger.

Sae wistfully she gaz'd on me,
　And lovelier was than ever ;
Quo' she, A sodger ance I lo'ed,
　Forget him shall I never :
Our humble cot, and hamely fare,
　Ye freely shall partake it,
That gallant badge—the dear cockade,
　Ye're welcome for the sake o't.

She gaz'd—she redden'd like a rose—
   Syne pale like ony lily ;
She sank within my arms, and cried
   Art thou my ain dear Willie ?
By Him who made yon sun and sky—
   By whom true love's regarded,
I am the man ; and thus may still
   True lovers be rewarded !

The wars are o'er, and I'm come hame,
   And find thee still true-hearted ;
Tho' poor in gear, we're rich in love,
   And mair we'se ne'er be parted.
Quo' she, My grandsire left me gowd,
   A mailen plenish'd fairly ;
And come, my faithful sodger lad,
   Thou'rt welcome to it dearly !

For gold the merchant ploughs the main,
   The farmer ploughs the manor ;
But glory is the sodger's prize,
   The sodger's wealth is honour :
The brave poor sodger ne'er despise,
   Nor count him as a stranger ;
Remember he's his country's stay
   In day and hour of danger.

THE DAY RETURNS.

TUNE—*Seventh of November.*

THE day returns, my bosom burns,
   The blissful day we twa did meet,
Tho' winter wild in tempest toil'd,
   Ne'er summer sun was half sae sweet.
Than a' the pride that loads the tide,
   And crosses o'er the sultry line ;
Than kingly robes, than crowns and globes,
   Heaven gave me more—it made thee mine !

While day and night can bring delight,
  Or nature aught of pleasure give,
While joys above my mind can move,
  For thee, and thee alone, I live !
When that grim foe of life below
  Comes in between to make us part,
The iron hand that breaks our band
  It breaks my bliss—it breaks my heart.

RAVING WINDS AROUND HER BLOWING.

TUNE—*Macgregor of Ruara's Lament.*

RAVING winds around her blowing,
Yellow leaves the woodlands strowing,
By a river hoarsely roaring,
Isabella stray'd deploring :—
" Farewell hours that late did measure
Sunshine days of joy and pleasure ;
Hail, thou gloomy night of sorrow,
Cheerless night, that knows no morrow !

" O'er the past too fondly wandering,
On the hopeless future pondering ;
Chilly grief my life-blood freezes,
Fell despair my fancy seizes.
Life, thou soul of every blessing,
Load to misery most distressing,
O how gladly I'd resign thee,
And to dark oblivion join thee ! "

THE YOUNG HIGHLAND ROVER.

TUNE—*Morag.*

LOUD blaw the frosty breezes,
  The snaw the mountains cover ;
Like winter on me seizes,
  Since my young Highland Rover
  Far wanders nations over.

Where'er he go, where'er he stray,
  May Heaven be his warden;
Return him safe to fair Strathspey,
  And bonnie Castle-Gordon!

The trees now naked groaning,
  Shall soon wi' leaves be hinging,
The birdies dowie moaning,
  Shall a' be blithely singing,
  And every flower be springing.
Sae I'll rejoice the lee-lang day,
  When by his mighty warden
My youth's return'd to fair Strathspey,
  And bonnie Castle-Gordon.

BRAVING ANGRY WINTER'S STORMS.

Tune—*Neil Gow's Lamentation for Abercairny.*

WHERE, braving angry winter's storms,
  The lofty Ochils rise,
Far in their shade my Peggy's charms
  First blest my wondering eyes;
As one who by some savage stream,
  A lonely gem surveys,
Astonish'd, doubly marks its beam,
  With art's most polished blaze.

Blest be the wild sequester'd shade,
  And blest the day and hour,
Where Peggy's charms I first survey'd,
  When first I felt their pow'r!
The tyrant death, with grim controul,
  May seize my fleeting breath;
But tearing Peggy from my soul
  Must be a stronger death.

HEY, THE DUSTY MILLER.

TUNE—*The Dusty Miller.*

HEY, the dusty miller,
  And his dusty coat ;
He will win a shilling,
  Or he spend a groat.
    Dusty was the coat,
      Dusty was the colour,
    Dusty was the kiss
      I got frae the miller.

Hey, the dusty miller,
  And his dusty sack ;
Leeze me on the calling
  Fills the dusty peck.
    Fills the dusty peck,
      Brings the dusty siller ;
    I wad gie my coatie
      For the dusty miller.

MY BONNIE MARY.

TUNE—*Go fetch to me a Pint o' Wine.*

Go fetch to me a pint o' wine,
  An' fill it in a silver tassie ;
That I may drink, before I go,
  A service to my bonnie lassie ;
The boat rocks at the pier o' Leith ;
  Fu' loud the wind blaws frae the ferry ;
The ship rides by the Berwick-law.
  And I maun leave my bonnie Mary.

The trumpets sound, the banners fly,
  The glittering spears are ranked ready ;
The shouts o' war are heard afar,
  The battle closes thick and bloody ;

But it's not the roar o' sea or shore
    Wad make me langer wish to tarry;
Nor shout o' war that's heard afar—
    It's leaving thee, my bonnie Mary.

WILLIE BREW'D A PECK O' MAUT.

TUNE—*Willie brew'd a Peck o' Maut.*

O, WILLIE brew'd a peck o' maut,
    And Rob and Allan cam' to pree;
Three blither hearts, that lee-lang night,
    Ye wadna find in Christendie.

> We are na fou, we're nae that fou,
>   But just a drappie in our e'e ;
> The cock may craw, the day may daw,
>   And aye we'll taste the barley bree.

> Here are we met, three merry boys,
>   Three merry boys, I trow, are we ;
> And mony a night we've merry been,
>   And mony mae we hope to be !

> It is the moon—I ken her horn,
>   That's blinkin in the lift sae hie ;
> She shines sae bright to wyle us hame,
>   But, by my sooth, she'll wait a wee !

> Wha first shall rise to gang awa',
>   A cuckold, coward loon is he !
> Wha last beside his chair shall fa',
>   He is the king amang us three !

> We are na fou, we're nae that fou,
>   But just a drappie in our e'e ;
> The cock may craw, the day may daw,
>   And aye we'll taste the barley bree.

THE WINTER IT IS PAST.

> THE winter it is past, and the summer's come at last,
>   And the little birds sing on ev'ry tree ;
> Now every thing is glad, while I am very sad,
>   Since my true love is parted from me.

> The rose upon the brier, by the waters running clear,
>   May have charms for the linnet or the bee ;
> Their little loves are blest, and their little hearts at rest,
>   But my true love is parted from me.

My love is like the sun, in the firmament does run,
   For ever is constant and true ;
But his is like the moon, that wanders up and down,
   And is every month changing anew.

All you that are in love, and cannot it remove,
   I pity the pains you endure :
For experience makes me know that your hearts are full o' woe,
   A woe that no mortal can cure.

RATTLIN', ROARIN' WILLIE.

Tune—*Rattlin', Roarin' Willie.*

O RATTLIN', roarin' Willie,
   O, he held to the fair,
An' for to sell his fiddle,
   An' buy some other ware ;
But parting wi' his fiddle,
   The saut tear blin't his e'e ;
And rattlin', roarin' Willie,
   Ye're welcome hame to me !

O Willie, come sell your fiddle,
   O sell your fiddle sae fine ;
O Willie, come sell your fiddle,
   And buy a pint o' wine !
If I should sell my fiddle,
   The warl' would think I was mad ;
For mony a rantin' day,
   My fiddle an' I hae had.

As I cam by Crochallan,
   I cannily keekit ben—
Rattlin', roarin' Willie
   Was sitting at yon board en' ;
Sitting at yon board en',
   And amang guid companie ;
Rattlin', roarin' Willie,
   Ye're welcome hame to me !

TO MARY IN HEAVEN.

Tune—*Death of Captain Cook.*

Thou ling'ring star, with less'ning ray,
  That lov'st to greet the early morn,
Again thou usher'st in the day
  My Mary from my soul was torn.
O Mary! dear departed shade!
  Where is thy place of blissful rest?
Seest thou thy lover lowly laid?
  Hear'st thou the groans that rend his breast?

That sacred hour can I forget?
  Can I forget the hallowed grove,
Where by the winding Ayr we met,
  To live one day of parting love?
Eternity will not efface
  Those records dear of transports past;
Thy image at our last embrace;
  Ah! little thought we 'twas our last!

Ayr, gurgling, kiss'd his pebbled shore,
  O'erhung with wild woods, thick'ning green;
The fragrant birch, and hawthorn hoar,
  Twin'd am'rous round the raptur'd scene;
The flow'rs sprang wanton to be prest,
  The birds sang love on every spray—
Till too, too soon, the glowing west,
  Proclaim'd the speed of winged day.

Still o'er these scenes my mem'ry wakes,
  And fondly broods with miser care!
Time but th' impression stronger makes,
  As streams their channels deeper wear.
My Mary, dear departed shade!
  Where is thy place of blissful rest?
Seest thou thy lover lowly laid?
  Hear'st thou the groans that rend his breast?

THE BONNIE BANKS OF AYR.

Tune—*Roslin Castle.*

The gloomy night is gath'ring fast,
Loud roars the wild, inconstant blast;
Yon murky cloud is foul with rain,
I see it driving o'er the plain;
The hunter now has left the moor,
The scatter'd coveys meet secure;
While here I wander, prest with care,
Along the lonely banks of Ayr.

The autumn mourns her rip'ning corn,
By early winter's ravage torn ;
Across her placid, azure sky,
She sees the scowling tempest fly :
Chill runs my blood to hear it rave—
I think upon the stormy wave,
Where many a danger I must dare,
Far from the bonnie banks of Ayr.

'Tis not the surging billow's roar,
'Tis not that fatal, deadly shore ;
'Tho' death in ev'ry shape appear,
The wretched have no more to fear !
But round my heart the ties are bound,
That heart transpierc'd with many a wound ;
These bleed afresh, those ties I tear,
To leave the bonnie banks of Ayr.

Farewell old Coïla's hills and dales,
Her heathy moors and winding vales ;
The scenes where wretched fancy roves,
Pursuing past, unhappy loves !
Farewell, my friends ! farewell, my foes !
My peace with these, my love with those—
The bursting tears my heart declare ;
Farewell, the bonnie banks of Ayr !

MY LOVELY NANCY.

Thine am I, my faithful fair,
  Thine, my lovely Nancy ;
Ev'ry pulse along my veins,
  Ev'ry roving fancy.

To thy bosom lay my heart,
  There to throb and languish :
Tho' despair had wrung its core,
  That would heal its anguish.

Take away these rosy lips,
  Rich with balmy treasure :
Turn away thine eyes of love,
  Lest I die with pleasure.

What is life when wanting love ?
  Night without a morning :
Love's the cloudless summer sun,
  Nature gay adorning.

MY HARRY WAS A GALLANT GAY.

TUNE—*Highlander's Lament.*

My Harry was a gallant gay,
  Fu' stately strode he on the plain ;
But now he's banish'd far away,
  I'll never see him back again.

      O for him back again !
        O for him back again !
    I wad gie a' Knockhaspie's land,
      For Highland Harry back again.

When a' the lave gae to their bed,
  I wander dowie up the glen ;
I set me down and greet my fill,
  And aye I wish him back again.

O were some villains hangit high,
  And ilka body had their ain !
Then I might see the joyfu' sight,
  My Highland Harry back again.

      O for him back again !
        O for him back again !
    I wad gie a' Knockhaspie's land
      For Highland Harry back again.

TO DAUNTON ME.

Tune—*To Daunton me.*

The blude red rose at Yule may blaw,
The simmer lilies bloom in snaw,
The frost may freeze the deepest sea ;
But an auld man shall never daunton me.

   To daunton me, and me so young,
   Wi' his fause heart and flatt'ring tongue,
   That is the thing you ne'er shall see ;
   For an auld man shall never daunton me.

For a' his meal, and a' his maut,
For a' his fresh beef and his saut,
For a' his gold and white monie,
An auld man shall never daunton me.

His gear may buy him kye and yowes,
His gear may buy him glens and knowes ;
But me he shall not buy nor fee,
For an auld man shall never daunton me.

He hirples twa-fauld as he dow,
Wi' his teethless gab and his auld beld pow,
And the rain dreeps down frae his red bleer'd e'e—
That auld man shall never daunton me.

   To daunton me, and me sae young,
   Wi' his fause heart and flatt'ring tongue,
   That is the thing you ne'er shall see ;
   For an auld man shall never daunton me.

TIBBIE DUNBAR.

Tune—*Johnny M'Gill.*

O, wilt thou go wi' me,
   Sweet Tibbie Dunbar?
O, wilt thou go wi' me,
   Sweet Tibbie Dunbar?

Wilt thou ride on a horse,
    Or be drawn in a car,
Or walk by my side,
    O sweet Tibbie Dunbar?

I care na thy daddie,
    His lands and his money,
I care na thy kin,
    Sae high and sae lordly:
But sae thou wilt hae me
    For better for waur—
And come in thy coatie,
    Sweet Tibbie Dunbar?

COME BOAT ME O'ER TO CHARLIE.

TUNE—*O'er the Water to Charlie.*

COME boat me o'er, come row me o'er,
    Come boat me o'er to Charlie;
I'll gie John Ross another bawbee,
    To boat me o'er to Charlie.

I lo'e weel my Charlie's name,
    Tho' some there be abhor him:
But O, to see auld Nick gaun hame,
    And Charlie's faes before him!

I swear and vow by moon and stars,
    And sun that shines so early,
If I had twenty thousand lives,
    I'd die as aft for Charlie.

    We'll o'er the water, and o'er the sea,
        We'll o'er the water to Charlie;
    Come weal, come woe, we'll gather and go,
        And live or die wi' Charlie!

THE BATTLE OF SHERIFF-MUIR.

Tune—*Cameronian Rant.*

" O CAM ye here the fight to shun,
   Or herd the sheep wi' me, man ?
Or were ye at the Sherra-muir,
   And did the battle see, man ?"
I saw the battle sair and teugh,
And reekin'-red ran mony a sheugh,
My heart, for fear, gaed sough for sough,
To hear the thuds, and see the cluds,
O' clans frae woods, in tartan duds,
   Wha glaum'd at kingdoms three, man.

The red-coat lads, wi' black cockades,
   To meet them were na slaw, man ;
They rush'd and push'd, and blude outgush'd,
   And mony a bouk did fa', man :
The great Argyle led on his files,
I wat they glanc'd for twenty miles :
They hack'd and hash'd, while broadswords clash'd.
And thro' they dash'd, and hew'd and smash'd,
   Till fey men died awa, man.

But had ye seen the philibegs,
   And skyrin tartan trews, man ;
When in the teeth they dar'd our Whigs
   And covenant true blues, man ;
In lines extended lang and large,
When baiginets o'erpower'd the targe,
And thousands hasten'd to the charge,
Wi' Highland wrath they frae the sheath
Drew blades o' death, till, out o' breath,
   They fled like frighted doos, man.

" O how deil, Tam, can that be true ?
   The chase gaed frae the north, man ;
I saw mysel' they did pursue
   The horsemen back to Forth, man ;

And at Dunblane, in my ain sight,
They took the brig wi' a' their might,
And straught to Stirling wing'd their flight;
But, cursed lot! the gates were shut;
And mony a huntit, poor red-coat,
  For fear amaist did swarf, man!"

"My sister Kate cam up the gate
  Wi' crowdie unto me, man;
She swore she saw some rebels run
  Frae Perth unto Dundee, man:
Their left-hand general had nae skill,
The Angus lads had nae good will
That day their neebours' blood to spill;
For fear by foes, that they should lose
Their cogs o' brose, they scar'd at blows,
  And hameward fast did flee, man."

They've lost some gallant gentleman,
  Amang the Highland clans, man;
"I fear my Lord Panmure is slain,"
  Or in his en'mies' hands, man:
Now wad ye sing this double fight,
Some fell for wrang, and some for right;
And mony bade the warld guid-night;
Say, pell, and mell, wi' muskets' knell,
How Tories fell, and Whigs to hell
  Flew off in frighted bands, man.

BEWARE O' BONNIE ANN.

Tune—*Ye Gallants bright.*

Ye gallants bright, I rede ye right,
  Beware o' bonnie Ann;
Her comely face sae fu' o' grace,
  Your heart she will trepan.

Her een sae bright, like stars by night,
　Her skin is like the swan ;
Sae jimply lac'd her genty waist,
　That sweetly ye might span.

Youth, grace, and love, attendant move,
　And pleasure leads the van :
In a' their charms, and conquering arms,
　They wait on bonnie Ann.
The captive bands may chain the hands,
　But love enslaves the man ;
Ye gallants braw, I rede you a',
　Beware o' bonnie Ann !

THE BLUE-EYED LASS.

I GAED a waefu' gate yestreen,
　A gate, I fear, I dearly rue ;
I gat my death frae twa sweet een,
　Twa lovely een o' bonnie blue.
'Twas not her golden ringlets bright ;
　Her lips, like roses, wet wi' dew,
Her heaving bosom, lily-white—
　It was her een sae bonnie blue.

She talk'd, she smil'd, my heart she wyl'd ;
　She charmed my soul—I wist na how ;
And aye the stound, the deadly wound,
　Came frae her een sae bonnie blue.
But spare to speak, and spare to speed ;
　She'll aiblins listen to my vow :
Should she refuse, I'll lay my dead
　To her twa een sae bonnie blue.

JOHN ANDERSON, MY JO.

JOHN Anderson, my jo, John,
　When we were first acquent ;
Your locks were like the raven,
　Your bonnie brow was brent ;

But now your brow is beld, John,
Your locks are like the snaw;
But blessings on your frosty pow,
John Anderson, my jo.

John Anderson, my jo, John,
  We clamb the hill thegither ;
And mony a canty day, John,
  We've had wi' ane anither :
Now we maun totter down, John,
  But hand in hand we'll go ;
And sleep thegither at the foot,
  John Anderson, my jo.

WHEN FIRST I SAW FAIR JEANIE'S FACE.

Air—*Maggie Lauder.*

WHEN first I saw fair Jeanie's face,
  I couldna tell what ail'd me,
My heart went fluttering pit-a-pat,
  My een they almost fail'd me.
She's aye sae neat, sae trim, sae tight,
  All grace does round her hover,
Ae look deprived me o' my heart,
  And I became a lover.

    She's aye, aye sae blithe, sae gay,
      She's aye sae blithe, and cheerie ;
    She's aye sae bonnie, blithe, and gay,
      Oh, gin I were her dearie !

Had I Dundas's whole estate,
  Or Hopetoun's wealth to shine in ;
Did warlike laurels crown my brow,
  Or humbler bays entwining—
I'd lay them a' at Jeanie's feet,
  Could I but hope to move her,
And prouder than a belted knight,
  I'd be my Jeanie's lover.
    She's aye, aye sae blithe, sae gay, etc.

But sair I fear some happier swain
  Has gain'd sweet Jeanie's favour :

If so, may ever bliss be hers,
  Though I maun never have her;
But gang she east, or gang she west,
  'Twixt Forth and Tweed all over,
While men have eyes, or ears, or taste,
  She'll always find a lover.
      She's aye, aye sae blithe, sae gay, etc.

THERE'S A YOUTH IN THIS CITY.

Tune—*Neil Gow's Lament.*

There's a youth in this city,
  It were a great pity
That he frae our lasses should wander awa';
  For he's bonnie an' braw,
  Weel favour'd witha',
And his hair has a natural buckle an' a'.
  His coat is the hue
  Of his bonnet sae blue:
His fecket is white as the new-driven snaw;
  His hose they are blae,
  And his shoon like the slae,
And his clear siller buckles they dazzle us a'.

  For beauty and fortune
  The laddie's been courtin';
Weel-featured, weel-tocher'd, weel-mounted, and braw;
  But chiefly the siller,
  That gars him gang till her, ·
The pennie's the jewel that beautifies a'.
  There's Meg wi' the mailen
  That fain wad a haen him; [1]
And Susie, whose daddy was laird o' the ha';
  There's lang-tocher'd Nancy
  Maist fetters his fancy—
But the laddie's dear sel' he lo'es dearest of a'..

BLOOMING NELLY.

Tune—*On a bank of Flowers.*

On a bank of flowers, in a summer day,
  For summer lightly drest,
The youthful blooming Nelly lay,
  With love and sleep opprest;
When Willie, wand'ring thro' the wood,
  Who for her favour oft had sued,
He gaz'd, he wish'd, he fear'd, he blush'd,
  And trembled where he stood.

Her closed eyes, like weapons sheath'd,
  Were seal'd in soft repose;
Her lips, still as she fragrant breath'd,
  It richer dy'd the rose.
The springing lilies sweetly prest,
  Wild—wanton, kiss'd her rival breast;
He gaz'd, he wish'd, he fear'd, he blush'd—
  His bosom ill at rest.

Her robes, light waving in the breeze,
  Her tender limbs embrace!
Her lovely form, her native ease,
  All harmony and grace!
Tumultuous tides his pulses roll,
  A faltering, ardent kiss he stole;
He gaz'd, he wish'd, he fear'd, he blush'd,
  And sigh'd his very soul.

As flies the partridge from the brake,
  On fear-inspired wings,
So Nelly, starting, half-awake,
  Away affrighted springs:
But Willie follow'd—as he should,
  He overtook her in the wood;
He vow'd, he pray'd, he found the maid
  Forgiving all and good.

LOGAN BRAES.

O Logan, sweetly didst thou glide
That day I was my Willie's bride!

And years sinsyne hae o'er us run,
Like Logan to the simmer sun.
But now thy flow'ry banks appear
Like drumlie winter, dark and drear,
While my dear lad maun face his faes,
Far, far frae me and Logan braes !

Again the merry month o' May
Has made our hills and valleys gay ;
The birds rejoice in leafy bowers,
The bees hum round the breathing flowers :
Blithe morning lifts his rosy eye,
And evening's tears are tears of joy :
My soul, delightless, a' surveys,
While Willie's far frae Logan braes.

Within yon milk-white hawthorn bush,
Amang her nestlings sits the thrush ;
Her faithfu' mate will share her toil,
Or wi' his song her cares beguile :
But I, wi' my sweet nurslings here,
Nae mate to help, nae mate to cheer,
Pass widow'd nights, and joyless days,
While Willie's far frae Logan braes.

O wae upon you, men o' state,
That brethren rouse to deadly hate !
As ye make mony a fond heart mourn,
Sae may it on your heads return !
How can your flinty hearts enjoy
The widow's tears, the orphan's cry !
But soon may peace bring happy days
And Willie hame to Logan braes !

COME REDE ME, DAME.

COME rede me, dame, come tell me, dame,
    And nane can tell mair truly,
What colour maun the man be of,
    To love a woman duly.

The carlin flew baith up and down,
    And leugh and answer'd ready,
I learn'd a sang in Annandale,
    A dark man for my lady.

But for a country quean like thee,
    Young lass, I tell thee fairly,
That wi' the white I've made a shift,
    And brown will do fu' rarely.

There's mickle love in raven locks,
    The flaxen ne'er grows youden,
There's kiss and hause me in the brown,
    And glory in the gowden.

GUIDWIFE COUNT THE LAWIN.

Tune—*Guidwife count the Lawin.*

Gane is the day, and mirk's the night,
But we'll ne'er stray for fau't o' light,
For ale and brandy's stars and moon,
And blude-red wine's the rising sun.

    Then guidwife count the lawin,
        The lawin, the lawin;
    Then guidwife count the lawin,
        And bring a coggie mair !

There's wealth and ease for gentlemen,
And semple-folk maun fecht and fen';
But here we're a' in ae accord,
For ilka man that's drunk's a lord.

My coggie is a haly pool,
That heals the wounds o' care and dool;
And pleasure is a wanton trout,
An' ye drink but deep ye'll find him out.

    Then guidwife count the lawin,
        The lawin, the lawin;
    Then guidwife count the lawin,
        And bring a coggie mair!

THE BATTLE OF KILLIECRANKIE.

TUNE—*Killiecrankie.*

WHARE hae ye been sae braw, lad?
  Whare hae ye been sae brankie, O?
O, whare hae ye been sae braw, lad?
  Cam ye by Killiecrankie, O?
An' ye had been whare I hae been,
  Ye wadna been sae cantie, O;
An' ye had seen what I hae seen,
  On the braes o' Killiecrankie, O.

I fought at land, I fought at sea;
  At hame I fought my auntie, O;
But I met the Devil an' Dundee,
  On the braes o' Killiecrankie, O.
The bauld Pitcur fell in a furr,
  An' Clavers got a clankie, O;
Or I had fed an Athole gled,
  On the braes o' Killiecrankie, O.

EPPIE ADAIR.

TUNE—*My Eppie.*

AN' O! my Eppie,
My jewel, my Eppie!
Wha wadna be happy
  Wi' Eppie Adair?
By love, and by beauty,
By law, and by duty,
I swear to be true to
  My Eppie Adair!

An' O! my Eppie,
My jewel, my Eppie!
Wha wadna be happy
  Wi' Eppie Adair?

A' pleasure exile me,
Dishonour defile me,
If e'er I beguile thee,
　My Eppie Adair !

O WHISTLE, AND I'LL COME TO YOU.

O WHISTLE, and I'll come to you, my lad,
O whistle, and I'll come to you, my lad :
Tho' father and mither and a' should gae mad,
O whistle, and I'll come to you, my lad.

But warily tent, when you come to court me,
And come na unless the back-yett be a-jee;
Syne up the back-stile, and let naebody see,
And come as ye were na comin' to me,
And come as ye were na comin' to me.

At kirk, or at market, whene'er ye meet me,
Gang by me as tho' that ye car'd na a flie;
But steal me a blink o' your bonnie black e'e,
Yet look as ye were na lookin' at me,
Yet look as ye were na lookin' at me.

Aye vow and protest that ye care na for me,
And whiles ye may lightly my beauty a wee;
But court na anither, tho' jokin' ye be,
For fear that she wyle your fancy frae me,
For fear that she wyle your fancy frae me.

 O whistle, and I'll come to you, my lad,
 O whistle, and I'll come to you, my lad:
 Tho' father and mither and a' should gae mad,
 O whistle, and I'll come to you, my lad.

WOMEN'S MINDS.

Tune—For a' that.

THOUGH women's minds, like winter winds,
 May shift and turn, and a' that,
The noblest breast adores them maist,
 A consequence I draw that.

  For a' that, and a' that,
   And twice as muckle's a' that,
  The bonnie lass that I lo'e best,
   She'll be my ain for a' that.

Great love I bear to all the fair,
 Their humble slave, and a' that;
But lordly will, I hold it still,
 A mortal sin to thraw that.

But there is ane aboon the lave,
　Has wit, and sense, and a' that;
A bonnie lass, I like her best,
　And wha a crime dare ca' that?

WHISTLE O'ER THE LAVE O'T.

TUNE—*Whistle o'er the lave o't.*

FIRST when Maggy was my care,
Heaven, I thought, was in her air;
Now we're married—spier nae mair—
　Whistle o'er the lave o't.—
Meg was meek, and Meg was mild,
Bonnie Meg was nature's child;
Wiser men than me's beguil'd—
　Whistle o'er the lave o't.

How we live, my Meg and me,
How we love, and how we 'gree,
I care na by how few may see;
　Whistle o'er the lave o't.—
Wha I wish were maggots' meat,
Dish'd up in her winding-sheet,
I could write—but Meg maun see't—
　Whistle o'er the lave o't.

THE CAPTAIN'S LADY.

TUNE—*O mount and go.*

O MOUNT and go,
　Mount and make you ready;
O mount and go,
　And be the Captain's Lady.

When the drums do beat,
　And the cannons rattle,
Thou shalt sit in state,
　And see thy love in battle.

When the vanquish'd foe
　　Sues for peace and quiet,
To the shades we'll go,
　　And in love enjoy it.

　　　O mount and go,
　　　　Mount and make you ready ;
　　　O mount and go,
　　　　And be the Captain's Lady.

THE BANKS OF NITH.

TUNE—*Robie donna Gorach.*

THE Thames flows proudly to the sea,
　　Where royal cities stately stand ;
But sweeter flows the Nith, to me,
　　Where Cummins ance had high command :
When shall I see that honour'd land,
　　That winding stream I love so dear !
Must wayward fortune's adverse hand
　　For ever, ever keep me here ?

How lovely, Nith, thy fruitful vales,
　　Where spreading hawthorns gaily bloom !
How sweetly wind thy sloping dales,
　　Where lambkins wanton thro' the broom !
Tho' wandering, now, must be my doom,
　　Far from thy bonnie banks and braes,
May there my latest hours consume,
　　Amang the friends of early days !

TAM GLEN.

TUNE—*Tam Glen.*

My heart is a-breaking, dear Tittie !
　　Some counsel unto me come len',
To anger them a' is a pity,
　　But what will I do wi' Tam Glen !

I'm thinking, wi' sic a braw fallow,
   In poortith I might mak a fen' ;
What care I in riches to wallow,
   If I mauna marry Tam Glen ?

There's Lowrie the laird o' Drumeller,
   "Guid day to you, brute !" he comes ben :
He brags and he blaws o' his siller,
   But when will he dance like Tam Glen ?

My minnie does constantly deave me,
    And bids me beware o' young men ;
They flatter, she says, to deceive me,
    But wha can think sae o' Tam Glen ?

My daddie says, gin I'll forsake him,
    He'll gie me guid hunder marks ten :
But, if it's ordain'd I maun take him,
    O wha will I get but Tam Glen ?

Yestreen at the Valentine's dealing,
    My heart to my mou' gied a sten ;
For thrice I drew ane without failing,
    And thrice it was written—Tam Glen.

The last Halloween I lay waukin
    My droukit sark-sleeve, as ye ken ;
His likeness cam up the house staukin,
    And the very grey breeks o' Tam Glen.

Come counsel, dear Tittie ! don't tarry—
    I'll gie ye my bonnie black hen,
Gif ye will advise me to marry
    The lad I lo'e dearly, Tam Glen.

IT IS NA, JEAN, THY BONNIE FACE.

Tune—*The Maid's complaint.*

It is na, Jean, thy bonnie face,
    Nor shape, that I admire,
Altho' thy beauty and thy grace
    Might weel awake desire.
Something, in ilka part o' thee,
    To praise, to love, I find ;
But, dear as is thy form to me,
    Still dearer is thy mind.

Nae mair ungen'rous wish I hae,
  Nor stronger in my breast,
Than if I canna mak thee sae,
  At least to see thee blest.
Content am I, if heaven shall give
  But happiness to thee:
And, as wi' thee I'd wish to live,
  For thee I'd bear to die.

MY LOVE SHE'S BUT A LASSIE YET.

TUNE—*Lady Badinscoth's Reel.*

My love she's but a lassie yet,
  My love she's but a lassie yet;
We'll let her stand a year or twa,
  She'll no be half sae saucy yet.
I rue the day I sought her, O,
  I rue the day I sought her, O;
Wha gets her need na say she's woo'd,
  But he may say he's bought her, O!

Come, draw a drap o' the best o't yet,
  Come, draw a drap o' the best o't yet;
Gae seek for pleasure where ye will,
  But here I never miss'd it yet.
We're a' dry wi' drinkin' o't,
  We're a' dry wi' drinkin' o't;
The minister kiss'd the fiddler's wife,
  An' couldna preach for thinkin' o't.

LOVELY DAVIES.

TUNE—*Miss Muir.*

O HOW shall I, unskilfu', try
  The poet's occupation,
The tunefu' powers, in happy hours,
  That whispers inspiration?

Even they maun dare an effort mair
  Than aught they ever gave us,
Or they rehearse, in equal verse,
  The charms o' lovely Davies.

Each eye it cheers, when she appears,
  Like Phœbus in the morning,
When past the shower, and every flower
  The garden is adorning.
As the wretch looks o'er Siberia's shore,
  When winter-bound the wave is;
Sae droops our heart when we maun part
  Frae charming, lovely Davies.

Her smile's a gift, frae 'boon the lift,
  That maks us mair than princes;
A sceptred hand, a king's command,
  Is in her darting glances :
The man in arms, 'gainst female charms,
  Even he her willing slave is;
He hugs his chain, and owns the reign
  Of conquering, lovely Davies.

My muse to dream of such a theme,
  Her feeble pow'rs surrender;
The eagle's gaze alone surveys
  The sun's meridian splendour :
I wad in vain essay the strain,
  The deed too daring brave is;
I'll drap the lyre, and mute, admire
  The charms o' lovely Davies.

WANDERING WILLIE.

HERE awa, there awa, wandering Willie,
  Now tired with wandering, haud awa hame;
Come to my bosom, my ae only dearie,
  And tell me thou bring'st me my Willie the same.

Loud blew the cauld winter winds at our parting;
   It was na the blast brought the tear in my e'e:
Now welcome the simmer, and welcome my Willie,
   The simmer to nature, my Willie to me.

Ye hurricanes, rest in the cave o' your slumbers!
   O how your wild horrors a lover alarms!
Awaken, ye breezes, row gently, ye billows,
   And waft my dear laddie ance mair to my arms.

But if he's forgotten his faithfullest Nannie,
   O still flow between us, thou wide roaring main;
May I never see it, may I never trow it,
   But, dying, believe that my Willie's my ain!

MY NANNIE'S AWA.

TUNE—*There'll never be Peace, etc.*

Now in her green mantle blithe nature arrays,
And listens the lambkins that bleat o'er the braes,
While birds warble welcome in ilka green shaw;
But to me it's delightless—my Nannie's awa!

The snaw-drap and primrose our woodlands adorn,
And violets bathe in the weet o' the morn;
They pain my sad bosom, sae sweetly they blaw,
They mind me o' Nannie—and Nannie's awa!

Thou lav'rock that springs frae the dews of the lawn,
The shepherd to warn o' the grey-breaking dawn,
And thou mellow mavis that hails the night fa',
Give over for pity—my Nannie's awa!

Come autumn sae pensive, in yellow and grey,
And soothe me with tidings o' nature's decay:
The dark dreary winter, and wild driving snaw,
Alane can delight me—now Nannie's awa!

CA' THE EWES.

TUNE—*Ca' the Ewes to the Knowes.*

As I gaed down the water-side,
There I met my shepherd lad,
He row'd me sweetly in his plaid,
  And he ca'd me his dearie.

    Ca' the ewes to the knowes,
    Ca' them whare the heather grows,
    Ca' them whare the burnie rowes,
      My bonnie dearie !

Will ye gang down the water-side,
And see the waves sae sweetly glide,
Beneath the hazels spreading wide ?
  The moon it shines fu' clearly.

I was bred up at nae sic school,
My shepherd lad, to play the fool,
And a' the day to sit in dool,
  And naebody to see me.

Ye sall get gowns and ribbons meet,
Cauf-leather shoon upon your feet,
And in my arms ye'se lie and sleep,
  And ye sall be my dearie.

If ye'll but stand to what ye've said,
I'se gang wi' you, my shepherd lad,
And ye may rowe me in your plaid,
  And I sall bé your dearie.

While waters wimple to the sea ;
While day blinks in the lift sae hie ;
'Till clay-cauld death sall blin' my e'e,
  Ye sall be my dearie.

THE LAZY MIST.

THE lazy mist hangs from the brow of the hill,
Concealing the course of the dark winding rill;
How languid the scenes, late so sprightly, appear!
As autumn to winter resigns the pale year.
The forests are leafless, the meadows are brown,
And all the gay foppery of summer is flown:
Apart let me wander, apart let me muse,
How quick time is flying, how keen fate pursues!

How long I have liv'd—but how much liv'd in vain !
How little of life's scanty span may remain !
What aspects, old Time, in his progress, has worn !
What ties cruel fate in my bosom has torn !
How foolish, or worse, till our summit is gain'd !
And downward, how weaken'd, how darken'd, how pain'd,
This life's not worth having with all it can give—
For something beyond it poor man sure must live.

SWEET CLOSES THE EVENING.

TUNE—*Craigie-burn wood.*

SWEET closes the evening on Craigie-burn wood,
 And blithely awaukens the morrow;
But the pride of the spring in the Craigie-burn wood
 Can yield to me nothing but sorrow.

  Beyond thee, dearie, beyond thee, dearie,
   And oh, to be lying beyond thee;
  O sweetly, soundly, weel may he sleep
   That's laid in the bed beyond thee !

I see the spreading leaves and flowers,
 I hear the wild birds singing;
But pleasure they hae nane for me,
 While care my heart is wringing.

I canna tell, I maunna tell,
 I darena for your anger;
But secret love will break my heart,
 If I conceal it langer.

I see thee gracefu', straight, and tall,
 I see thee sweet and bonnie;
But oh, what will my torments be,
 If thou refuse thy Johnnie !

To see thee in anither's arms,
  In love to lie and languish,
'Twad be my dead, that will be seen,
  My heart wad burst wi' anguish.

But, Jeanie, say thou wilt be mine,
  Say, thou lo'es nane before me;
And a' my days o' life to come
  I'll gratefully adore thee.

    Beyond thee, dearie, beyond thee, dearie,
      And oh, to be lying beyond thee;
    O sweetly, soundly, weel may he sleep
      That's laid in the bed beyond thee!

THERE'LL NEVER BE PEACE 'TILL JAMIE COMES HAME.

TUNE—There are few gude fellows when Willie's awa.

By yon castle wa', at the close of the day,
I heard a man sing, tho' his head it was grey;
And as he was singing, the tears fast down came,
There'll never be peace till Jamie comes hame.

The church is in ruins, the state is in jars;
Delusions, oppressions, and murderous wars;
We darena weel say't, tho' we ken wha's to blame—
There'll never be peace till Jamie comes hame!

My seven braw sons for Jamie drew sword,
And now I greet round their green beds in the yerd.
It brak the sweet heart of my faithfu' auld dame—
There'll never be peace till Jamie comes hame.

Now life is a burthen that bows me down,
Sin' I tint my bairns, and he tint his crown;
But till my last moments my words are the same—
There'll never be peace till Jamie comes hame!

GLOOMY DECEMBER.

Tune—*Wandering Willie.*

Ance mair I hail thee, thou gloomy December !
  Ance mair I hail thee, wi' sorrow and care ;
Sad was the parting thou makes me remember,
  Parting wi' Nancy, oh ! ne'er to meet mair.
Fond lovers' parting is sweet painful pleasure,
  Hope beaming mild on the soft parting hour ;
But the dire feeling, oh farewell for ever !
  Is anguish unmingl'd, and agony pure.

Wild as the winter now tearing the forest,
  'Till the last leaf o' the summer is flown,
Such is the tempest has shaken my bosom,
  Since my last hope and last comfort is gone !
Still as I hail thee, thou gloomy December,
  Still shall I hail thee wi' sorrow and care ;
For sad was the parting thou makes me remember,
  Parting wi' Nancy, oh ! ne'er to meet mair.

BEHOLD THE HOUR.

Tune—*Oran-gaoil.*

Behold the hour, the boat arrive,
  Thou goest, thou darling of my heart !
Sever'd from thee can I survive ?
  But fate has will'd, and we must part.
I'll often greet this surging swell,
  Yon distant isle will often hail :
" E'en here I took the last farewell ;
  There, latest mark'd her vanish'd sail."

Along the solitary shore,
  While flitting sea-fowl round me cry,
Across the rolling, dashing roar,
  I'll westward turn my wistful eye :

Happy, thou Indian grove, I'll say,
  Where now my Nancy's path may be!
While thro' thy sweets she loves to stray,
  O, tell me, does she muse on me?

OPEN THE DOOR TO ME, O!

O, open the door, some pity to show,
  O, open the door to me, O!
Tho' thou hast been false, I'll ever prove true,
  O, open the door to me, O!

Cauld is the blast upon my pale cheek,
  But caulder thy love for me, O!
The frost that freezes the life at my heart
  Is nought to my pains frae thee, O!

The wan moon is setting behind the white wave,
  And time is setting with me, O!
False friends, false love, farewell! for mair
  I'll ne'er trouble them, nor thee, O!

She has open'd the door, she has open'd it wide;
  She sees his pale corse on the plain, O!
My true love! she cried, and sank down by his side,
  Never to rise again, O!

WAR SONG.

AIR—*Oran an Doig; or, the Song of Death.*

Scene—A field of battle. Time of the day, evening. The wounded and dying of the
victorious army are supposed to join in the following song:—

FAREWELL, thou fair day, thou green earth, and ye skies,
  Now gay with the broad setting sun!
Farewell loves and friendships, ye dear tender ties!
  Our race of existence is run!

Thou grim king of terrors, thou life's gloomy foe!
　Go, frighten the coward and slave!
Go teach them to tremble, fell tyrant! but know,
　No terrors hast thou to the brave!

Thou strik'st the dull peasant,—he sinks in the dark,
　Nor saves e'en the wreck of a name;—
Thou strik'st the young hero—a glorious mark!
　He falls in the blaze of his fame!

In the field of proud honour—our swords in our hands,
　Our king and our country to save—
While victory shines on life's last ebbing sands
　Oh! who would not die with the brave!

AE FOND KISS.

TUNE—*Rory Dall's Port.*

AE fond kiss, and then we sever;
Ae fareweel, and then, for ever!
Deep in heart-wrung tears I'll pledge thee,
Warring sighs and groans I'll wage thee,
Who shall say that fortune grieves him,
While the star of hope she leaves him?
Me, nae cheerfu' twinkle lights me;
Dark despair around benights me.

I'll ne'er blame my partial fancy,
Naething could resist my Nancy;
But to see her was to love her;
Love but her, and love for ever.—
Had we never lov'd sae kindly,
Had we never lov'd sae blindly,
Never met—or never parted,
We had ne'er been broken-hearted.

Fare thee weel, thou first and fairest !
Fare thee weel, thou best and dearest !
Thine be ilka joy and treasure,
Peace, enjoyment, love, and pleasure !
Ae fond kiss, and then we sever ;
Ae fareweel, alas ! for ever !
Deep in heart-wrung tears I'll pledge thee,
Warring sighs and groans I'll wage thee.

BONNIE LESLEY.

O saw ye bonnie Lesley,
   As she gaed o'er the border?
She's gane, like Alexander,
   To spread her conquests farther.

To see her is to love her,
   And love but her for ever ;
For Nature made her what she is,
   And never made anither !

Thou art a queen, fair Lesley,
   Thy subjects we, before thee :
Thou art divine, fair Lesley,
   The hearts o' men adore thee.

The Deil he could na scaith thee,
   Nor aught that wad belang thee ;
He'd look into thy bonnie face,
   And say, " I canna wrang thee."

The powers aboon will tent thee ;
   Misfortune sha' na steer thee :
Thou'rt like themselves sae lovely,
   That ill they'll ne'er let near thee.

Return again, fair Lesley,
   Return to Caledonie !
That we may brag we hae a lass
   There's nane again sae bonnie.

A RED, RED ROSE.

TUNE—*Graham's Strathspey.*

O, MY luve's like a red, red rose,
   That's newly sprung in June :
O, my luve's like the melodie
   That's sweetly play'd in tune.

As fair art thou, my bonnie lass,
   So deep in luve am I :
And I will luve thee still, my dear,
   'Till a' the seas gang dry.

''Till a' the seas gang dry, my dear,
   And the rocks melt wi' the sun :
I will luve thee still, my dear,
   While the sands o' life shall run.

And fare thee weel, my only luve !
   And fare thee weel a-while !
And I will come again, my luve,
   Tho' it were ten thousand mile.

SIMMER'S A PLEASANT TIME.

TUNE—*Aye waukin O.*

SIMMER'S a pleasant time,
   Flow'rs of every colour ;
The water rins o'er the heugh,
   And I long for my true lover.

    Aye waukin O,
      Waukin still and wearie ;
    Sleep I can get nane
      For thinkin' on my dearie.

When I sleep I dream,
   When I wauk I'm eerie ;
Sleep I can get nane
   For thinkin' on my dearie.

Lanely night comes on,
   A' the lave are sleepin' ;
I think on my bonnie lad,
   And I bleer my een wi' greetin'.

    Aye waukin O,
      Waukin still and wearie ;
    Sleep I can get nane
      For thinkin' on my dearie.

THE BONNIE WEE THING.

TUNE—*Bonnie wee Thing.*

BONNIE wee thing, cannie wee thing,
　Lovely wee thing, wert thou mine,
I wad wear thee in my bosom,
　Lest my jewel I should tine.
Wishfully I look and languish
　In that bonnie face o' thine;
And my heart it stounds wi' anguish,
　Lest my wee thing be na mine.

Wit, and grace, and love, and beauty,
　In ae constellation shine;
To adore thee is my duty,
　Goddess o' this soul o' mine!
Bonnie wee thing, cannie wee thing,
　Lovely wee thing, wert thou mine,
I wad wear thee in my bosom,
　Lest my jewel I should tine!

BESS AND HER SPINNING-WHEEL.

TUNE—*The sweet Lass that lo'es me.*

O LEEZE me on my spinning-wheel,
And leeze me on my rock and reel;
Frae tap to tae that cleeds me bien,
And haps me fiel and warm at e'en!
I'll set me down and sing and spin,
While laigh descends the simmer sun,
Blest wi' content, and milk and meal—
O leeze me on my spinning-wheel!

On ilka hand the burnies trot,
And meet below my theekit cot;
The scented birk and hawthorn white,
Across the pool their arms unite,
Alike to screen the birdie's nest,
And little fishes' caller rest:

The sun blinks kindly in the biel',
Where blithe I turn my spinning-wheel.

On lofty aiks the cushats wail,
And echo cons the doolfu' tale ;
The lintwhites in the hazel braes,
Delighted, rival ither's lays :
The craik amang the clover hay,
The paitrick whirrin' o'er the ley,
The swallow jinkin round my shiel,
Amuse me at my spinning-wheel.

Wi' sma' to sell, and less to buy,
Aboon distress, below envy,
O wha wad leave this humble state,
For a' the pride of a' the great ?
Amid their flaring, idle toys,
Amid their cumbrous, dinsome joys,
Can they the peace and pleasure feel
Of Bessy at her spinning-wheel ?

NITHSDALE'S WELCOME HAME.

THE noble Maxwells and the powers,
    Are coming o'er the border,
And they'll gae big Terreagle's towers,
    And set them a' in order.
And they declare Terreagle's fair,
    For their abode they chuse it ;
There's no a heart in a' the land
    But's lighter at the news o't.

Tho' stars in skies may disappear,
    And angry tempests gather ;
The happy hour may soon be near
    That brings us pleasant weather :
The weary night o' care and grief
    May hae a joyfu' morrow ;
So dawning day has brought relief—
    Farcweel our night o' sorrow !

AULD LANG SYNE.

SHOULD auld acquaintance be forgot,
    And never brought to min' ?
Should auld acquaintance be forgot,
    And days o' lang syne ?

        For auld lang syne, my dear,
            For auld lang syne,
        We'll tak a cup o' kindness yet,
            For auld lang syne !

We twa hae run about the braes,
   And pu'd the gowans fine;
But we've wander'd mony a weary foot,
   Sin auld lang syne.

We twa hae paidl't i' the burn,
   Frae mornin' sun till dine:
But seas between us braid hae roar'd,
   Sin auld lang syne.

And here's a hand, my trusty fiere,
    And gie's a hand o' thine ;
And we'll tak a right guid willie-waught,
    For auld lang syne !

And surely ye'll be your pint stoup,
    And surely I'll be mine ;
And we'll tak a cup o' kindness yet,
    For auld lang syne !

     For auld lang syne, my dear,
      For auld lang syne,
     We'll tak a cup o' kindness yet,
      For auld lang syne !

O, FOR ANE-AND-TWENTY, TAM !

TUNE—*The Moudiewort.*

AN' O, for ane-and-twenty, Tam !
    An' hey, sweet ane-and-twenty, Tam !
I'll learn my kin a rattlin' sang,
    An I saw ane-and-twenty, Tam.

They snool me sair, and haud me down,
    And gar me look like bluntie, Tam ;
But three short years will soon wheel roun'—
    And then comes ane-and-twenty, Tam.

A gleib o' lan', a claut o' gear,
    Was left me by my auntie, Tam ;
At kith or kin I need na spier,
    An I saw ane-and-twenty, Tam.

They'll hae me wed a wealthy coof,
    'Tho' I mysel' hae plenty, Tam ;
But hear'st thou laddie—there's my loof—
    I'm thine at ane-and-twenty, Tam.

    An' O, for ane-and-twenty, Tam !
     An' hey, sweet ane-and-twenty, Tam !
    I'll learn my kin a rattlin' sang,
     An I saw ane-and-twenty, Tam.

FAIR ELIZA.

A Gaelic Air.

Turn again, thou fair Eliza,
    Ae kind blink before we part,
Rue on thy despairing lover!
    Canst thou break his faithfu' heart?
Turn again, thou fair Eliza;
    If to love thy heart denies,
For pity hide the cruel sentence
    Under friendship's kind disguise!

'Thee, dear maid, hae I offended?
    The offence is loving thee:
Canst thou wreck his peace for ever
    Wha for thine wad gladly dee?
While the life beats in my bosom,
    Thou shalt mix in ilka throe;
Turn again, thou lovely maiden,
    Ae sweet smile on me bestow.

Not the bee upon the blossom,
    In the pride o' sunny noon;
Not the little sporting fairy,
    All beneath the simmer moon;
Not the poet, in the moment
    Fancy lightens in his e'e,
Kens the pleasure, feels the rapture,
    That thy presence gies to me.

O LUVE WILL VENTURE IN.

Tune—*The Posie.*

O luve will venture in
    Where it daurna weel be seen
O luve will venture in
    Where wisdom aince has been;

2 G

But I will down yon river rove,
  Amang the wood sae green,
And a' to pu' a posie
  To my ain dear May.

The primrose I will pu',
  The firstling of the year ;
And I will pu' the pink,
  The emblem o' my dear ;
For she's the pink o' womankind,
  And blooms without a peer—
And a' to be a posie
  To my ain dear May.

I'll pu' the budding rose,
  When Phœbus peeps in view,
For its like a baumy kiss
  O' her sweet, bonnie mou' ;
The hyacinth's for constancy,
  Wi' its unchanging blue—
And a' to be a posie
  To my ain dear May.

The lily it is pure,
  And the lily it is fair,
And in her lovely bosom
  I'll place the lily there ;
The daisy's for simplicity,
  And unaffected air—
And a' to be a posie
  To my ain dear May.

The hawthorn I will pu',
  Wi' its locks o' siller grey,
Where, like an aged man,
  It stands at break of day.
But the songster's nest within the bush
  I winna tak away—
And a' to be a posie
  To my ain dear May.

The woodbine I will pu',
　　When the ev'ning star is near,
And the diamond draps o' dew
　　Shall be her een sae clear;
The violet's for modesty,
　　Which weel she fa's to wear—
And a' to be a posie
　　To my ain dear May.

I'll tie the posie round
　　Wi' the silken band of love,
And I'll place it in her breast,
　　And I'll swear, by a' above,
That to my latest draught o' life
　　The band shall ne'er remove—
And this will be a posie
　　To my ain dear May.

ANNA, THY CHARMS.

Tune—*Bonnie Mary.*

Anna, thy charms my bosom fire,
　　And waste my soul with care;
But, ah! how bootless to admire,
　　When fated to despair!
Yet in thy presence, lovely fair,
　　To hope may be forgiv'n;
For sure 'twere impious to despair,
　　So much in sight of heav'n

SHE'S FAIR AND FAUSE.

Tune—*She's fair and fause.*

She's fair and fause that causes my smart,
　　I lo'ed her meikle and lang;
She's broken her vow, she's broken my heart,
　　And I may e'en gae hang.

A coof cam in wi' routh o' gear,
And I hae tint my dearest dear;
But woman is but warld's gear,
 Sae let the bonnie lassie gang.

Whae'er ye be that woman love,
 To this be never blind,
Nae ferlie 'tis tho' fickle she prove,
 A woman has't by kind.
O woman, lovely woman fair!
An angel form's fa'n to thy share,
'Twad been o'er meikle to gien thee mair—
 I mean an angel mind.

FRAE THE FRIENDS AND LAND I LOVE.

FRAE the friends and land I love,
 Driv'n by fortune's felly spite,
Frae my best belov'd I rove,
 Never mair to taste delight;
Never mair maun hope to find
 Ease frae toil, relief frae care:
When remembrance racks the mind,
 Pleasures but unveil despair.

Brightest climes shall mirk appear,
 Desert ilka blooming shore,
Till the fates, nae mair severe,
 Friendship, love, and peace restore;
Till Revenge, wi' laurell'd head,
 Bring our banish'd hame again;
And ilka loyal bonnie lad
 Cross the seas and win his ain.

THE BANKS OF THE DEVON.

How pleasant the banks of the clear winding Devon,
 With green-spreading bushes, and flowers blooming fair!
But the bonniest flower on the banks of the Devon
 Was once a sweet bud, on the braes of the Ayr.

Mild be the sun on this sweet blushing flower,
　In the gay rosy morn, as it bathes in the dew!
And gentle the fall of the soft vernal shower,
　That steals on the evening each leaf to renew.

O spare the dear blossom, ye orient breezes,
   With chill hoary wing, as ye usher the dawn !
And far be thou distant, thou reptile, that seizes
   The verdure and pride of the garden and lawn !
Let Bourbon exult in his gay gilded lilies,
   And England, triumphant, display her proud rose :
A fairer than either adorns the green valleys,
   Where Devon, sweet Devon, meandering flows.

MY AIN KIND DEARIE, O.

TUNE—*The Lea-Rig.*

WHEN o'er the hill the eastern star
   Tells bughtin-time is near, my jo ;
And owsen frae the furrow'd field
   Return sae dowf and weary, O ;
Down by the burn, where scented birks
   Wi' dew are hanging clear, my jo ;
I'll meet thee on the lea-rig,
   My ain kind dearie, O !

In mirkest glen, at midnight hour,
   I'd rove, and ne'er be eerie, O ;
If thro' that glen I gaed to thee,
   My ain kind dearie, O !
Altho' the night were ne'er sae wild,
   And I were ne'er sae wearie, O,
I'd meet thee on the lea-rig,
   My ain kind dearie, O !

The hunter lo'es the morning sun,
   To rouse the mountain deer, my jo ;
At noon the fisher seeks the glen,
   Along the burn to steer, my jo ;
Gie me the hour o' gloamin grey,
   It maks my heart sae cheerie, O,
To meet thee on the lea-rig,
   My ain kind dearie, O !

MY WIFE'S A WINSOME WEE THING.

SHE is a winsome wee thing,
She is a handsome wee thing,
She is a bonnie wee thing,
This sweet wee wife o' mine.

I never saw a fairer,
I never lo'ed a dearer;
And neist my heart I'll wear her,
For fear my jewel tine.

She is a winsome wee thing,
She is a handsome wee thing,
She is a bonnie wee thing,
This sweet wee wife o' mine.

The warld's wrack we share o't,
The warstle and the care o't;
Wi' her I'll blithely bear it,
And think my lot divine.

THE GALLANT WEAVER.

TUNE—*The Weavers' March.*

WHERE Cart rins rowin' to the sea,
By mony a flow'r and spreading tree,
There lives a lad, the lad for me,
He is a gallant weaver.
Oh, I had wooers aught or nine,
They gied me rings and ribbons fine;
And I was fear'd my heart would tine
And I gied it to the weaver.

My daddie signed my tocher-band,
To gie the lad that has the land;
But to my heart I'll add my hand,
And gie it to the weaver.
While birds rejoice in leafy bowers;
While bees delight in op'ning flowers;
While corn grows green in simmer showers,
I'll love my gallant weaver.

THE BANKS O' DOON.

FIRST VERSION.

Ye flowery banks o' bonnie Doon,
  How can ye bloom sae fair?
How can ye chant, ye little birds,
  And I sae fu' o' care?

Thou'll break my heart, thou bonnie bird,
  That sings upon the bough;
Thou minds me o' the happy days
  When my fause luve was true.

Thou'll break my heart, thou bonnie bird,
  That sings beside thy mate;
For sae I sat, and sae I sang,
  And wist na o' my fate.

Aft hae I rov'd by bonnie Doon,
  To see the woodbine twine,
And ilka bird sang o' its love;
  And sae did I o' mine.

Wi' lightsome heart I pu'd a rose,
  Frae aff its thorny tree;
And my fause luver staw the rose,
  But left the thorn wi' me.

THE BANKS O' DOON.

SECOND VERSION.

TUNE—*Caledonian Hunt's Delight.*

Ye banks and braes o' bonnie Doon,
  How can you bloom sae fresh and fair?
How can ye chant, ye little birds,
  And I sae weary, fu' o' care?
Thou'll break my heart, thou warbling bird,
  That wantons thro' the flowering thorn:
Thou minds me o' departed joys,
  Departed—never to return!

Oft hae I rov'd by bonnie Doon,
　To see the rose and woodbine twine ;
And ilka bird sang o' its luve,
　And fondly sae did I o' mine,
Wi' lightsome heart I pu'd a rose,
　Fu' sweet upon its thorny tree ;
And my fause luver stole my rose,
　But, ah ! he left the thorn wi' me.

THE BONNIE LAD THAT'S FAR AWA.

Tune—*Owre the Hills and far awa.*

O how can I be blithe and glad,
　Or how can I gang brisk and braw,
When the bonnie lad that I lo'e best
　Is o'er the hills and far awa ?
When the bonnie lad that I lo'e best
　Is o'er the hills and far awa ?

It's no the frosty winter wind,
   It's no the driving drift and snaw;
But aye the tear comes in my e'e,
   To think on him that's far awa.
But aye the tear comes in my e'e,
   To think on him that's far awa.

My father pat me frae his door,
   My friends they hae disown'd me a',
But I hae ane will tak' my part,
   The bonnie lad that's far awa.
But I hae ane will tak' my part,—
   The bonnie lad that's far awa.

A pair o' gloves he bought for me,
   And silken snoods he gae me twa;
And I will wear them for his sake,
   The bonnie lad that's far awa.
And I will wear them for his sake,—
   The bonnie lad that's far awa.

O weary winter soon will pass,
   And spring will cleed the birken-shaw;
And my young babie will be born,
   And he'll be hame that's far awa.
And my young babie will be born,
   And he'll be hame that's far awa.

SMILING SPRING COMES IN REJOICING.

TUNE—*Bonnie Bell.*

THE smiling spring comes in rejoicing,
   And surly winter grimly flies;
Now crystal clear are the falling waters,
   And bonnie blue are the sunny skies;
Fresh o'er the mountains breaks forth the morning,
   The ev'ning gilds the ocean's swell;
All creatures joy in the sun's returning,
   And I rejoice in my bonnie Bell.

The flowery spring leads sunny summer,
  And yellow autumn presses near,
Then in his turn comes gloomy winter,
  Till smiling spring again appear.
Thus seasons dancing, life advancing,
  Old Time and Nature their changes tell,
But never ranging, still unchanging,
  I adore my bonnie Bell.

MY TOCHER'S THE JEWEL.

TUNE—*My Tocher's the Jewel.*

O MEIKLE thinks my luve o' my beauty,
  And meikle thinks my luve o' my kin ;
But little thinks my luve I ken brawlie
  My tocher's the jewel has charms for him.
It's a' for the apple he'll nourish the tree ;
  It's a' for the hiney he'll cherish the bee ;
My laddie's sae meikle in luve wi' the siller,
  He canna hae luve to spare for me.

Your proffer o' luve's an airl-penny,
  My tocher's the bargain ye wad buy ;
But an ye be crafty, I am cunnin',
  Sae ye wi' anither your fortune maun try.
Ye're like to the timmer o' yon rotten wood,
  Ye're like to the bark o' yon rotten tree,
Ye'll slip frae me like a knotless thread,
  And ye'll crack your credit wi' mae nor me.

SAW YE MY PHELY.

TUNE—*When she cam ben she bobbit.*

O SAW ye my dear, my Phely ?
O saw ye my dear, my Phely ?
She's down i' the grove, she's wi' a new love,
  She winna come hame to her Willy.

What says she, my dearest, my Phely ?
What says she, my dearest, my Phely ?
She lets thee to wit that she has thee forgot,
    And for ever disowns thee, her Willy.

O had I ne'er seen thee, my Phely !
O had I ne'er seen thee, my Phely !
As light as the air, and fause as thou's fair—
    Thou's broken the heart o' thy Willy.

THE CHARMING MONTH OF MAY.

IT was the charming month of May,
When all the flow'rs were fresh and gay,
One morning, by the break of day,
    The youthful, charming Chloe ;
From peaceful slumber she arose,
Girt on her mantle and her hose,
And o'er the flowery mead she goes,
    The youthful, charming Chloe.
        Lovely was she by the dawn,
            Youthful Chloe, charming Chloe,
        Tripping o'er the pearly lawn,
            The youthful, charming Chloe.

The feather'd people you might see,
Perch'd all around, on every tree,
In notes of sweetest melody,
    They hail the charming Chloe ;
Till, painting gay the eastern skies,
The glorious sun began to rise,
Out-rivall'd by the radiant eyes
    Of youthful, charming Chloe.
        Lovely was she by the dawn,
            Youthful Chloe, charming Chloe,
        Tripping o'er the pearly lawn,
            . The youthful, charming Chloe.

FAREWELL, THOU STREAM.

Farewell, thou stream that winding flows
　Around Eliza's dwelling!
O mem'ry! spare the cruel throes
　Within my bosom swelling:
Condemn'd to drag a hopeless chain,
　And yet in secret languish,
To feel a fire in every vein,
　Nor dare disclose my anguish.

Love's veriest wretch, unseen, unknown,
　I fain my griefs would cover;
The bursting sigh, th' unweeting groan,
　Betray the hapless lover.
I know thou doom'st me to despair,
　Nor wilt, nor canst, relieve me;
But O, Eliza, hear one prayer—
　For pity's sake forgive me!

The music of thy voice I heard,
　Nor wist while it enslav'd me;
I saw thine eyes, yet nothing fear'd,
　'Till fears no more had sav'd me:
Th' unwary sailor thus aghast,
　The wheeling torrent viewing;
'Mid circling horrors sinks at last
　In overwhelming ruin.

O PHILLY, HAPPY BE THAT DAY.

Tune—*The Sow's Tail.*

HE.

O Philly, happy be that day,
When, roving through the gather'd hay,
My youthfu' heart was stown away,
　And by thy charms, my Philly.

SHE.

O Willy, aye I bless the grove
Where first I own'd my maiden love,
Whilst thou didst pledge the Powers above
    To be my ain dear Willy.

HE.

As songsters of the early year
Are ilka day mair sweet to hear,
So ilka day to me mair dear
    And charming is my Philly.

SHE.

As on the brier the budding rose
Still richer breathes and fairer blows,
So in my tender bosom grows
    The love I bear my Willy.

HE.

The milder sun and bluer sky
That crown my harvest cares wi' joy,
Were ne'er sae welcome to my eye
    As is a sight o' Philly.

SHE.

The little swallow's wanton wing,
Tho' wafting o'er the flowery spring,
Did ne'er to me sic tidings bring
    As meeting o' my Willy.

HE.

The bee that thro' the sunny hour
Sips nectar in the opening flower,
Compar'd wi' my delight is poor,
    Upon the lips o' Philly.

SHE.

The woodbine in the dewy weet
When evening shades in silence meet,
Is nocht sae fragrant or sae sweet
    As is a kiss o' Willy.

HE.

Let fortune's wheel at random rin,
And fools may tine, and knaves may win ;
My thoughts are a' bound up in ane,
    And that's my ain dear Philly.

SHE.

What's a' the joys that gowd can gie ?
I care na wealth a single flie ;
The lad I love's the lad for me,
    And that's my ain dear Willy.

CHLORIS.

My Chloris, mark how green the groves,
    The primrose banks how fair ;
The balmy gales awake the flowers,
    And wave thy flaxen hair.

The lav'rock shuns the palace gay,
    And o'er the cottage sings ;

For nature smiles as sweet, I ween,
  To shepherds as to kings.

Let minstrels sweep the skilfu' string
  In lordly lighted ha' :
The shepherd stops his simple reed,
  Blithe, in the birken shaw.

The princely revel may survey
  Our rustic dance wi' scorn ;
But are their hearts as light as ours,
  Beneath the milk-white thorn ?

The shepherd, in the flow'ry glen,
  In shepherd's phrase will woo :
The courtier tells a finer tale—
  But is his heart as true ?

These wild-wood flowers I've pu'd, to deck
  That spotless breast o' thine :
The courtier's gems may witness love—
  But 'tis na love like mine.

HOW LANG AND DREARY IS THE NIGHT.

Tune—*Cauld Kail in Aberdeen.*

How lang and dreary is the night,
  When I am frae my dearie ;
I restless lie frae e'en to morn,
  Though I were ne'er sae weary.

    For oh ! her lanely nights are lang ;
      And oh, her dreams are eerie ;
    And oh, her widow'd heart is sair,
      That's absent frae her dearie.

When I think on the lightsome days
  I spent wi' thee, my dearie ;

And now what seas between us roar—
  How can I be but eerie ?

How slow ye move, ye heavy hours !
  The joyless day how dreary !
It was na sae ye glinted by,
  When I was wi' my dearie.

    For oh, her lanely nights are lang ;
      And oh, her dreams are eerie ;
    And oh, her widow'd heart is sair,
      That's absent frae her dearie.

TO CHLORIS.

'Tis friendship's pledge, my young, fair friend,
  Nor thou the gift refuse,
Nor with unwilling ear attend
  The moralising muse.

Since thou, in all thy youth and charms,
  Must bid the world adieu,
(A world 'gainst peace in constant arms)
  To join the friendly few.

Since, thy gay morn of life o'ercast,
  Chill came the tempest's lower ;
(And ne'er misfortune's eastern blast
  Did nip a fairer flower.)

Since life's gay scenes must charm no more,
  Still much is left behind ;
Still nobler wealth hast thou in store—
  The comforts of the mind !

Thine is the self-approving glow,
  On conscious honour's part ;
And, dearest gift of heaven below,
  Thine friendship's truest heart.

The joys refin'd of sense and taste,
  With every muse to rove :
And doubly were the poet blest,
  These joys could he improve.

AH, CHLORIS.

Tune—*Major Graham.*

Ah, Chloris! since it may na be
  That thou of love wilt hear ;
If from the lover thou maun flee,
  Yet let the friend be dear.

Altho' I love my Chloris mair
  Than ever tongue could tell ;
My passion I will ne'er declare,
  I'll say, I wish thee well.

Tho' a' my daily care thou art,
  And a' my nightly dream,
I'll hide the struggle in my heart,
  And say it is esteem.

LET NOT WOMAN E'ER COMPLAIN.

Tune—*Duncan Gray.*

Let not woman e'er complain
  Of inconstancy in love ;
Let not woman e'er complain
  Fickle man is apt to rove :
Look abroad through nature's range,
Nature's mighty law is change ;
Ladies, would it not be strange,
  Man should then a monster prove ?

Mark the winds, and mark the skies ;
  Ocean's ebb, and ocean's flow ;
Sun and moon but set to rise,
  Round and round the seasons go :

Why then ask of silly man
To oppose great nature's plan?
We'll be constant while we can—
    You can be no more, you know.

AFTON WATER.

Tune—*The Yellow-haired Laddie.*

Flow gently, sweet Afton! among thy green braes,
Flow gently, I'll sing thee a song in thy praise;
My Mary's asleep by thy murmuring stream—
Flow gently, sweet Afton, disturb not her dream.

Thou stock-dove, whose echo resounds thro' the glen,
Ye wild whistling blackbirds in yon thorny den;
Thou green-crested lapwing, thy screaming forbear—
I charge you disturb not my slumbering fair.

How lofty, sweet Afton! thy neighbouring hills,
Far mark'd with the courses of clear winding rills;
There daily I wander as noon rises high,
My flocks and my Mary's sweet cot in my eye.

How pleasant thy banks and green valleys below,
Where wild in the woodlands the primroses blow!
There oft as mild ev'ning weeps over the lea,
The sweet-scented birk shades my Mary and me.

The crystal stream, Afton, how lovely it glides!
And winds by the cot where my Mary resides!
How wanton thy waters her snowy feet lave,
As gathering sweet flow'rets she stems thy clear wave.

Flow gently, sweet Afton! among thy green braes,
Flow gently, sweet river, the theme of my lays!
My Mary's asleep by thy murmuring stream—
Flow gently, sweet Afton! disturb not her dream.

CONTENTED WI' LITTLE.

TUNE—*Lumps o' Pudding.*

CONTENTED wi' little, and cantie wi' mair,
Whene'er I foregather wi' sorrow and care,
I gie them a skelp, as they're creeping alang,
Wi' a cog o' guid swats, and an auld Scottish sang.

I whiles claw the elbow o' troublesome thought;
But man is a sodger, and life is a faught;
My mirth and guid humour are coin in my pouch,
And my freedom's my lairdship nae monarch dare touch.

A towmond o' trouble, should that be my fa',
A night o' guid fellowship sowthers it a': ·
When at the blithe end o' our journey at last,
Wha the deil ever thinks o' the road he has past!

Blind chance, let her snapper and stoyte on her way;
Be't to me, be't frae me, e'en let the jade gae:
Come ease, or come travail; come pleasure or pain;
My warst word is—"Welcome, and welcome again!"

THE HIGHLAND LADDIE.

TUNE—*If thou'lt play me fair play.*

THE bonniest lad that e'er I saw,
  Bonnie laddie, Highland laddie,
Wore a plaid, and was fu' braw,
  Bonnie Highland laddie.
On his head a bonnet blue,
  Bonnie laddie, Highland laddie:
His royal heart was firm and true,
  Bonnie Highland laddie.

Trumpets sound, and cannons roar,
  Bonnie lassie, Lawland lassie;
And a' the hills wi' echoes roar,
  Bonnie Lawland lassie.
Glory, honour, now invite,
  Bonnie lassie, Lawland lassie,
For freedom and my king to fight,
  Bonnie Lawland lassie.

The sun a backward course shall take,
  Bonnie laddie, Highland laddie;
Ere aught thy manly courage shake,
  Bonnie Highland laddie.
Go! for yoursel' procure renown,
  Bonnie laddie, Highland laddie;
And for your lawful king, his crown,
  Bonnie Highland laddie.

CALEDONIA.

Tune—*Caledonian Hunt's Delight.*

THERE was once a day—but old Time then was young—,
 That brave Caledonia, the chief of her line,
From some of your northern deities sprung,
 (Who knows not that brave Caledonia's divine ?)
From Tweed to the Orcades was her domain,
 To hunt, or to pasture, or do what she would :
Her heav'nly relations there fixed her reign,
 And pledg'd her their godheads to warrant it good.

A lambkin in peace, but a lion in war,
 The pride of her kindred the heroine grew :
Her grandsire, old Odin, triumphantly swore,
 "Whoe'er shall provoke thee th' encounter shall rue !"
With tillage or pasture at times she would sport
 To feed her fair flocks by her green rustling corn ;
But chiefly the woods were her fav'rite resort,
 Her darling amusement the hounds and the horn.

Long quiet she reign'd ; till thitherward steers
 A flight of bold eagles from Adria's strand :
Repeated, successive, for many long years,
 They darken'd the air, and they plunder'd the land :
Their pounces were murder, and terror their cry,
 They'd conquer'd and ruin'd a world beside ;
She took to her hill, and her arrows let fly—
 The daring invaders they fled or they died.

The fell Harpy-raven took wing from the north,
 The scourge of the seas, and the dread of the shore !
The wild Scandinavian boar issu'd forth,
 To wanton in carnage, and wallow in gore ;
O'er countries and kingdoms their fury prevail'd,
 No arts could appease them, no arms could repel ;
But brave Caledonia in vain they assail'd,
 As Largs well can witness, and Loncartie tell.

The Cameleon-savage disturb'd her repose,
  With tumult, disquiet, rebellion, and strife;
Provok'd beyond bearing, at last she arose,
  And robb'd him at once of his hopes and his life:
The Anglian lion, the terror of France,
  Oft prowling, ensanguin'd the Tweed's silver flood:
But, taught by the bright Caledonian lance,
  He learned to fear in his own native wood.

Thus bold, independent, unconquer'd, and free,
  Her bright course of glory for ever shall run:
For brave Caledonia immortal must be;
  I'll prove it from Euclid as clear as the sun.
Rectangle-triangle, the figure we'll choose,
  The upright is Chance, and old Time is the base;
But brave Caledonia's the hypothenuse;
  Then, ergo, she'll match them and match them always.

THE FAREWELL.

TUNE—*It was a' for our rightfu' king.*

IT was a' for our rightfu' king,
  We left fair Scotland's strand;
It was a' for our rightfu' king
  We e'er saw Irish land, my dear,
  We e'er saw Irish land.

Now a' is done that men can do,
  And a' is done in vain;
My love and native land farewell,
  For I maun cross the main, my dear,
  For I maun cross the main.

He turned him right, and round about,
  Upon the Irish shore;
And gae his bridle-reins a shake,
  With adieu for evermore, my dear,
  With adieu for evermore.

The sodger frae the wars returns,
  The sailor frae the main ;
But I hae parted frae my love,
  Never to meet again, my dear,
  Never to meet again.

When day is gane, and night is come,
  And a' folk bound to sleep ;
I think on him that's far awa',
  The lee-lang night, and weep, my dear,
  The lee-lang night, and weep.

HER FLOWING LOCKS.

TUNE—*Unknown.*

HER flowing locks, the raven's wing,
Adown her neck and bosom hing ;
How sweet unto that breast to cling,
  And round that neck entwine her !
Her lips are roses wat wi' dew,
O, what a feast her bonnie mou' !
Her cheeks a mair celestial hue,
  A crimson still diviner.

O STEER HER UP.

TUNE—*O steer her up and haud her gaun.*

O STEER her up and haud her gaun—
  Her mither's at the mill, jo ;
An' gin she winna tak' a man,
  E'en let her tak' her will, jo :
First shore her wi' a kindly kiss,
  And ca' anither gill, jo,
An' gin she tak' the thing amiss,
  E'en let her flyte her fill, jo.

O steer her up, and be na blate,
  An' gin she tak' it ill, jo,
Then lea'e the lassie till her fate,
  An' time nae langer spill, jo :

Ne'er break your heart for ae rebut,
  But think upon it still, jo ;
That gin the lassie winna do't,
  Ye'll fin' anither will, jo.

FOR THE SAKE OF SOMEBODY.

TUNE—*For the sake of Somebody.*

My heart is sair—I dare na tell—
  My heart is sair for Somebody ;
I could wake a winter night
  For the sake o' Somebody.

2 K

Oh-hon ! for Somebody !
Oh-hey ! for Somebody !
I could range the world around,
For the sake o' Somebody !

Ye Powers that smile on virtuous love,
O, sweetly smile on Somebody !
Frae ilka danger keep him free,
And send me safe my Somebody.
Oh-hon ! for Somebody !
Oh-hey ! for Somebody !
I wad do—what wad I not ?
For the sake o' Somebody ?

THE HIGHLAND WIDOW'S LAMENT.

OH ! I am come to the low countrie,
Och-on, och-on, och-rie !
Without a penny in my purse,
To buy a meal to me.

It was na sae in the Highland hills,
Och-on, och-on, och-rie !
Nae woman in the country wide
Sae happy was as me.

For then I had a score o' kye,
Och-on, och-on, och-rie !
Feeding on yon hills so high,
And giving milk to me.

And there I had three score o' yowes,
Och-on, och-on, och-rie !
Skipping on yon bonnie knowes,
And casting woo' to me.

I was the happiest of a' the clan,
Sair, sair may I repine ;
For Donald was the brawest man,
And Donald he was mine.

Till Charlie Stuart cam' at last,
  Sae far to set us free ;
My Donald's arm was wanted then
  For Scotland and for me.

Their waefu' fate what need I tell,
  Right to the wrang did yield :
My Donald and his Country fel'
  Upon Culloden-field.

Ochon, O Donald, O !
  Och-on, och-on, och-rie !
Nae woman in the warld wide
  Sae wretched now as me.

CANST THOU LEAVE ME THUS, MY KATY?

TUNE—*Roy's Wife.*

Is this thy plighted, fond regard,
  Thus cruelly to part, my Katy?
Is this thy faithful swain's reward—
  An aching, broken heart, my Katy?

    Canst thou leave me thus, my Katy?
    Canst thou leave me thus, my Katy?
    Well thou know'st my aching heart—
    And canst thou leave me thus for pity?

Farewell ! and ne'er such sorrows tear
  That fickle heart of thine, my Katy !
Thou may'st find those will love thee dear—
  But not a love like mine, my Katy !

    Canst thou leave me thus, my Katy?
    Canst thou leave me thus, my Katy?
    Well thou know'st my aching heart—
    And canst thou leave me thus for pity?

AMANG THE TREES WHERE HUMMING BEES.

TUNE—*The King of France, he rode a Race.*

AMANG the trees, where humming bees
　　At buds and flowers were hinging, O,
Auld Caledon drew out her drone,
　　And to her pipe was singing, O ;
'Twas pibroch, sang, strathspey, or reels,
　　She dirl'd them aff fu' clearly, O,
When there cam a yell o' foreign squeels,
　　That dang her tapsalteerie, O.

Their capon craws and queer ha ha's,
　　They made our lugs grow eerie, O ;
The hungry bike did scrape and pike,
　　'Till we were wae and weary, O ;
But a royal ghaist wha ance was cas'd
　　A prisoner aughteen year awa,
He fir'd a fiddler in the north
　　That dang them tapsalteerie, O.

MY HEART'S IN THE HIGHLANDS.

TUNE—*Faille na Miosg.*

My heart's in the Highlands, my heart is not here ;
My heart's in the Highlands a chasing the deer ;
Chasing the wild deer, and following the roe—
My heart's in the Highlands, wherever I go.
Farewell to the Highlands, farewell to the North,
The birthplace of valour, the country of worth ;
Wherever I wander, wherever I rove,
The hills of the Highlands for ever I love.

Farewell to the mountains high cover'd with snow ;
Farewell to the straths and green valleys below ;
Farewell to the forests and wild hanging woods ;
Farewell to the torrents and loud-pouring floods.

My heart's in the Highlands, my heart is not here,
My heart's in the Highlands a chasing the deer ;
Chasing the wild deer, and following the roe—
My heart's in the Highlands, wherever I go.

CASSILLIS' BANKS.

Tune—*Unknown.*

Now bank an' brae are claith'd in green,
  An' scatter'd cowslips sweetly spring ;
By Girvan's fairy-haunted stream
  The birdies flit on wanton wing.
To Cassillis' banks when e'ening fa's,
  There wi' my Mary let me flee,
There catch her ilka glance of love,
  The bonnie blink o' Mary's e'e !

The chield wha boasts o' warld's walth
  Is aften laird o' meikle care ;
But Mary she is a' mine ain—
  Ah ! fortune canna gie me mair !
Then let me range by Cassillis' banks,
  Wi' her, the lassie dear to me,
And catch her ilka glance o' love,
  The bonnie blink o' Mary's e'e !

THE WINTER OF LIFE.

Tune—*Gil Morice.*

But lately seen in gladsome green,
  The woods rejoic'd the day ;
Thro' gentle showers the laughing flowers
  In double pride were gay :
But now our joys are fled
  On winter blasts awa !
Yet maiden May, in rich array,
  Again shall bring them a'.

But my white pow, nae kindly thowe,
  Shall melt the snaws of age ;
My trunk of eild, but buss or bield,
  Sinks in Time's wintry rage.

Oh ! age has weary days,
  And nights o' sleepless pain !
Thou golden time o' youthfu' prime,
  Why com'st thou not again ?

BANNOCKS O' BARLEY.

Tune—*The Killogie.*

Bannocks o' bear meal,
  Bannocks o' barley ;
Here's to the Highlandman's
  Bannocks o' barley.
Wha in a brulzie,
  Will first cry a parley ?
Never the lads wi'
  The bannocks o' barley !

Bannocks o' bear meal,
  Bannocks o' barley ;
Here's to the Highlandman's
  Bannocks o' barley !
Wha in his wae-days
  Were loyal to Charlie ?
Wha but the lads wi'
  The bannocks o' barley ?

SAE FAR AWA.

Tune—*Dalkeith Maiden Bridge.*

O, sad and heavy should I part,
  But for her sake sae far awa ;
Unknowing what my way may thwart,
  My native land sae far awa.
Thou that of a' things Maker art,
  That form'd this Fair sae far awa,
Gie body strength, then I'll ne'er start
  At this my way sae far awa.

How true is love to pure desert,
　So love to her, sae far awa :
And nocht can heal my bosom's smart,
　While, oh! she is sae far awa.
Nane other love, nane other dart,
　I feel but her's, sae far awa ;
But fairer never touch'd a heart
　Than her's, the Fair sae far awa.

THERE WAS A BONNIE LASS.

AN UNFINISHED SKETCH.

THERE was a bonnie lass,
　And a bonnie, bonnie lass,
And she lo'ed her bonnie laddie dear,
　Till war's loud alarms
　Tore her laddie frae her arms,
Wi' mony a sigh and a tear.

　Over sea, over shore,
　Where the cannons loudly roar,
He still was a stranger to fear ;
　And nocht could him quail,
　Or his bosom assail,
But the bonnie lass he lo'ed sae dear.

YOUNG JAMIE, PRIDE OF A' THE PLAIN.

TUNE—*The Carlin o' the Glen.*

YOUNG Jamie, pride of a' the plain,
Sae gallant and sae gay a swain ;
Thro' a' our lasses he did rove,
And reign'd resistless king of love :
But now wi' sighs and starting tears,
He strays among the woods and briers ;
Or in the glens and rocky caves,
His sad complaining dowie raves.

I wha sae late did range and rove,
And chang'd with every moon my love,
I little thought the time was near
Repentance I should buy sae dear :
The slighted maids my torments see,
And laugh at a' the pangs I dree ;
While she, my cruel, scornfu' Fair,
Forbids me e'er to see her mair !

O AYE MY WIFE SHE DANG ME.

TUNE—*My wife she dang me.*

O AYE my wife she dang me,
    An' aft my wife did bang me,
If ye gie a woman a' her will,
    Gude faith, she'll soon o'er-gang ye.

On peace and rest my mind was bent,
  And fool I was I married ;
But never honest man's intent
  As cursedly miscarried.

Some sairie comfort still at last,
  When a' their days are done, man ;
My pains o' hell on earth are past,
  I'm sure o' bliss aboon, man.
O aye my wife she dang me,
  And aft my wife did bang me,
If ye gie a woman a' her will,
  Gude faith, she'll soon o'er-gang ye.

O LASSIE, ART THOU SLEEPING YET?

Tune—*Let me in this ae Night.*

O Lassie, art thou sleeping yet,
Or art thou waking, I would wit ?
For love has bound me hand and foot,
  And I would fain be in, jo.

      O let me in this ae night,
        This ae, ae, ae night,
      For pity's sake this ae night,
        O rise and let me in, jo !

Thou hear'st the winter wind and weet,
Nae star blinks thro' the driving sleet :
Tak pity on my weary feet,
  And shield me frae the rain, jo.

The bitter blast that round me blaws,
Unheeded howls, unheeded fa's :
The cauldness o' thy heart's the cause
  Of a' my grief and pain, jo.

      O let me in this ae night,
        This ae, ae, ae night ;
      For pity's sake this ae night,
        O rise and let me in, jo !

HER ANSWER.

O tell na me o' wind and rain,
Upbraid na me wi' cauld disdain!
Gae back the gate ye cam again,
  I winna let ye in, jo.

    I tell you now this ae night,
      This ae, ae, ae night;
    And ance for a' this ae night,
      I winna let you in, jo.

The snellest blast, at mirkest hours,
That round the pathless wand'rer pours,
Is nocht to what poor she endures,
  That's trusted faithless man, jo.

The sweetest flower that deck'd the mead,
Now trodden like the vilest weed;
Let simple maid the lesson read,
  The weird may be her ain, jo.

The bird that charm'd his summer-day
Is now the cruel fowler's prey;
Let witless, trusting woman say
  How aft her fate's the same, jo.

    I tell you now this ae night,
      This ae, ae, ae night;
    And ance for a' this ae night,
      I winna let you in, jo!

ADDRESS TO THE WOOD-LARK.

TUNE—*Where'll bonnie Ann lie.*
  Or, Loch-Eroch side.

O STAY, sweet warbling wood-lark, stay,
Nor quit for me the trembling spray,
A hapless lover courts thy lay,
  Thy soothing, fond complaining.

Again, again that tender part,
That I may catch thy melting art ;
For surely that wad touch her heart
　　Wha kills me wi' disdaining.

Say, was thy little mate unkind,
And heard thee as the careless wind ?
Oh, nocht but love and sorrow join'd
　　Sic notes o' wo could wauken.

Thou tells o' never-ending care ;
O' speechless grief and dark despair :
For pity's sake, sweet bird, nae mair !
　　Or my poor heart is broken !

ON CHLORIS BEING ILL.

TUNE—*Ay wakin' O.*

CAN I cease to care ?
　　Can I cease to languish ?
While my darling fair
　　Is on the couch of anguish ?

　　Long, long the night,
　　　　Heavy comes the morrow,
　　While my soul's delight
　　　　Is on her bed of sorrow.

Every hope is fled,
　　Every fear is terror ;
Slumber even I dread,
　　Every dream is horror.

Hear me, Pow'rs divine !
　　Oh, in pity hear me !
Take aught else of mine,
　　But my Chloris spare me !

　　Long, long the night,
　　　　Heavy comes the morrow,
　　While my soul's delight
　　　　Is on her bed of sorrow.

THE DUMFRIES VOLUNTEERS.

Tune—Push about the Forum.

Does haughty Gaul invasion threat?
  Then let the louns beware, Sir;
There's wooden walls upon our seas,
  And volunteers on shore, Sir.
The Nith shall rin to Corsincon,
  The Criffel sink in Solway,
Ere we permit a foreign foe
    On British ground to rally!
      We'll ne'er permit a foreign foe
        On British ground to rally.

O let us not, like snarling curs,
  In wrangling be divided;
Till, slap! come in an unco loun,
  And wi' a rung decide it.
Be Britain still to Britain true,
  Amang oursels united;
For never but by British hands
  Maun British wrangs be righted!
    For never, etc.

The kettle o' the kirk and state,
  Perhaps a clout may fail in't;
But deil a foreign tinkler loun
  Shall ever ca' a nail in't.
Our fathers' bluid the kettle bought;
  And wha wad dare to spoil it?
By heavens! the sacrilegious dog
  Shall fuel be to boil it!
    By heavens, etc.

The wretch that wad a tyrant own,
  And the wretch, his true-sworn brother,
Wha would set the mob aboon the throne,
  May they be damn'd together!

Wha will not sing, "God save the King,"
Shall hang as high's the steeple ;
But while we sing, "God save the King,"
We'll ne'er forget the People.
                    But while we sing, etc.

FRAGMENT.—CHLORIS.

Tune—*Caledonian Hunt's Delight.*

Why, why tell thy lover,
   Bliss he never must enjoy ?
Why, why undeceive him,
   And give all his hopes the lie ?

O why, while fancy, raptur'd, slumbers,
   Chloris, Chloris all the theme,
Why, why wouldst thou, cruel,
   Wake thy lover from his dream ?

WHEN ROSY MAY COMES IN WI' FLOWERS.

Tune—*The Gardener wi' his paidle.*

When rosy May comes in wi' flowers,
To deck her gay, green-spreading bowers,
Then busy, busy, are his hours—
   The gard'ner wi' his paidle.
The crystal waters gently fa' ;
The merry birds are lovers a' ;
The scented breezes round him blaw—
   The gard'ner wi' his paidle.

When purple morning starts the hare
To steal upon her early fare,
Then thro' the dews he maun repair—
   The gard'ner wi' his paidle.

When day, expiring in the west,
The curtain draws of nature's rest,
He flies to her arms he lo'es the best —
'The gard'ner wi' his paidle.

O WAT YE WHA'S IN YON TOWN.

TUNE—*I'll aye ca' in by yon Town.*

Now haply down yon gay green shaw
  She wanders by yon spreading tree :
How blest ye flow'rs that round her blaw,
  Ye catch the glances o' her e'e !

    O, wat ye wha's in yon town,
      Ye see the e'enin' sun upon ?
    The fairest dame's in yon town,
      That e'enin' sun is shining on.

How blest ye birds that round her sing,
  And welcome in the blooming year !
And doubly welcome be the spring,
  The season to my Lucy dear.

The sun blinks blithe on yon town,
  And on yon bonnie braes of Ayr ;
But my delight's in yon town,
  And dearest bliss, is Lucy fair.

Without my love, not a' the charms
  O' Paradise could yield me joy ;
But gie me Lucy in my arms,
  And welcome Lapland's dreary sky !

My cave wad be a lover's bower,
  Tho' raging winter rent the air ;
And she a lovely little flower,
  That I wad tent and shelter there.

O, sweet is she in yon town,
  The sinkin' sun's gane down upon ;
A fairer than's in yon town
  His setting beam ne'er shone upon.

If angry fate is sworn my foe,
  And suffering I am doom'd to bear ;

I careless quit aught else below,
   But spare me—spare me, Lucy dear !

For while life's dearest blood is warm,
   Ae thought frae her shall ne'er depart,
And she—as fairest is her form !
   She has the truest, kindest heart !
      O, wat ye wha's in yon town,
         Ye see the e'enin' sun upon ?
      The fairest dame's in yon town
         That e'enin' sun is shining on.

THE CARLES OF DYSART.

TUNE—*Hey, ca' thro'.*

UP wi' the carles o' Dysart
   And the lads o' Buckhaven,
And the kimmers o' Largo,
   And the lasses o' Leven.
      Hey, ca' thro', ca' thro',
         For we hae mickle ado ;
      Hey, ca' thro', ca' thro',
         For we hae mickle ado.

We hae tales to tell,
   And we hae sangs to sing ;
We hae pennies to spend,
   And we hae pints to bring.

We'll live a' our days,
   And them that come behin',
Let them do the like,
   And spend the gear they win.
      Hey, ca' thro', ca' thro',
         For we hae mickle ado ;
      Hey, ca' thro', ca' thro',
         For we hae mickle ado.

FORLORN, MY LOVE, NO COMFORT NEAR.

Tune—*Let me in this ae Night.*

FORLORN, my love, no comfort near,
Far, far from thee I wander here ;
Far, far from thee, the fate severe
   At which I most repine, love.

     O wert thou, love, but near me ;
     But near, near, near me ;
     How kindly thou wouldst cheer me,
       And mingle sighs with mine, love !

Around me scowls a wintry sky,
That blasts each bud of hope and joy ;
And shelter, shade, nor home have I,
   Save in those arms of thine, love.

Cold, alter'd friendship's cruel part,
To poison fortune's ruthless dart—
Let me not break thy faithful heart,
   And say that fate is mine, love.

But dreary tho' the moments fleet,
O let me think we yet shall meet !
That only ray of solace sweet
   Can on thy Chloris shine, love.

     O wert thou, love, but near me ;
     But near, near, near me ;
     How kindly thou wouldst cheer me,
       And mingle sighs with mine, love !

I'LL AYE CA' IN BY YON TOWN.

Tune—*I'll gae nae mair to yon Town.*

I'LL aye ca' in by yon town,
   And by yon garden green, again ;
I'll aye ca' in by yon town,
   And see my bonnie Jean again.

There's nane sall ken, there's nane sall guess,
   What brings me back the gate again ;
But she, my fairest faithfu' lass,
   And stownlins we sall meet again.

She'll wander by the aiken tree,
   When trystin-time draws near again ;
And when her lovely form I see,
   O haith, she's doubly dear again !
I'll aye ca' in by yon town,
   And by yon garden green again ;
I'll aye ca' in by yon town,
   And see my bonnie Jean again.

CALEDONIA.

Tune—Humours of Glen.

THEIR groves o' sweet myrtle let foreign lands reckon,
   Where bright-beaming summers exalt their perfume;
Far dearer to me yon lone glen o' green breckan,
   Wi' the burn stealing under the lang yellow broom:
Far dearer to me are yon humble broom bowers,
   Where the blue-bell and gowan lurk lowly unseen;
For there, lightly tripping amang the wild flowers,
   A-listening the linnet, aft wanders my Jean.

Tho' rich is the breeze in their gay sunny valleys,
   And cauld CALEDONIA's blast on the wave,
Their sweet-scented woodlands that skirt the proud palace,
   What are they?—The haunt o' the tyrant and slave!
The slave's spicy forests, and gold-bubbling fountains,
   The brave Caledonian views wi' disdain;
He wanders as free as the winds of his mountains,
   Save love's willing fetters, the chains o' his Jean.

O BONNIE WAS YON ROSY BRIER.

O BONNIE was yon rosy brier,
   That blooms sae far frae haunt o' man;
And bonnie she, and ah, how dear!
   It shaded frae the e'enin' sun.

Yon rosebuds in the morning dew,
   How pure amang the leaves sae green;
But purer was the lover's vow
   They witness'd in their shade yestreen.

All in its rude and prickly bower,
   That crimson rose, how sweet and fair!
But love is far a sweeter flower
   Amid life's thorny path o' care.

The pathless wild, and wimpling burn,
  Wi' Chloris in my arms, be mine;
And I the world, nor wish, nor scorn,
  Its joys and griefs alike resign.

NOW SPRING HAS CLAD THE GROVE IN GREEN.

A SCOTTISH SONG.

Now spring has clad the grove in green,
  And strew'd the lea wi' flowers:
The furrow'd, waving corn is seen
  Rejoice in fostering showers;
While ilka thing in nature join
  Their sorrows to forego,
O why thus all alone are mine
  The weary steps of woe?

The trout within yon wimpling burn
  Glides swift, a silver dart,
And safe beneath the shady thorn
  Defies the angler's art:
My life was ance that careless stream,
  That wanton trout was I;
But love, wi' unrelenting beam,
  Has scorch'd my fountains dry.

The little flow'ret's peaceful lot,
  In yonder cliff that grows,
Which, save the linnet's flight, I wot,
  Nae ruder visit knows,
Was mine; till love has o'er me past,
  And blighted a' my bloom,
And now beneath the with'ring blast
  My youth and joy consume.

The waken'd lav'rock warbling springs,
  And climbs the early sky,
Winnowing blithe her dewy wings
  In morning's rosy eye;

As little reckt I sorrow's power,
    Until the flow'ry snare
O' witching love, in luckless hour,
    Made me the thrall o' care.

O had my fate been Greenland snows,
    Or Afric's burning zone,
Wi' man and nature leagu'd my foes,
    So Peggy ne'er I'd known !
The wretch whase doom is, " hope nae mair,"
    What tongue his woes can tell !
Within whase bosom, save despair,
    Nae kinder spirits dwell.

'TWAS NA HER BONNIE BLUE E'E.

TUNE—*Laddie lie near me.*

'Twas na her bonnie blue e'e was my ruin ;
Fair tho' she be, that was ne'er my undoing :
'Twas the dear smile when naebody did mind us,
'Twas the bewitching, sweet, stown glance o' kindness.

Sair do I fear that to hope is denied me,
Sair do I fear that despair maun abide me !
But tho' fell fortune should fate us to sever,
Queen shall she be in my bosom for ever.

Mary, I'm thine wi' a passion sincerest,
And thou hast plighted me love o' the dearest !
And thou'rt the angel that never can alter—
Sooner the sun in his motion would falter.

HOW CRUEL ARE THE PARENTS.

TUNE—*John Anderson, my Jo.*

How cruel are the parents
    Who riches only prize,
And, to the wealthy booby,
    Poor woman sacrifice !

Meanwhile the hapless daughter
  Has but a choice of strife ;—
To shun a tyrant father's hate,
  Become a wretched wife.

The rav'ning hawk pursuing,
  The trembling dove thus flies,
To shun impelling ruin
  Awhile her pinion tries ;
Till of escape despairing,
  No shelter or retreat,
She trusts the ruthless falconer,
  And drops beneath his feet !

JESSY.

Tune—*Here's a Health to them that's awa.*

Here's a health to ane I lo'e dear !
  Here's a health to ane I lo'e dear !
Thou art sweet as the smile when fond lovers meet,
  And soft as their parting tear—Jessy !

Altho' thou maun never be mine,
  Altho' even hope is denied ;
'Tis sweeter for thee despairing
  Than aught in the world beside—Jessy !

I mourn through the gay, gaudy day,
  As, hopeless, I muse on thy charms ;
But welcome the dream o' sweet slumber,
  For then I am lock't in thy arms—Jessy !

I guess by the dear angel smile,
  I guess by the love-rolling e'e ;
But why urge the tender confession,
  'Gainst fortune's fell cruel decree !—Jessy !

Here's a health to ane I lo'e dear !
  Here's a health to ane I lo'e dear !
Thou art sweet as the smile when fond lovers meet,
  And soft as their parting tear—Jessy !

LAST MAY A BRAW WOOER.

TUNE—*The Lothian Lassie.*

LAST May a braw wooer cam down the lang glen,
   And sair wi' his love he did deave me;
I said there was naething I hated like men,
   The deuce gae wi'm, to believe, believe me,
   The deuce gae wi'm, to believe me!

He spak o' the darts in my bonnie black een,
  And vow'd for my love he was deein;
I said he might dee when he liked, for Jean,
  The Lord forgie me for leein, for leein,
  The Lord forgie me for leein!

A weel-stocked mailen—himsel' for the laird—
  And marriage aff-hand, were his proffers:
I never loot on that I kenn'd it, or car'd,
  But thought I might hae waur offers, waur offers,
  But thought I might hae waur offers.

But what wad ye think? in a fortnight or less—
  The deil tak his taste to gae near her!
He up the lang loan to my black cousin Bess,
  Guess ye how, the jad! I could bear her, could
      bear her,
  Guess ye how, the jad! I could bear her.

But a' the neist week, as I freeted wi' care,
  I gaed to the tryste o' Dalgarnock,
And wha but my fine fickle lover was there!
  I glowr'd as I'd seen a warlock, a warlock,
  I glowr'd as I'd seen a warlock.

But owre my left shouther I gae him a blink,
  Lest neebors might say I was saucy;
My wooer he caper'd as he'd been in drink,
  And vow'd I was his dear lassie, dear lassie,
  And vow'd I was his dear lassie.

I spier'd for my cousin fu' couthy and sweet,
  Gin she had recovered her hearin',
And how her new shoon fit her auld shachl't feet,
  But, heavens! how he fell a swearin', a swearin',
  But, heavens! how he fell a swearin'!

He begged, for Gudesake, I wad be his wife,
  Or else I wad kill him wi' sorrow ;
Sae, e'en to preserve the poor body his life,
  I think I maun wed him to-morrow, to-morrow,
  I think I maun wed him to-morrow.

HUNTING SONG.

TUNE—*I rede you beware at the hunting.*

THE heather was blooming, the meadows were mawn,
Our lads gaed a-hunting ae day at the dawn,
O'er moors and o'er mosses, and mony a glen,
At length they discover'd a bonnie moor-hen.

  I rede you beware at the hunting, young men ;
  I rede you beware at the hunting, young men ;
  Tak' some on the wing, and some as they spring,
  But cannily steal on a bonnie moor-hen.

Sweet brushing the dew from the brown heather-bells,
Her colours betrayed her on yon mossy fells ;
Her plumage outlustr'd the pride o' the spring,
And O, as she wantoned gay on the wing.

Auld Phœbus himsel', as he peep'd o'er the hill,
In spite, at her plumage he tried his skill ;
He levell'd his rays where she bask'd on the brae—
His rays were outshone, and but mark'd where she lay.

They hunted the valley, they hunted the hill,
The best of our lads, wi' the best o' their skill ;
But still as the fairest she sat in their sight,
Then, whirr ! she was over, a mile at a flight.

  I rede you beware at the hunting, young men ;
  I rede you beware at the hunting, young men ;
  Tak' some on the wing, and some as they spring,
  But cannily steal on a bonnie moor-hen.

MARK YONDER POMP.

TUNE.—*Deil tak' the wars.*

MARK yonder pomp of costly fashion,
  Round the wealthy, titled bride :
But when compar'd with real passion,
  Poor is all that princely pride,
    What are the showy treasures ?
    What are the noisy pleasures ?
The gay gaudy glare of vanity and art :
    The polish'd jewel's blaze
    May draw the wond'ring gaze,
    And courtly grandeur bright
    The fancy may delight,
But never, never can come near the heart.

But, did you see my dearest Chloris
  In simplicity's array ;
Lovely as yonder sweet opening flower is,
  Shrinking from the gaze of day ?
    O then, the heart alarming,
    And all resistless charming,
In Love's delightful fetters she chains the willing soul !
    Ambition would disown
    The world's imperial crown,
    Even Avarice would deny
    His worshipp'd deity,
And feel thro' ev'ry vein Love's raptures roll.

OH, WERT THOU IN THE CAULD BLAST.

TUNE—*The Lass o' Livingstone.*

OH, wert thou in the cauld blast
  On yonder lea, on yonder lea,
My plaidie to the angry airt,
  I'd shelter thee, I'd shelter thee :

Or did misfortune's bitter storms
  Around thee blaw, around thee blaw,
Thy bield should be my bosom,
  To share it a', to share it a'.

Or were I in the wildest waste,
  Sae bleak and bare, sae bleak and bare,
The desert were a paradise,
  If thou wert there, if thou wert there :
Or were I monarch o' the globe,
  Wi' thee to reign, wi' thee to reign,
The brightest jewel in my crown
  Wad be my queen, wad be my queen.

HEY FOR A LASS WI' A TOCHER.

TUNE—*Balinamona Ora.*

⁎AWA wi' your witchcraft o' beauty's alarms,
The slender bit beauty you grasp in your arms :
O gie me the lass that has acres o' charms,
O gie me the lass wi' the weel-stockit farms,

  Then hey for a lass wi' a tocher,
  Then hey for a lass wi' a tocher ;
  Then hey for a lass wi' a tocher,
    The nice yellow guineas for me.

Your beauty's a flower, in the morning that blows,
And withers the faster, the faster it grows ;
But the rapturous charm o' the bonnie green knowes,
Ilk spring they're new deckit wi' bonnie white yowes.

And e'en when this beauty your bosom has blest,
The brightest o' beauty may cloy, when possest ;
But the sweet yellow darlings wi' Geordie imprest,
The langer ye hae them—the mair they're carest.

  Then hey for a lass wi' a tocher,
  Then hey for a lass wi' a tocher ;
  Then hey for a lass wi' a tocher,
    The nice yellow guineas for me.

COUNTRY LASSIE.

TUNE—The Country Lass.

IN simmer, when the hay was mawn,
   And corn wav'd green in ilka field,
While clover blooms white o'er the lea,
   And roses blaw in ilka bield ;
Blithe Bessie in the milking shiel,
   Says—I'll be wed, come o't what will ;
Out spak a dame in wrinkled eild—
   O' guid advisement comes nae ilL

It's ye hae wooers mony ane,
   And, lassie, ye're but young, ye ken ;
Then wait a wee, and cannie wale,
   A routhie but, a routhie ben :

There's Johnnie o' the Buskie-glen,
   Fu' is his barn, fu' is his byre;
Tak this frae me, my bonnie hen,
   It's plenty beets the lover's fire.

For Johnnie o' the Buskie-glen,
   I dinna care a single flie;
He lo'es sae weel his craps and kye,
   He has nae love to spare for me:
But blithe's the blink o' Robie's e'e,
   And weel I wat he lo'es me dear:
Ae blink o' him I wad na gie
   For Buskie-glen and a' his gear.

O thoughtless lassie, life's a faught;
   The canniest gate, the strife is sair:
But aye fu' han't is fechtin best,
   An' hungry care's an unco care:
But some will spend, and some will spare,
   An' wilfu' folk maun hae their will;
Syne as ye brew, my maiden fair,
   Keep mind that ye maun drink the yill.

O, gear will buy me rigs o' land,
   And gear will buy me sheep and kye;
But the tender heart o' leesome love,
   The gowd and siller canna buy;
We may be poor—Robie and I,
   Light is the burden love lays on;
Content and love bring peace and joy—
   What mair hae queens upon a throne?

SWEETEST MAY.

Sweetest May, let love inspire thee;
Take a heart which he desires thee;
As thy constant slave regard it;
For its faith and truth reward it.

Proof o' shot to birth or money,
Not the wealthy, but the bonnie ;
Not high-born, but noble-minded,
In love's silken band can bind it !

THIS IS NO MY AIN LASSIE.

Tune—*This is no my ain house.*

I SEE a form, I see a face,
Ye weel may wi' the fairest place ;
It wants, to me, the witching grace,
   The kind love that's in her e'e.

     O this is no my ain lassie,
       Fair tho' the lassie be ;
     O weel ken I my ain lassie,
       Kind love is in her e'e.

She's bonnie, blooming, straight, and tall,
And lang has had my heart in thrall ;
And aye it charms my very saul,
   The kind love that's in her e'e.

A thief sae pawkie is my Jean,
To steal a blink, by a' unseen ;
But gleg as light are lovers' een,
   When kind love is in the e'e.

It may escape the courtly sparks,
It may escape the learned clerks ;
But weel the watching lover marks
   The kind love that's in her e'e.

     O this is no my ain lassie,
       Fair tho' the lassie be ;
     O weel ken I my ain lassie,
       Kind love is in her e'e.

O WHA IS SHE THAT LO'ES ME.

Tune—*Morag.*

O WHA is she that lo'es me,
 And has my heart a-keeping?
O sweet is she that lo'es me,
 As dews o' simmer weeping,
 In tears the rose-buds steeping!

  O that's the lassie o' my heart,
   My lassie ever dearer;
  O that's the queen o' womankind,
   And ne'er a ane to peer her.

If thou shalt meet a lassie,
 In grace and beauty charming,
That e'en thy chosen lassie,
 Erewhile thy breast sae warming,
 Had ne'er sic powers alarming;
   O that's, etc.

If thou hadst heard her talking,
 And thy attentions plighted,
That ilka body talking,
 But her by thee is slighted,
 And thou art all delighted;
   O that's, etc.

If thou hast met this fair one;
 When frae her thou hast parted,
If every other fair one,
 But her, thou hast deserted,
 And thou art broken-hearted;

  O that's the lassie o' my heart,
   My lassie ever dearer;
  O that's the queen o' womankind,
   And ne'er a ane to peer her.

MUSING ON THE ROARING OCEAN.

TUNE—Druimion dubh.

Musing on the roaring ocean,
  Which divides my love and me ;
Wearying Heaven in warm devotion,
  For his weal where'er he be.

Hope and fear's alternate billow
  Yielding late to nature's law,

Whisp'ring spirits round my pillow
　　Talk of him that's far awa.

Ye whom sorrow never wounded,
　　Ye who never shed a tear,
Care-untroubled, joy-surrounded,
　　Gaudy day to you is dear.

Gentle night, do thou befriend me ;
　　Downy sleep, the curtain draw ;
Spirits kind, again attend me,
　　Talk of him that's far awa !

O POORTITH CAULD.

Tune—*I had a horse.*

O POORTITH cauld, and restless love,
　　Ye wreck my peace between ye ;
Yet poortith a' I could forgive,
　　An 'twere na' for my Jeannie.

　　　O why should fate sic pleasure have,
　　　　Life's dearest bands untwining ?
　　　Or why sae sweet a flower as love
　　　　Depend on fortune's shining !

This warld's wealth when I think on,
　　Its pride, and a' the lave o't—
Fie, fie on silly coward man,
　　That he should be the slave o't !

Her een sae bonnie blue betray
　　How she repays my passion ;
But prudence is her o'erword aye,
　　She talks of rank and fashion.

O wha can prudence think upon,
　　And sic a lassie by him ?
O wha can prudence think upon,
　　And sae in love as I am !

How blest the humble cotter's fate !
  He woos his simple dearie ;
The silly bogles, wealth and state,
  Can never make them eerie.

    O why should fate sic pleasure have,
      Life's dearest bands untwining !
    Or why sae sweet a flower as love
      Depend on fortune's shining ?

LADY MARY ANN.

TUNE—*Craigston's growing.*

O, LADY Mary Ann
  Looks o'er the castle wa',
She saw three bonnie boys
  Playing at the ba' ;
The youngest he was
  The flower amang them a'—
My bonnie laddie's young,
  But he's growin' yet.

O father ! O father !
  An ye think it fit,
We'll send him a year
  To the college yet :
We'll sew a green ribbon
  Round about his hat,
And that will let them ken
  He's to marry yet.

Lady Mary Ann
  Was a flower i' the dew,
Sweet was its smell,
  And bonnie was its hue ;
And the langer it blossom'd
  The sweeter it grew ;
For the lily in the bud
  Will be bonnier yet.

Young Charlie Cochrane
  Was the sprout of an aik ;
Bonnie and bloomin'
  And straught was its make :
The sun took delight
  To shine for its sake,
And it will be the brag
  O' the forest yet.

The simmer is gane
  When the leaves they were green,
And the days are awa
  That we hae seen ;
But far better days
  I trust will come again,
For my bonnie laddie's young,
  But he's growin' yet.

O LAY THY LOOF IN MINE, LASS.

TUNE—*Cordwainer's March.*

O LAY thy loof in mine, lass,
In mine, lass, in mine, lass ;
And swear on thy white hand, lass,
  That thou wilt be my ain.
A slave to love's unbounded sway,
He aft has wrought me meikle wae ;
But now he is my deadly fae,
  Unless thou be my ain.

There's mony a lass has broke my rest,
That for a blink I hae lo'ed best ;
But thou art queen within my breast,
  For ever to remain.
O lay thy loof in mine, lass,
In mine, lass, in mine, lass ;
And swear on thy white hand, lass,
  That thou wilt be my ain.

UP IN THE MORNING EARLY.

Up in the morning's no for me,
  Up in the morning early;
When a' the hills are cover'd wi' snaw,
  I'm sure it's winter fairly.

Cauld blaws the wind frae east to west,
  The drift is driving sairly;
Sae loud and shrill I hear the blast,
  I'm sure it's winter fairly.

The birds sit chittering in the thorn,
   A' day they fare but sparely;
And lang's the night frae e'en to morn—
   I'm sure its winter fairly.

     Up in the morning's no for me,
       Up in the morning early;
     When a' the hills are cover'd wi' snaw,
       I'm sure it's winter fairly.

SHE SAYS SHE LO'ES ME BEST OF A'.

TUNE—*Onagh's Waterfall.*

SAE flaxen were her ringlets,
   Her eyebrows of a darker hue,
Bewitchingly o'er-arching
   Twa laughing een o' bonnie blue.
Her smiling, sae wiling,
   Wad make a wretch forget his woe;
What pleasure, what treasure,
   Unto these rosy lips to grow!
Such was my Chloris' bonnie face,
   When first her bonnie face I saw;
And aye my Chloris' dearest charm,
   She says she lo'es me best of a'.

Like harmony her motion;
   Her pretty ankle is a spy,
Betraying fair proportion,
   Wad mak a saint forget the sky.
Sae warming, sae charming,
   Her faultless form and gracefu' air;
Ilk feature—auld nature
   Declar'd that she could do nae mair.
Her's are the willing chains o' love,
   By conquering beauty's sovereign law
And aye my Chloris' dearest charm,
   She says she lo'es me best of a'.

Let others love the city,
   And gaudy show at sunny noon ;
Gie me the lonely valley,
   The dewy eve, and rising moon ;
Fair beaming, and streaming,
   Her silver light the boughs amang ;
While falling, recalling,
   The amorous thrush concludes his sang :
There, dearest Chloris, wilt thou rove
   By wimpling burn and leafy shaw,
And hear my vows o' truth and love,
   And say thou lo'est me best of a' ?

THE LAST TIME I CAME O'ER THE MOOR.

THE last time I came o'er the moor,
   I left my love behind me ;
Ye powers, what pain do I endure,
   When soft ideas mind me.
Soon as the ruddy morn display'd
   The beaming day ensuing,
I met betimes my lovely maid
   In fit retreats for wooing.

Beneath the cooling shade we lay,
   Gazing and chastely sporting ;
We kiss'd and promis'd time away,
   Till night spread her black curtain.
I pitied all beneath the skies,
   Ev'n kings, when she was nigh me ;
In rapture I beheld her eyes,
   Which could but ill deny me.

Should I be call'd where cannons roar,
   Where mortal steel may wound me ;
Or cast upon some foreign shore,
   Where danger may surround me ;

Yet hopes again to see my love,
    And feast on glowing kisses,
Shall make my cares at distance move,
    In prospect of such blisses.

In all my soul there's not one place
    To let a rival enter;
Since she excels in ev'ry grace,
    In her my love shall centre:
Sooner the seas shall cease to flow,
    Their waves the Alps shall cover,
On Greenland ice shall roses grow,
    Before I cease to love her.

The next time I go o'er the moor,
    She shall a lover find me;
And that my faith is firm and pure,
    Tho' I left her behind me :
Then Hymen's sacred bonds shall chain
    My heart to her fair bosom;
There, while my being does remain,
    My love more fresh shall blossom."

THE LOVELY LASS OF INVERNESS.

Tune—*The Lass of Inverness.*

THE lovely lass o' Inverness
    Nae joy nor pleasure can she see;
For e'en and morn she cries, alas !
    And aye the saut tear blin's her e'e :
Drumossie moor—Drumossie day—
    A waefu' day it was to me !
For there I lost my father dear,
    My father dear, and brethren three.

Their winding sheet the bluidy clay,
    Their graves are growing green to see :
And by them lies the dearest lad
    That ever blest a woman's e'e !

Now wae to thee, thou cruel lord,
    A bluidy man I trow thou be !
For mony a heart thou hast made sair
    That ne'er did wrang to thine or thee.

A HIGHLAND LAD MY LOVE WAS BORN.

TUNE—*O an ye were dead, gudeman.*

A HIGHLAND lad my love was born,
The Lawland laws he held in scorn :
But he still was faithfu' to his clan,
My gallant braw John Highlandman.

    Sing, hey my braw John Highlandman !
    Sing, ho my braw John Highlandman !
    There's not a lad in a' the lan'
    Was match for my John Highlandman.

With his philibeg an' tartan plaid,
An' guid claymore down by his side,
The ladies' hearts he did trepan,
My gallant braw John Highlandman.
                Sing, hey, etc.

We ranged a' from Tweed to Spey,
An' liv'd like lords and ladies gay ;
For a Lawland face he fearèd none,
My gallant braw John Highlandman.
                Sing, hey, etc.

They banish'd him beyond the sea,
But, ere the bud was on the tree,
Adown my cheeks the pearls ran,
Embracing my John Highlandman.
                Sing, hey, etc.

But, oh ! they catch'd him at the last,
And bound him in a dungeon fast ;
My curse upon them every one,
They've hang'd my braw John Highlandman.
                Sing, hey, etc.

And now a widow, I must mourn
The pleasures that will ne'er return ;
Nae comfort but a hearty can,
When I think on John Highlandman.

Sing, hey, etc.

DAMON AND SYLVIA.

TUNE—*The tither morn, as I forlorn.*

YON wand'ring rill, that marks the hill,
   And glances o'er the brae, Sir,
Slides by a bower, where mony a flower,
   Sheds fragrance on the day, Sir.

There Damon lay, with Sylvia gay,
   To love they thought nae crime, Sir ;
The wild-birds sang, the echoes rang,
   While Damon's heart beat time, Sir.

AULD ROB MORRIS.

THERE'S auld Rob Morris that wons in yon glen,
He's the king o' guid fellows and wale of auld men ;
He has gowd in his coffers, he has owsen and kine,
And ae bonnie lassie, his darling and mine.

She's fresh as the morning, the fairest in May ;
She's sweet as the ev'ning amang the new hay ;
As blithe and as artless as lambs on the lea,
And dear to my heart as the light to my e'e.

But oh ! she's an heiress,—auld Robin's a laird,
And my daddie has nought but a cot-house and yard ;
A wooer like me maunna hope to come speed ;
The wounds I must hide that will soon be my dead.

The day comes to me, but delight brings me nane ;
The night comes to me, but my rest it is gane :
I wander my lane like a night-troubl'd ghaist,
And I sigh as my heart it wad burst in my breast.

O had she but been of a lower degree,
I then might hae hop'd she'd hae smil'd upon me !
O, how past describing had then been my bliss,
As now my distraction no words can express !

O TIBBIE, I HAE SEEN THE DAY.

TUNE—*Invercauld's reel.*

O TIBBIE, I hae seen the day,
   Ye wadna been sae shy ;
For laik o' gear ye lightly me,
   But, trowth, I care na by.

Yestreen I met you on the moor,
Ye spak na, but gaed by like stoure ;
Ye geck at me because I'm poor,
   But fient a hair care I.

I doubt na, lass, but ye may think,
Because ye hae the name o' clink,
That ye can please me at a wink,
   Whene'er ye like to try.

But sorrow tak him that's sae mean,
Altho' his pouch o' coin were clean,
Wha follows ony saucy quean
   That looks sae proud and high.

Altho' a lad were e'er sae smart,
If that he want the yellow dirt,
Ye'll cast your head anither airt,
   And answer him fu' dry.

But if he hae the name o' gear,
Ye'll fasten to him like a brier,
Tho' hardly he, for sense or lear,
   Be better than the kye.

But, Tibbie, lass, tak my advice,
Your daddie's gear maks you sae nice;
The deil a ane wad spier your price,
   Were ye as poor as I.

There lives a lass in yonder park,
I would nae gie her in her sark,
For thee, wi' a' thy thousan' mark!
   Ye needna look sae high.

ADOWN WINDING NITH.

ADOWN winding Nith I did wander,
   To mark the sweet flowers as they spring;
Adown winding Nith I did wander,
   Of Phillis to muse and to sing.

     Awa wi' your belles and your beauties,
      They never wi' her can compare:
     Whaever has met wi' my Phillis,
      Has met wi' the queen o' the fair.

The daisy amus'd my fond fancy,
  So artless, so simple, so wild ;
Thou emblem, said I, o' my Phillis !
  For she is simplicity's child.

The rose-bud's the blush o' my charmer,
  Her sweet balmy lip when 'tis prest :
How fair and how pure is the lily,
  But fairer and purer her breast !

Yon knot of gay flowers in the arbour,
  They ne'er wi' my Phillis can vie :
Her breath is the breath o' the woodbine,
  Its dewdrop o' diamond, her eye.

Her voice is the song of the morning,
  That wakes thro' the green-spreading grove,
When Phœbus peeps over the mountains,
  On music, and pleasure, and love.

But beauty how frail and how fleeting,
  The bloom of a fine summer's day !
While worth in the mind o' my Phillis
  Will flourish without a decay.

    Awa wi' your belles and your beauties,
      They never wi' her can compare :
    Whaever has met wi' my Phillis
      Has met wi' the queen o' the fair.

THE LOVER'S MORNING SALUTE TO HIS MISTRESS.

Tune—*Deil tak the Wars.*

Sleep'st thou, or wak'st thou, fairest creature ?
  Rosy morn now lifts his eye,
Numbering ilka bud which nature
  Waters wi' the tears o' joy :
  Now thro' the leafy woods,
And by the reeking floods,

Wild nature's tenants, freely, gladly stray;
    The lintwhite in his bower
    Chants o'er the breathing flower;
    The lav'rock to the sky
    Ascends wi' sangs o' joy,
While the sun and thou arise to bless the day.

Phœbus, gilding the brow o' morning,
    Banishes ilk darksome shade,
Nature gladdening and adorning;
    Such to me my lovely maid.
    When absent frae my fair,
    The murky shades o' care
With starless gloom o'ercast my sullen sky;
    But when, in beauty's light,
    She meets my ravish'd sight,
    When thro' my very heart
    Her beaming glories dart—
'Tis then I wake to life, to light, and joy.

LOVELY POLLY STEWART.

TUNE—*Ye're welcome, Charlie Stewart.*

O LOVELY Polly Stewart!
    O charming Polly Stewart!
There's ne'er a flower that blooms in May
    That's half sae fair as thou art.
The flower it blaws, it fades and fa's,
    And art can ne'er renew it;
But worth and truth eternal youth
    Will gie to Polly Stewart.

May he whose arms shall fauld thy charms,
    Possess a leal and true heart;
To him be given to ken the heaven
    He grasps in Polly Stewart.
O lovely Polly Stewart!
    O charming Polly Stewart!
There's ne'er a flower that blooms in May
    That's half sae sweet as thou art.

IS THERE, FOR HONEST POVERTY.

TUNE—For a' that, and a' that.

Is there, for honest poverty,
   That hangs his head, and a' that?
The coward-slave, we pass him by,
   We dare be poor for a' that!
For a' that, and a' that,
   Our toil's obscure, and a' that;
The rank is but the guinea-stamp,
   The man's the gowd for a' that!

What tho' on hamely fare we dine,
   Wear hoddin grey, and a' that,

Gie fools their silks, and knaves their wine,
  A man's a man for a' that !
For a' that, and a' that,
  Their tinsel show, and a' that ;
The honest man, though e'er sae poor,
  Is king o' men for a' that !

Ye see yon birkie ca'd—a lord,
  Wha struts, and stares, and a' that,
Though hundreds worship at his word,
  He's but a coof for a' that :
For a' that, and a' that,
  His riband, star, and a' that ;
The man of independent mind
  He looks and laughs at a' that !

A king can mak a belted knight,
  A marquis, duke, and a' that ;
But an honest man's aboon his might,
  Guid faith he maunna fa' that !
For a' that, and a' that,
  Their dignities, and a' that,
The pith o' sense, and pride o' worth,
  Are higher ranks than a' that,

Then let us pray that come it may—
  As come it will for a' that—
That sense and worth, o'er a' the earth,
  · May bear the gree, and a' that ;
For a' that, and a' that,
  It's comin' yet for a' that,
That man to man, the warld o'er,
  Shall brothers be for a' that ?

O SAW YE MY DEARIE.

O saw ye my dearie, my Eppie M'Nab ?
O saw ye my dearie, my Eppie M'Nab ?

She's down in the yard, she's kissin' the laird,
She winna come hame to her ain Jock Rab.
O come thy ways to me, my Eppie M'Nab!
O come thy ways to me, my Eppie M'Nab!
Whate'er thou hast done, be it late, be it soon,
'Thou's welcome again to thy ain Jock Rab.

What says she, my dearie, my Eppie M'Nab?
What says she, my dearie, my Eppie M'Nab?
She lets thee to wit, that she has thee forgot,
And for ever disowns thee, her ain Jock Rab.
O had I ne'er seen thee, my Eppie M'Nab!
O had I ne'er seen thee, my Eppie M'Nab!
As light as the air, as fause as thou's fair,
Thou's broken the heart o' thy ain Jock Rab.

CA' THE YOWES.

Ca' the yowes to the knowes,
Ca' them whare the heather grows,
Ca' them whare the burnie rowes—
  My bonnie dearie !
Hark the mavis' evening sang
Sounding Clouden's woods amang !
Then a-faulding let us gang,
  My bonnie dearie.

We'll gae down by Clouden side,
Thro' the hazels spreading wide,
O'er the waves that sweetly glide
  To the moon sae clearly.

Yonder Clouden's silent towers,
Where at moonshine midnight hours,
O'er the dewy bending flowers,
  Fairies dance sae cheery.

Ghaist nor bogle shalt thou fear ;
Thou'rt to love and heaven sae dear,
Nocht of ill may come thee near,
  My bonnie dearie.

Fair and lovely as thou art,
Thou hast stown my very heart;
I can die—but canna part—
    My bonnie dearie!
        Ca' the yowes to the knowes,
        Ca' them whare the heather grows,
        Ca' them whare the burnie rowes—
        My bonnie dearie!

FAIREST MAID ON DEVON BANKS.

TUNE—*Rothemurche.*

FAIREST maid on Devon banks,
    Crystal Devon, winding Devon,
Wilt thou lay that frown aside,
    And smile as thou wert wont to do!

Full well thou know'st I love thee dear!
Could'st thou to malice lend an ear?
O! did not love exclaim "Forbear,
    Nor use a faithful lover so."

Then come, thou fairest of the fair,
Those wonted smiles, O let me share;
And by thy beauteous self I swear
    No love but thine my heart shall know.

    Fairest maid on Devon banks,
        Crystal Devon, winding Devon,
    Wilt thou lay that frown aside,
        And smile as thou were wont to do?

OUT OVER THE FORTH.

TUNE—*Charlie Gordon's welcome Hame.*

OUT over the Forth I look to the north,
    But what is the north and its Highlands to me?
The south nor the east gie ease to my breast,
    The far foreign land, or the wild-rolling sea.

But I look to the west, when I gae to rest,
  That happy my dreams and my slumbers may be ;
For far in the west lives he I lo'e best,
  The lad that is dear to my babie and me.

LORD GREGORY.

O MIRK, mirk is this midnight hour,
  And loud the tempest's roar ;
A waefu' wanderer seeks thy tow'r—
  Lord Gregory, ope thy door !

An exile frae her father's ha',
  And a' for loving thee;
At least some pity on me shaw,
  If love it may na be.

Lord Gregory, mind'st thou not the grove
  By bonnie Irwin-side,
Where first I own'd that virgin-love
  I lang, lang had denied?

How aften didst thou pledge and vow
  Thou wad for aye be mine;
And my fond heart, itsel' sae true,
  It ne'er mistrusted thine.

Hard is thy heart, Lord Gregory,
  And flinty is thy breast—
Thou dart of heaven that flashest by,
  O wilt thou give me rest!

Ye mustering thunders from above,
  Your willing victim see!
But spare and pardon my fause love,
  His wrangs to heaven and me!

AS I WAS A-WAND'RING.

Tune—*Rinn M'eudial mo Mhealladh.—A Gaelic Air.*

As I was a-wand'ring ae midsummer e'enin',
  The pipers and youngsters were makin' their game;
Amang them I spied my faithless fause lover,
  Which bled a' the wound o' my dolour again.

Weel, since he has left me, may pleasure gae wi' him;
  I may be distress'd, but I winna complain;
I'll flatter my fancy I may get anither,
  My heart it shall never be broken for ane.

I couldna get sleeping till dawin for greetin',
  The tears trickl'd down like the hail and the rain:
Had I na got greetin', my heart wad a broken,
  For, oh! love forsaken's a tormenting pain!

Although he has left me for greed o' the siller,
  I dinna envy him the gains he can win ;
I rather wad bear a' the lade o' my sorrow
  Than ever hae acted sae faithless to him.

Weel, since he has left me, may pleasure gae wi' him,
  I may be distress'd, but I winna complain ;
I'll flatter my fancy I may get anither,
  My heart it shall never be broken for ane.

HERE'S A HEALTH TO THEM THAT'S AWA.

TUNE—*Here's a health to them that's awa.*

HERE's a health to them that's awa,
Here a health to them that's awa ;
And wha winna wish guid luck to our cause,
May never guid luck be their fa' !
It's guid to be merry and wise,
It's guid to be honest and true,
It's guid to support Caledonia's cause,
And bide by the buff and the blue.

Here's a health to them that's awa,
Here's a health to them that's awa,
Here's a health to Charlie the chief o' the clan,
Altho' that his band be but sma'.
May liberty meet wi' success !
May prudence protect her frae evil !
May tyrants and tyranny tine in the mist,
And wander their way to the devil !

Here's a health to them that's awa,
Here's a health to them that's awa ;
Here's a health to Tammie the Norland laddie,
That lives at the lug o' the law !
Here's freedom to him that wad read,
Here's freedom to him that wad write !
There's nane ever fear'd that the truth should be heard
But they wham the truth wad indite.

Here's a health to them that's awa,
Here's a health to them that's awa ;

Here's Chieftain M'Leod, a chieftain worth gowd,
Tho' bred amang mountains o' snaw !
Here's a health to them that's awa,
Here's a health to them that's awa ;
And wha winna wish guid luck to our cause,
May never guid luck be their fa' !

HIGHLAND MARY.

Tune—*Katherine Ogie.*

YE banks and braes and streams around
    The castle o' Montgomery,
Green be your woods, and fair your flowers,
    Your waters never drumlie !
There simmer first unfaulds her robes,
    And there they langest tarry ;
For there I took the last fareweel
    O' my sweet Highland Mary.

How sweetly bloom'd the grey green birk !
    How rich the hawthorn's blossom !
As underneath their fragrant shade,
    I clasp'd her to my bosom !
The golden hours, on angel wings,
    Flew o'er me and my dearie ;
For dear to me, as light and life,
    Was my sweet Highland Mary !

Wi' mony a vow, and lock'd embrace,
    Our parting was fu' tender ;
And, pledging aft to meet again,
    We tore ourselves asunder ;
But, oh ! fell Death's untimely frost,
    That nipt my flower sae early !—
Now green's the sod, and cauld's the clay,
    That wraps my Highland Mary !

Oh, pale, pale now, those rosy lips,
    I aft hae kiss'd sae fondly !
And clos'd for aye the sparklin glance
    That dwelt on me sae kindly !

And mouldering now in silent dust
That heart that lo'ed me dearly—
But still within my bosom's core
Shall live my Highland Mary!

BLITHE HAE I BEEN.

Tune—*Liggeram Cosh.*

Blithe hae I been on yon hill,
  As the lambs before me ;
Careless ilka thought and free,
  As the breeze flew o'er me.
Now nae langer sport and play,
  Mirth or sang can please me ;
Lesley is sae fair and coy,
  Care and anguish seize me.

Heavy, heavy is the task,
  Hopeless love declaring ; ·
Trembling, I dow nocht but glow'r,
  Sighing, dumb, despairing !
If she winna ease the thraws
  In my bosom swelling ;
Underneath the grass-green sod,
  Soon maun be my dwelling.

HERE'S TO THY HEALTH, MY BONNIE LASS.

Tune—*Laggan Burn.*

Here's to thy health, my bonnie lass,
  Guid night, and joy be wi' thee ;
I'll come nae mair to thy bower-door,
  To tell thee that I lo'e thee.
O dinna think, my pretty pink,
  But I can live without thee :
I vow and swear, I dinna care,
  How lang ye look about ye.

Thou'rt aye sae free informing me
  Thou hast nae mind to marry ;
I'll be as free informing thee
  Nae time hae I to tarry.

I ken thy frien's try ilka means
  Frae wedlock to delay thee ;
Depending on some higher chance—
  But fortune may betray thee.

I ken they scorn my low estate,
  But that does never grieve me ;
But I'm as free as ony he,
  Sma' siller will relieve me.
I'll count my health my greatest wealth,
  Sae long as I'll enjoy it :
I'll fear nae scant, I'll bode nae want,
  As lang's I get employment.

But far-off fowls hae feathers fair,
  And aye until ye try them :
Tho' they seem fair, still have a care,
  They may prove waur than I am.
But at twal at night, when the moon shines bright,
  My dear, I'll come and see thee ;
For the man that lo'es his mistress weel
  Nae travel makes him weary.

MY SPOUSE NANCY.

Husband, husband, cease your strife,
  Nor longer idly rave, sir ;
Tho' I am your wedded wife,
  Yet I am not your slave, sir.
" One of two must still obey,
  Nancy, Nancy ;
Is it man, or woman, say,
  My spouse, Nancy ?"

If 'tis still the lordly word,
  Service and obedience ;
I'll desert my sov'reign lord,
  And so good-bye allegiance !

"Sad will I be so bereft,
 Nancy, Nancy;
Yet I'll try to make a shift,
 My spouse, Nancy."

My poor heart then break it must,
 My last hour I'm near it:
When you lay me in the dust,
 Think, think, how you will bear it.
"I will hope and trust in heaven,
 Nancy, Nancy;
Strength to bear it will be given,
 My spouse, Nancy."

Well, sir, from the silent dead,
 Still I'll try to daunt you;
Ever round your midnight bed
 Horrid sprites shall haunt you.
"I'll wed another, like my dear
 Nancy, Nancy;
Then all hell will fly for fear,
 My spouse, Nancy."

HERE IS THE GLEN.

Tune—*Banks of Cree.*

HERE is the glen, and here the bower,
 All underneath the birchen shade;
The village-bell has told the hour—
 O what can stay my lovely maid?

'Tis not Maria's whispering call;
 'Tis not the balmy-breathing gale,
Mixt with some warbler's dying fall,
 The dewy star of eve to hail.

It is Maria's voice I hear!
 So calls the woodlark in the grove,
His little faithful mate to cheer,
 At once 'tis music—and 'tis love.

And art thou come ? and art thou true ?
O welcome, dear to love and me !
And let us all our vows renew
Along the flow'ry banks of Cree.

MARY MORISON.

Tune—*Bide ye yet.*

O Mary, at thy window be,
It is the wish'd, the trysted hour !
Those smiles and glances let me see
That make the miser's treasure poor :

How blithely wad I bide the stoure,
  A weary slave frae sun to sun ;
Could I the rich reward secure,
  The lovely Mary Morison.

Yestreen, when to the trembling string,
  The dance gaed thro' the lighted ha',
To thee my fancy took its wing,
  I sat, but neither heard nor saw :
Tho' this was fair, and that was braw,
  And yon the toast of a' the town,
I sigh'd, and said, amang them a',
  " Ye are na Mary Morison."

O Mary, canst thou wreck his peace
  Wha for thy sake would gladly dee ?
Or canst thou break that heart of his
  Whase only faut is loving thee ?
If love for love thou wilt na gie,
  At least be pity to me shown ;
A thought ungentle canna be
  The thought o' Mary Morison.

HAPPY FRIENDSHIP.

Here around the ingle bleezing,
  Wha sae happy and sae free ;
Tho' the northern wind blaws freezing,
  Frien'ship warms baith you and me.

    Happy we are a' thegither,
      Happy we'll be yin an' a',
    Time shall see us a' the blither
      Ere we rise to gang awa.

See the miser o'er his treasure,
  Gloating wi' a greedy e'e !
Can he feel the glow o' pleasure
  That around us here we see !

Can the peer, in silk and ermine,
  Ca' his conscience half his own ;
His claes are spun an' edged wi' vermin,
  Tho' he stan' afore a throne !

Thus then let us a' be tassing
  Aff our stoups o' gen'rous flame ;
An', while roun' the board 'tis passing,
  Raise a sang in frien'ship's name.

Frien'ship makes us a' mair happy,
  Frien'ship gies us a' delight ;
Frien'ship consecrates the drappie,
  Frien'ship brings us here to-night.

    Happy we've been a' thegither,
      Happy we've been yin an' a',
    Time shall find us a' the blither
     When we rise to gang awa'.

A VISION.

As I stood by yon roofless tower,
  Where the wa'-flower scents the dewy air,
Where the howlet mourns in her ivy bower,
  'And tells the midnight moon her care ;

The winds were laid, the air was still,
  The stars they shot alang the sky ;
The fox was howling on the hill,
  And the distant-echoing glens reply.

The stream, adown its hazelly path,
  Was rushing by the ruin'd wa's,
Hasting to join the sweeping Nith,
  Whose distant roaring swells and fa's.

The cauld blue north was streaming forth
  Her lights, wi' hissing, eerie din ;
Athort the lift they start and shift,
  Like fortune's favours, tint as win.

By heedless chance I turn'd mine eyes,
  And, by the moonbeam, shook to see
A stern and stalwart ghaist arise,
  Attir'd as minstrels wont to be.

Had I a statue been o' stane,
  His daring look had daunted me ;
And on his bonnet grav'd was plain,
  The sacred posie—" Liberty !"

And frae his harp sic strains did flow,
  Might rous'd the slumb'ring dead to hear :
But, oh ! it was a tale of woe,
  As ever met a Briton's ear !

He sang wi' joy his former day,
  He, weeping, wail'd his latter times ;
But what he said it was nae play,—
  I winna ventur't in my rhymes.

COME, LET ME TAKE THEE.

TUNE—*Cauld Kail.*

COME, let me take thee to my breast,
  And pledge we ne'er shall sunder ;
And I shall spurn as vilest dust
  The warld's wealth and grandeur :
And do I hear my Jeanie own
  That equal transports move her ?
I ask for dearest life alone
  That I may live to love her.

Thus in my arms, wi a' thy charms,
  I clasp my countless treasure ;
I'll seek nae mair o' heaven to share,
  Than sic a moment's pleasure :
And by thy een, sae bonnie blue,
  I swear I'm thine for ever !
And on thy lips I seal my vow,
  And break it shall I never !

YON WILD MOSSY MOUNTAINS.

Yon wild mossy mountains sae lofty and wide,
That nurse in their bosom the youth o' the Clyde,

Where the grouse lead their coveys thro' the heather to feed,
And the shepherd tents his flock as he pipes on his reed.
  Where the grouse lead their coveys thro' the heather to feed,
  And the shepherd tents his flock as he pipes on his reed.

Not Gowrie's rich valleys, nor Forth's sunny shores,
To me hae the charms o' yon wild, mossy moors;
For there, by a lanely, sequester'd clear stream,
Resides a sweet lassie, my thought and my dream.
  For there, by a lanely, sequester'd clear stream,
  Resides a sweet lassie, my thought and my dream.

Amang thae wild mountains shall still be my path,
Ilk stream foaming down its ain green, narrow strath;
For there, wi' my lassie, the day-lang I rove,
While o'er us, unheeded, flee the swift hours o' love.
  For there, wi' my lassie, the day-lang I rove,
  While o'er us, unheeded, flee the swift hours o' love.

She is not the fairest, altho' she is fair;
O' nice education but sma' is her share;
Her parentage humble as humble can be;
But I lo'e the dear lassie because she lo'es me.
  Her parentage humble as humble can be,
  But I lo'e the dear lassie because she lo'es me.

To beauty what man but maun yield him a prize,
In her armour of glances, and blushes, and sighs?
And when wit and refinement hae polish'd her darts,
They dazzle our een as they flee to our hearts.
  And when wit and refinement hae polish'd her darts, ·
  They dazzle our een, as they flee to our hearts.

But kindness, sweet kindness, in the fond sparkling e'e,
Has lustre outshining the diamond to me;
And the heart-beating love, as I'm clasp'd in her arms,
O, these are my lassie's all-conquering charms!
  And the heart-beating love, as I'm clasped in her arms,
  O, these are my lassie's all-conquering charms!

JOCKEY'S TA'EN THE PARTING KISS.

Tune—*Bonnie Lassie, tak a man.*

Jockey's ta'en the parting kiss,
   O'er the mountains he is gane;
And with him is a' my bliss,
   Nought but griefs with me remain.
Spare my love, ye winds that blaw,
   Plashy sleets and beating rain!
Spare my love, thou feathery snaw,
   Drifting o'er the frozen plain!

When the shades of evening creep
   O'er the day's fair, gladsome e'e,
Sound and safely may he sleep,
   Sweetly blithe his waukening be!
He will think on her he loves,
   Fondly he'll repeat her name;
For where'er he distant roves,
   Jockey's heart is still at hame.

DAINTY DAVIE.

Now rosy May comes in wi' flowers,
To deck her gay, green-spreading bowers,
And now comes in my happy hours,
   To wander wi' my Davie.

      Meet me on the warlock knowe,
         Dainty Davie, dainty Davie,
      There I'll spend the day wi' you,
         My ain dear dainty Davie.

The crystal waters round us fa',
The merry birds are lovers a',
The scented breezes round us blaw
   A-wandering wi' my Davie.

When purple morning starts the hare,
'To steal upon her early fare,
Then thro' the dews I will repair,
　To meet my faithfu' Davie.

When day, expiring in the west,
The curtain draws o' nature's rest,
I flee to his arms I lo'e best,
　And that's my ain dear Davie.

　　　Meet me on the warlock knowe,
　　　　Bonnie Davie, dainty Davie,
　　　There I'll spend the day wi' you,
　　　　My ain dear dainty Davie.

WILL YE GO TO THE INDIES, MY MARY?

Tune—*Ewe-bughts.*

TO MARY CAMPBELL.

Will ye go to the Indies, my Mary,
　And leave auld Scotia's shore?
Will ye go to the Indies, my Mary,
　Across the Atlantic's roar?

O sweet grows the lime and the orange,
　And the apple on the pine;
But a' the charms o' the Indies
　Can never equal thine.

I hae sworn by the Heavens to my Mary,
　I hae sworn by the Heavens to be true;
And sae may the Heavens forget me,
　When I forget my vow!

O plight me your faith, my Mary,
　And plight me your lily-white hand;
O plight me your faith, my Mary,
　Before I leave Scotia's strand.

We hae plighted our troth, my Mary,
　In mutual affection to join;
And curst be the cause that shall part us!
　The hour and the moment o' time!

BY ALLAN STREAM.

Tune—*Allan Water.*

By Allan stream I chanc'd to rove
  While Phœbus sank beyond Benledi;
The winds were whispering through the grove,
  The yellow corn was waving ready:

I listen'd to a lover's sang,
　And thought on youthfu' pleasures many;
And aye the wild wood echoes rang—
　O dearly do I love thee, Annie.

O happy be the woodbine bower,
　Nae nightly bogle make it eerie;
Nor ever sorrow stain the hour,
　The place and time I met my dearie!
Her head upon my throbbing breast,
　She, sinking, said, " I'm thine for ever!"
While mony a kiss the seal imprest,
　The sacred vow,—we ne'er should sever.

The haunt o' spring's the primrose brae,
　The simmer joys the flocks to follow;
How cheery, thro' her shortening day,
　Is autumn, in her weeds o' yellow!
But can they melt the glowing heart,
　Or chain the soul in speechless pleasure,
Or thro' each nerve the rapture dart,
　Like meeting her, our bosom's treasure?

THERE WAS A LASS, AND SHE WAS FAIR.

Tune—Bonnie Jean.

There was a lass, and she was fair,
　At kirk and market to be seen;
When a' the fairest maids were met,
　The fairest maid was bonnie Jean.

And aye she wrought her mammie's wark,
　And aye she sang sae merrilie;
The blithest bird upon the bush
　Had ne'er a lighter heart than she.

But hawks will rob the tender joys
　That bless the little lintwhite's nest:
And frost will blight the fairest flowers,
　And love will break the soundest rest.

Young Robie was the brawest lad,
  The flower and pride of a' the glen;
And he had owsen, sheep, and kye,
  And wanton naigies nine or ten.

He gaed wi' Jeanie to the tryste,
  He danc'd wi' Jeanie on the down;
And, lang ere witless Jeanie wist,
  Her heart was tint, her peace was stown.

As in the bosom o' the stream,
  The moonbeam dwells at dewy e'en;
So trembling, pure, was tender love
  Within the breast o' bonnie Jean.

And now she works her mammie's wark,
  And aye she sighs wi' care and pain;
Yet wist na what her ail might be,
  Or what wad mak her weel again.

But did na Jeanie's heart loup light,
  And did na joy blink in her e'e,
As Robie tauld a tale o' love
  Ae e'enin on the lily lea?

The sun was sinking in the west,
  The birds sang sweet in ilka grove;
His cheek to hers he fondly prest,
  And whisper'd thus his tale o' love:

"O Jeanie fair, I lo'e thee dear;
  O canst thou think to fancy me?
Or wilt thou leave thy mammie's cot,
  And learn to tent the farms wi' me?

"At barn or byre thou shalt na drudge,
  Or naething else to trouble thee;
But stray amang the heather-bells,
  And tent the waving corn wi' me."

Now what could artless Jeanie do?
She had nae will to say him na:
At length she blush'd a sweet consent,
And love was aye between them twa.

GALA WATER.

There's braw, braw lads on Yarrow braes,
That wander thro' the blooming heather;
But Yarrow braes nor Ettrick shaws
Can match the lads o' Gala Water.

But there is ane, a secret ane,
Aboon them a' I lo'e him better;
And I'll be his, and he'll be mine,
The bonnie lad o' Gala Water.

Altho' his daddie was nae laird,
And tho' I hae nae meikle tocher;
Yet rich in kindest, truest love,
We'll tent our flocks by Gala Water.

It ne'er was wealth, it ne'er was wealth,
That coft contentment, peace, or pleasure;
The bands and bliss o' mutual love,
O that's the chiefest warld's treasure!

LINES ON A MERRY PLOUGHMAN.

As I was a wand'ring ae morning in spring,
I heard a merry ploughman sae sweetly to sing;
And as he was singin' thae words he did say,
There's nae life like the Ploughman in the month o' sweet
May.—

The lav'rock in the morning she'll rise frae her nest,
And mount to the air wi' the dew on her breast;
And wi' the merry Ploughman she'll whistle and sing;
And at night she'll return to her nest back again.

BRUCE'S ADDRESS TO HIS ARMY AT BANNOCKBURN.

Scots, wha hae wi' WALLACE bled,
Scots, wham BRUCE has aften led ;
Welcome to your gory bed,
   Or to Victory !

Now's the day, and now's the hour ;
See the front o' battle lour ;
See approach proud Edward's pow'r—
   Chains and slavery !

Wha will be a traitor-knave ?
Wha can fill a coward's grave ?
Wha sae base as be a slave ?
   Let him turn and flee !

Wha for SCOTLAND's king and law,
FREEDOM's sword will strongly draw ;
Free-man stand, or Free-man fa' ?
   Let him follow me !

By Oppression's woes and pains !
By your sons in servile chains !
We will drain our dearest veins,
   But they shall be free !

Lay the proud usurpers low !
Tyrants fall in every foe !
LIBERTY's in every blow !—
   Let us do, or die !

WHEN I THINK ON THE HAPPY DAYS.

WHEN I think on the happy days
   I spent wi' you, my dearie ;
And now what lands between us lie,
   How can I be but eerie !

How slow ye move, ye heavy hours,
   As ye were wae and weary !
It was na sae ye glinted by
   When I was wi' my dearie.

O MALLY'S MEEK, MALLY'S SWEET.

As I was walking up the street,
　A barefit maid I chanc'd to meet ;
But O the road was very hard
　For that fair maiden's tender feet.

　　O Mally's meek, Mally's sweet,
　　　Mally's modest and discreet,
　　Mally's rare, Mally's fair,
　　　Mally's every way complete.

It were mair meet, that those fine feet
　Were weel lac'd up in silken shoon,
And 'twere mair fit that she should sit
　Within yon chariot gilt aboon.

Her yellow hair, beyond compare,
　Comes trinkling down her swan-white neck ;
And her two eyes, like stars in skies,
　Would keep a sinking ship frae wreck.

　　O Mally's meek, Mally's sweet,
　　　Mally's modest and discreet,
　　Mally's rare, Mally's fair,
　　　Mally's every way complete.

DELUDED SWAIN, THE PLEASURE.

Deluded swain, the pleasure
　The fickle fair can give thee
Is but a fairy treasure—
　Thy hopes will soon deceive thee.

The billows on the ocean,
　The breezes idly roaming,
The clouds' uncertain motion—
　They are but types of woman.

Oh! art thou not ashamed
  To doat upon a feature?
If man thou would'st be named,
  Despise the silly creature.

Go, find an honest fellow ;
  Good claret set before thee :
Hold on till thou art mellow,
  And then to bed in glory.

FAIR JENNY.

TUNE—*Saw ye my Father?*

WHERE are the joys I have met in the morning,
  That danc'd to the lark's early song?
Where is the peace that awaited my wand'ring,
  At ev'ning the wild woods among?

No more a-winding the course of yon river,
  And marking sweet flow'rets so fair:
No more I trace the light footsteps of pleasure,
  But sorrow and sad sighing care.

Is it that summer's forsaken our valleys,
  And grim, surly winter is near?
No, no ! the bees' humming round the gay roses,
  Proclaim it the pride of the year.

Fain would I hide, what I fear to discover,
  Yet long, long too well have I known
All that has caused this wreck in my bosom,
  Is Jenny, fair Jenny alone.

Time cannot aid me, my griefs are immortal,
  Nor hope dare a comfort bestow :
Come then, enamour'd and fond of my anguish
  Enjoyment I'll seek in my woe.

PHILLIS THE FAIR.

Tune—Robin Adair.

While larks with little wing
  Fann'd the pure air,
Tasting the breathing spring,
  Forth I did fare :
Gay the sun's golden eye
  Peep'd o'er the mountains high ;
Such thy morn ! did I cry,
  Phillis the fair.

In each bird's careless song,
  Glad did I share ;
While yon wild flowers among,
  Chance led me there :
Sweet to the opening day,
  Rosebuds bent the dewy spray ;
Such thy bloom ! did I say,
  Phillis the fair.

Down in a shady walk
  Doves cooing were ;
I marked the cruel hawk
  Caught in a snare :
So kind may fortune be,
Such make his destiny !
He who would injure thee,
  Phillis the fair.

THOU HAST LEFT ME EVER.

TUNE—*Fee him, Father.*

THOU hast left me ever, Jamie !
  Thou hast left me ever ;
Thou hast left me ever, Jamie !
  Thou hast left me ever.
Aften hast thou vow'd that death
  Only should us sever ;
Now thou'st left thy lass for aye—
  I maun see thee never, Jamie,
    I'll see thee never !

Thou hast me forsaken, Jamie !
  Thou hast me forsaken ;
Thou hast me forsaken, Jamie !
  Thou hast me forsaken.
Thou canst love anither jo,
  While my heart is breaking :
Soon my weary een I'll close—
  Never mair to waken, Jamie,
    Ne'er mair to waken !

NOTES.

———◆———

Note 1.—*The Cotter's Saturday Night.*   P. 5.

Gilbert Burns gives the following distinct account of the origin of this poem :—

"Robert had frequently remarked to me that he thought there was something peculiarly venerable in the phrase, 'Let us worship God!' used by a decent, sober head of a family, introducing family-worship. To this sentiment of the author the world is indebted for 'The Cotter's Saturday Night. When Robert had not some pleasure in view in which I was not thought fit to participate, we used frequently to walk together, when the weather was favourable, on the Sunday afternoons, those precious breathing-times to the labouring part of the community—and enjoyed such Sundays as would make one regret to see their number abridged. It was in one of these walks that I first had the pleasure of hearing the author repeat 'The Cotter's Saturday Night.' I do not recollect to have read or heard anything by which I was more highly electrified. The fifth and sixth stanzas, and the eighteenth, thrilled with peculiar ecstasy through my soul. The cotter, in the 'Saturday Night,' is an exact copy of my father in his manners, his family devotion, and exhortations ; yet the other parts of the description do not apply to our family. None of us were 'at service out among the farmers roun'.' Instead of our depositing our 'sair-won penny-fee' with our parents, my father laboured hard, and lived with the most rigid economy, that he might be able to keep his children at home, thereby having an opportunity of watching the progress of our young minds, and forming in them early habits of piety and virtue ; and from this motive alone did he engage in farming, the source of all his difficulties and distresses."

Note 2.—*Tam O' Shanter.*   P. 17.

Captain Grose, in the introduction to his "Antiquities of Scotland," says,—"To my *ingenious* friend, Mr. Robert Burns, I have been seriously obligated ; he was not only at the pains of making out what was most worthy of notice in Ayrshire, the country honoured by his birth, but he also wrote, expressly for this work, the *pretty tale* annexed to Alloway Church." This pretty tale was "Tam O' Shanter," certainly the most popular of all our poet's works. In a letter to Captain Grose, Burns gives the legend which formed the groundwork of the poem :—"On a market-day in the town of Ayr, a farmer from Carrick, and consequently whose way lay by the very gate of Alloway kirkyard, in order to cross the river Doon at the old bridge, which is about two or three hundred yards further on than the said gate, had been detained by his business, till by the time he reached Alloway it was the wizard hour, between night and morning. Though he was terrified with a blaze streaming from the kirk, yet it is a well-known fact that to turn back on these occasions is running by far the greatest risk of mischief—he prudently advanced on his road. When he had reached the gate of the kirkyard he was surprised and entertained, through the ribs and arches of an old Gothic window, which still faces the highway, to see a dance of witches merrily footing it round their old sooty blackguard master, who was keeping them all alive with the power of his bagpipe. The farmer, stopping his horse to observe them a little, could plainly descry the faces of many old women of his acquaintance and neighbourhood. How the gentleman was dressed tradition does not say, but that the ladies were all in their smocks ; and one of them happening unluckily to have a smock which was considerably too short to answer all the purpose of that piece of dress, our farmer was so tickled that he involuntarily burst out, with a loud laugh, 'Weel luppen, Maggie wi' the short sark !' and, recollecting himself, instantly spurred his horse to the top of his speed. I need not mention the universally-known fact that no diabolical power can pursue you beyond the middle of a running stream. Lucky it was for the poor farmer that the river Doon was so near, for notwithstanding the speed of his horse, which was a good one, against he reached the middle of the arch of the bridge, and consequently the middle of the stream, the pursuing vengeful hags were so close at his heels that one of them actually sprang to seize him ; but it was too late: nothing was on her side of the stream but the horse's tail, which immediately gave way at her infernal grip, as if blasted by a stroke of lightning ; but the farmer was beyond her reach.   However, the unsightly tailless condition of the vigorous steed was, to the last hour of the noble creature's life, an awful warning to the Carrick farmers not to stay too late in Ayr markets."

Note 3.—*Lament of Mary Queen of Scots.*   P: 35.

This poem is said to have been written at the instigation of Lady Winifred Maxwell Constable, daughter of William Maxwell, Earl of Nithsdale, who rewarded him with a present of a valuable snuff-box, having a portrait of Queen Mary on the lid.   In a letter to Graham of Fintray, enclosing a copy of "The Lament," the poet says :—"Whether it is that the story of our Mary Queen of Scots has a peculiar effect on the feelings of a poet, or whether I have, in the enclosed ballad, succeeded beyond my usual poetic success, I know not, but it has pleased me beyond any effort of my Muse for a good while past."

Note 4.—*The Twa Dogs.*   P. 37.

Gilbert Burns says,—"The tale of the 'Twa Dogs' was composed after the resolution of publishing was nearly taken.   Robert had a dog, which he called Luath, that was a great favourite.   The dog had been killed by the wanton cruelty of some person the night before my father's death.   Robert said to me that he should like to confer such immortality as he could bestow on his old friend Luath, and that he had a great mind to introduce something into the book under the title of 'Stanzas to the Memory of a Quadruped Friend ;' but this plan was given up for the poem as it now stands.   Cæsar was merely the creature of the poet's imagination, created for the purpose of holding chat with his favourite Luath."   The factor who stood for his portrait here was the same of whom he writes to Dr. Moore in 1787 :—"My indignation yet boils at the scoundrel factor's insolent threatening letters, which used to set us all in tears."

Note 5.—*Elegy on Captain Matthew Henderson.*   P. 46.

In a letter to Dr. Moore, dated February 1791, the poet says :—"The Elegy on Captain Henderson is a tribute to the memory of a man I loved much.   Poets have in this the same advantage as Roman Catholics : they can be of service to their friends after they have passed that bourne where all other kindness ceases to be of any avail.   Whether, after all, either the one or the other be of any real service to the dead is, I fear, very problematical ; but I am sure they are highly gratifying to the living.   Captain Henderson was a retired soldier, of agreeable manners and upright character, who had a lodging in Carrubber's Close, Edinburgh, and mingled with the best society of the city : he dined regularly at Fortune's Tavern, and was a member of the Capillaire Club, which was composed of all who inclined to the witty and the joyous.

Note 6.—*Death and Dying Words of Poor Mailie.*   P. 55.

"The circumstances of the poor sheep," says Gilbert Burns, "were pretty much as Robert has described them.   He had, partly by way of frolic, bought a ewe and two lambs from a neighbour, and she was tethered in a field adjoining the house at Lochlea.   He and I were going out with our teams, and our two younger brothers to drive for us, at mid-day, when Hugh Wilson, a curious-looking, awkward boy, clad in plaiding, came to us with much anxiety in his face, with the information that the ewe had entangled herself in the tether, and was lying in the ditch.   Robert was much tickled with Hughoc's appearance and postures on the occasion.   Poor Mailie was set to rights, and when we returned from the plough in the evening, he repeated to me her 'Death and Dying Words' pretty much in the way they now stand."

Note 7.—*Macpherson's Farewell.*   P. 59.

"James Macpherson was a noted Highland freebooter of uncommon personal strength, and an excellent performer on the violin.   After holding the counties of Aberdeen, Banff, and Moray in fear for some years, he was seized by Duff of Braco, ancestor of the Earl of Fife, and tried before the sheriff of Banffshire (November 7, 1700), along with certain gipsies who had been taken in his company.   In the prison, while he lay under sentence of death, he composed a song and an appropriate air, the former commencing thus :—

> ' I've spent my time in rioting,
>   Debauch'd my health and strength,
> I squander'd fast as pillage came,
>   And fell to shame at length.
>
> ' But dantonly, and wantonly,
>   And rantingly I'll gae ;
> I'll play a tune, and dance it roun'
>   Beneath the gallows tree.'

When brought to the place of execution, on the Gallows-hill of Banff (Nov. 16), he played the tune on his violin, and then asked if any friend was present who would accept the instrument as a gift at his hands. No one coming forward, he indignantly broke the violin on his knee, and threw away the fragments ; after which he submitted to his fate. The traditionary accounts of Macpherson's immense prowess are justified by his sword, which is still preserved in Duff House, at Banff, and is an implement of great length and weight—as well as by his bones, which were found a few years ago, and were allowed by all who saw them to be much stronger than the bones of ordinary men."

NOTE 8.—*Halloween.*   P. 76.

a Certain little, romantic, rocky, green hills, in the neighbourhood of the ancient seat of the Earls of Cassilis.—*B*.

b A noted cavern near Colean House, called the Cove of Colean ; which, as well as Cassilis Downans, is famed in country story for being a favourite haunt of fairies.—*B*.

c The famous family of that name, the ancestors of Robert Bruce, the great deliverer of his country, were Earls of Carrick.—*B*.

d The first ceremony of Halloween is pulling each a stock or plant of kail. They must go out, hand-in-hand, with eyes shut, and pull the first they meet with ; its being big or little, straight or crooked, is prophetic of the size and shape of the grand object of all their spells—the husband or wife. If any yird, or earth, stick to the root, that is tocher, or fortune, and the taste of the custoc—that is, the heart of the stem—is indicative of the natural temper and disposition. Lastly, the stems, or to give them their ordinary appellation, the runts, are placed somewhere above the head of the door ; and the Christian names of the people whom chance brings into the house, are, according to the priority of placing the runts, the names in question.—*B*.

e They go to the barn-yard and pull each, at three several times, a stalk of oats. If the third stalk wants the top-pickle—that is, the grain at the top of the stalk, the party in question will come to the marriage-bed anything but a maid.—*B*.

f When the corn is in a doubtful state, by being too green or wet, the stack-builder, by means of old timber, etc., makes a large apartment in his stack, with an opening in the side which is fairest exposed to the wind : this he calls a fause-house.—*B*.

g Burning the nuts is a famous charm. They name the lad and lass to each particular nut, as they lay them in the fire, and, accordingly as they burn quietly together, or start from beside one another, the course and issue of the courtship will be.—*B*.

h Whoever would, with success, try this spell, must strictly observe these directions :—Steal out, all alone, to the kiln, and darkling throw into the pot a clue of blue yarn ; wind it in a new clue of the old one ; and, towards the latter end, something will hold the thread ; demand "Wha hauds?"—*i.e.* who holds ? An answer will be returned from the kiln-pot, by naming the Christian and surname of your future spouse.—*B*.

i Take a candle, and go alone to a looking glass ; eat an apple before it, and some traditions say, you should comb your hair all the time ; the face of your conjugal companion *to be*, will be seen in the glass, as if peeping over your shoulder.—*B*.

k Steal out unperceived, and sow a handful of hemp-seed, harrowing it with anything you can conveniently draw after you. Repeat now and then, "Hemp-seed, I saw thee ; hemp-seed I saw thee ; and him (or her) that is to be my true love, come after me and pou thee." Look over your left shoulder, and you will see the appearance of the person invoked, in the attitude of pulling hemp. Some traditions say, "Come after me and shaw thee," that is, show thyself ; in which case it simply appears. Others omit the harrowing, and say, "Come after me, and harrow thee."—*B*.

l This charm must likewise be performed unperceived and alone. You go to the barn, and open both doors, taking them off the hinges, if possible ; for there is danger that the being about to appear may shut the doors, and do you some mischief. Then take that instrument used in winnowing the corn, which in our country dialect we call a wecht ; and go through all the attitudes of letting down corn against the wind. Repeat it three times ; and the third time an apparition will pass through the barn, in at the windy door, and out at the other, having both the figure in question and the appearance of retinue marking the employment or station in life.—*B.*

m Take an opportunity of going unnoticed to a bean-stack, and fathom it three times round. The last fathom of the last time you will catch in your arms the appearance of your future conjugal yoke-fellow.—*B.*

n You go out, one or more, for this is a social spell, to a south-running spring or rivulet, where "three lairds' lands meet," and dip your left shirt-sleeve. Go to bed in sight of a fire, and hang your wet sleeve before it to dry. Lie awake; and sometime near midnight an apparition having the exact figure of the grand object in question will come and turn the sleeve, as if to dry the other side of it.—*B.*

o Take three dishes: put clean water in one, foul water in another, leave the third empty: blindfold a person, and lead him to the hearth where the dishes are ranged; he (or she) dips the left hand; if by chance in the clean water, the future husband or wife will come to the bar of matrimony a maid; if in the foul, a widow; if in the empty dish, it foretells, with equal certainty, no marriage at all. It is repeated three times, and every time the arrangement of the dishes is altered.—*B.*

p Sowens—the shell of the corn (called in the rural districts, shellings) is steeped in water until all the fine meal particles are extracted; the liquid is then strained off, and boiled with milk or butter until it thickens.

Note 9.—*Tam Samson's Elegy.* P. 85.

"The hero of this poem was a respectable old nursery-seedsman in Kilmarnock, greatly addicted to sporting, and one of the poet's earliest friends, who loved curling on the ice in winter, and shooting on the moors in the season. When no longer able to march over hill and hag in quest of

'Paitricks, teals, moor-pouts, and plivers,'

he loved to lie on the lang settle, and listen to the deeds of others on field and flood; and when a good tale was told, he would cry, 'Hech, man! three at a shot; that was famous!' Some one having informed Tam, in his old age, that Burns had written a poem—'a gay queer ane'—concerning him, he sent for the bard, and, in something like wrath, requested to hear it; he smiled grimly at the relation of his exploits, and then cried out, 'I'm no dead yet, Robin—I'm worth ten dead fowk; wherefore should ye say that I am dead?' Burns took the hint, retired to the window for a minute or so, and, coming back, recited the 'Per Contra,'

'Go, Fame, and canter like a filly,'

with which Tam was so delighted that he rose unconsciously, rubbed his hands, and exclaimed, 'That'll do—ha! ha!—that'll do!' He survived the poet, and the epitaph is inscribed on his gravestone in the churchyard of Kilmarnock."

Note 10.—*The Vision.* P. 99.

a The town of Ayr. *b* The Wallaces.—*B.* *c* Sir William Wallace.—*B.*

d Adam Wallace of Richardton, cousin to the immortal preserver of Scottish independence.—*B.*

e Wallace, Laird of Craigie, who was second in command, under Douglas, Earl of Ormond, at the famous battle on the banks of Sark, fought in 1448. That glorious victory was principally owing to the judicious conduct and intrepid valour of the gallant Laird of Craigie, who died of his wounds after the action.—*B.*

f Coilus, King of the Picts, from whom the district of Kyle, is said to take its name, lies buried, as tradition says, near the family seat of the Montgomeries of Coilsfield, where his burial-place is still shown.—*B.*

g Barskimming, the seat of the late Lord Justice-Clerk.—*B.* (Sir Thomas Miller of Glenlee, afterwards President of the Court of Session.)

h The Rev. Dr. Matthew Stewart, the celebrated mathematician, and his son, Mr. Dugald Stewart, the elegant expositor of the Scottish school of metaphysics, are here meant, their villa of Catrine being situated on the Ayr. *i* Colonel Fullarton.—*B.*

Note 11.—*Verses on Seeing a Wounded Hare.* P. 118.

This poem was founded on a real incident. James Thomson, a neighbour of the poet's, states that having shot at and wounded a hare, it ran past the poet, who happened to be near. "He cursed me, and said he would not mind throwing me into the water; and I'll warrant he could hae done't, though I was both young and strong."

GLOSSARY.

The *ch* and *gh* have always the guttural sound. The sound of the English diphthong *oo*, is commonly spelled *ou*. The French *u*, a sound which often occurs in the Scottish language, is marked *oo*, or *ui*. The *a* in genuine Scottish words, except when forming a diphthong, or followed by *e* mute after a single consonant, sounds generally like the broad English *a* in *wall*. The Scottish diphthong *æ*, always, and *ea* very often, sound like the French *e* masculine. The Scottish diphthong *ey* sounds like the Latin *ei*.

ABEIGH, at a shy distance
Aboon, above, up
Abread, abroad, in sight
Abreed, in breadth
Ae, one
Aff loof, off-hand, unpremeditated
Agley, off the right line, wrong
Aiblins, perhaps
Ain, own
Airn, iron
Aith, an oath
Aits, oats
Aiver, an old horse
Aizle, a hot cinder
Alake, alas
Amaist, almost
An', and
An, if
Ance, once
Ane, one, and
Anent, over against
Anither, another
Arle-penny, airles, earnest money
Ase, ashes
Asklent, asquint, aslant
Asteer, abroad, stirring
Athart, athwart
Aught, possession; as, In a' my aught, In all my possession
Auld lang syne, olden time, days of other years
Auld, old
Auldfarren or Auld Farrant, sagacious, cunning, prudent
Ava, at all
Awn, the beard of barley, oats, etc.
Awnie, bearded
Ayont, beyond

BACKETS, ash-boxes
Backlins, coming, coming back, returning
Bad, did bid
Baide, endured, did stay
Baggie, the belly
Banie, having large bones, stout
Bairn, a child
Bairntime, a family of children, a brood
Ban, to swear
Bane, bone
Bang, to beat, to strive

Bannock, a kind of thick cake of bread, a small jannock, or loaf made of oat-meal
Bardie, diminutive of bard
Barefit, barefooted
Barmie, of, or like, barm
Batch, a crew, a gang
Bats, bots
Baudrons, a cat
Bauld, bold
Bawk, bank
Basn't, having a white stripe down the face
Be, to let be; to give over, to cease
Bear, barley
Beastie, diminutive of beast
Beet, to add fuel to fire
Beld, bald
Belyve, by and by
Ben, into the spence or parlour, a spence
Bethankit, grace after meat
Beuk, a book
Bicker, a kind of wooden dish, a short race
Biel or Bield, shelter
Bien, wealthy, plentiful
Big, to build
Biggin, building, a house
Biggit, built
Bill, a bull
Billie, a brother, a young fellow
Bing, a heap of grain, potatoes, etc.
Birk, birch
Birken-shaw, Birchen-wood-shaw, a small wood
Birkie, a clever fellow
Birring, the noise of partridges, etc. when they spring
Bit, crisis, nick of time
Bizz, a bustle, to buzz
Blastie, a shrivelled dwarf, a term of contempt
Blate, bashful, sheepish
Bladd, a flat piece of anything, to slap
Blaw, to blow, to boast
Bleerit, bleared, sore with rheum
Bleert and blin', bleared and blind
Blellum, an idle talking fellow
Blether, bladder, to talk idly, nonsense
Bleth'rin', talking idly

Blink, a little while, a smiling look, to look kindly, to shine by fits
Blinker, a term of contempt
Blinkin, smirking
Blue-gown, one of those beggars who formerly got annually, on the king's birthday, a blue cloak or gown, with a badge
Bluid, blood
Bluntie, a sniveller, a stupid person
Blype, a shred, a large piece
Bock, to vomit, to gush intermittently
Bocked, gushed, vomited
Bodle, a small copper coin
Bogles, spirits, hobgoblins
Bonnie or Bonny, handsome, beautiful
Boord, a board
Boortree, the shrub elder, planted much of old in hedges of barnyards, etc.
Boost, behaved, must needs
Bore, a hole in the wall
Botch, an angry tumour
Bousing, drinking
Bow-kail, cabbage
Bowt, bended, crooked
Brackens, fern
Brae, a declivity, a precipice, the slope of a hill
Braindg't, reeled forward
Brnaik, a kind of harrow
Braindge, to run rashly forward
Brak, broke, made insolvent
Branks, a kind of wooden curb for horses
Brash, a sudden illness
Brats, coarse clothes, rags, etc.
Brattle, a short race, hurry, fury
Braw, fine, handsome
Brawly or Brawlie, very well, finely, heartily
Braxie, a diseased sheep
Breastie, diminutive of breast
Breastit, did spring up or forward
Breef, an invulnerable or irresistible spell
Breeks, breeches
Brent, smooth
Brewin', brewing
Bree, juice, liquid

Brig, a bridge
Brunstane, brimstone
Brisket, the breast, the bosom
Brither, a brother
Brock, a badger
Brogue, a hum, a trick
Broo, broth, a trick
Broose, broth; a race at country weddings, who shall first reach the bridegroom's house on returning from church
Browster-wives, ale-house wives
Brugh, a burgh
Bruilzie, a broil, a combustion
Brunt, did burn, burnt
Brust, to burst, burst
Buchan-bullers, the boiling of the sea among the rocks of Buchan
Buckskin, an inhabitant of Virginia
Bught, a sheep-pen
Bughtin-time, the time of collecting the sheep in the pens to be milked
Buirdly, stout made, broad made
Bum-clock, a humming beetle that flies in the summer evenings
Bumming, humming as bees
Bummle, to blunder
Bummler, a blunderer
Bunker, a window-seat
Burdies, diminutive of birds
Bure, did bear
Burn, water, a rivulet
Burnewin, i.e. burn the wind, a blacksmith
Burnie, diminutive of burn
Buskie, bushy
Buskit, dressed
Busks, dresses
Bussle, a bustle, to bustle
Buss, shelter
But, bot, with, without
But an' ben, a small house of kitchen and room
By himsell, lunatic, distracted
Byke, a bee-hive
Byre, a cow-stable, a sheep-pen

Ca', to call, to name, to drive
Ca't or Ca'd, called, driven, calved
Cadger, a carrier
Cadie or Caddie, a young fellow, a porter or messenger
Caff, chaff
Caird, a tinker
Cairn, a loose heap of stones
Calf-ward, a small enclosure for calves
Callan, a boy
Caller, fresh, sound, refreshing
Canie or Cannie, gentle, mild, dexterous
Cannilie, dexterously, gently
Cantie or Canty, cheerful, merry
Cantrip, a charm, a spell
Cape-stane, cope-stone
Careerin', moving cheerfully
Carle, an old man
Carlin, a stout old woman
Cartes, cards
Caudron, a caldron
Cauk and keel, chalk and red clay
Caup, a wooden drinking vessel
Cesses, taxes
Chanter, a part of a bagpipe
Chap, a person, a fellow
Chaup, a stroke, a blow
Cheekit, checked
Cheep, a chirp, to chirp

Chiel or Cheel, a young fellow
Chimla or Chimlie, a fire-grate, a fire-place
Chimla-lug, the fireside
Chittering, shivering, trembling
Chockin', choking
Chow, to chew; Cheek for chow, side by side
Chuffie, fat-faced
Clachan, a small village about a church, a hamlet
Claise or Claes, clothes
Claivers, nonsense, not sense
Clap, clapper of a mill
Clarkit, wrote
Clash, an idle tale, the story of the day
Clatter, to tell idle stories, an idle story
Claught, snatched at, laid hold of
Clat, to clean, to scrape
Clauted, scraped
Clavers, idle stories
Claw, to scratch
Cleed, to clothe
Cleeds, clothes
Cleekit, having caught
Clinkin, jerking, clinking
Clinkumbell, he who rings the church-bell
Clips, shears
Clishmaclaver, idle conversation
Clock, to hatch, a beetle
Clockin, hatching
Cloot, the hoof of a cow, sheep, etc.
Clootie, an old name for the devil
Clour, a bump or swelling after a blow
Cluds, clouds
Coble, a fishing boat
Cocknernony, a lock of hair tied upon a girl's head, a cap
Coft, bought
Cog, a wooden dish
Coggie, diminutive of cog
Collie, a shepherd's dog
Collieshangie, quarrelling, an uproar
Cood, the cud
Coof, a blockhead, ninny
Cookit, appeared and disappeared by fits
Coost, did cast
Coot, the ankle or foot
Cootie, a wooden kitchen dish,— also those fowls whose legs are clad with feathers are said to be cootie
Corbies, a species of the crow
Core, Corps, party, clan
Corn'd, fed with oats
Cotter, the inhabitant of a cot-house, or cottager
Couthie, kind, loving
Cowe, to terrify, to keep under, to lop, to cut, fright, a branch of furze, broom, etc.
Cowp, to barter, tumble over, a gang
Cowpit, tumbled
Cowrin, cowering
Cowt, a colt
Cozie, snug
Coziely, snugly
Crabbit, crabbed, fretful
Crack, conversation, to converse
Crackin, conversing
Craft or Croft, a field near a house (in old husbandry)

Craiks, cries or calls incessantly, a bird
Crambo-clink or Crambo-jingle, rhymes, doggrel verses
Crankous, fretful, captious
Cranreuch, the hoar frost
Crap, a crop, to crop
Craw, the crow of a cock, a rook
Creel, a basket, to have one's wits in a creel, to be crazed, to be fascinated
Creepie-stool, the same as cutty-stool
Creeshie, greasy
Crood or Croud, to coo as a dove
Croon, a hollow and continued moan, to make a noise like the continued roar of a bull, to hum a tune
Crooning, humming
Crouchie, crook-backed
Croose, cheerful, courageous
Crousely, cheerfully, courageously
Crowdie, a mixture of oatmeal and boiled water, sometimes from the broth of beef, mutton, etc.
Crowdie-time, breakfast time
Crowlin, crawling
Crummock, a cow with crooked horns
Crump, hard and brittle, spoken of bread
Crunt, a blow on the head with a cudgel
Cuif, a blockhead, a ninny
Cummock, a short staff with a crooked head
Curchie, a curtsey
Curler, a player at a game on the ice, called curling
Curling, a game on the ice
Curmurring, murmuring
Curpin, the cropper
Cushat, the dove or wood-pigeon
Cutty, short, a short spoon or tobacco pipe
Cutty-stool, the stool of repentance

Daddie, father
Daffin, merriment, foolishness
Daft, merry, giddy, foolish
Daimen, rare, now and then: daimen-icker, an ear of corn, here and there
Dainty, pleasant, good humoured, agreeable
Daise or Daze, to stupify
Dales, plains, valleys
Darg or Dark, a day's labour
Darklins, darkling
Daud, to thrash, to abuse
Daur, to dare
Daurt, dared
Davoc, David
Dawd, a large piece
Dawtit or Dawtet, fondled, caressed
Dearies, diminutive of dears
Dearthfu', dear
Deave, to deafen
Deil-ma-care, no matter, for all that.
Deleerit, delirious
Descrive, to describe
Dight, to wipe, to clean corn from chaff
Dight, to clean from chaff
Ding, to overcome, to push

Dink, neat, tidy, trim
Dinna, do not
Dirl, a slight tremulous stroke or pain
Dizen or Dizz'n, a dozen
Doited, stupid, dull
Dolt, stupid, crazed
Donsie, unlucky
Dool, sorrow; to sing dool, to lament, to mourn
Doos, doves
Dorty, saucy, nice
Douce or Douse, sober, wise, prudent
Doucely, soberly, prudently
Dought, was or were able
Dour and din, sullen and sallow
Doure, stout, durable, sullen, stubborn
Dow, am or are able, can
Dowff, pithless, wanting force
Dowie, worn with grief, fatigue, care, half asleep
Downa, am or are not able, cannot
Doylt, stupid
Dozent, stupified, impotent
Draigle, to soil by trailing, to draggle among water, etc.
Draunting, drawling, of a slow enunciation
Dreep, to ooze, to drop
Dreigh, tedious, long about it
Dribble, drizzling, slaver
Drift, a drove
Drone, part of a bagpipe
Droop-rumpl't, that droops at the crupper
Droukit, wet
Drounting, drawling
Drouth, thirst, drought
Drucken, drunken
Drumly, muddy
Drummock, meal and water mixed in a raw state
Drunt, pet, sour humour
Dub, a small pond
Duds, rags, clothes
Duddie, ragged
Dung, worsted, pushed, driven
Dunted, beaten, boxed
Dush, to butt as a ram, etc.

Eerie, frighted, dreading spirits
Eild, old age
Elbuck, the elbow
Eldritch, ghastly, frightful
Eller, an elder or church officer
Especial, especially
Ettle, to try, to attempt
Eydent, diligent

Faddom't, measured
Fairin, a present brought from a fair
Fallow, fellow
Fand, did find
Farl, a cake of oaten bread, etc.
Fash, trouble, care, to trouble, to care for
Fashed, troubled
Fasteren e'en, Fasten's even, Shrove Tuesday
Fauld, a fold, to fold
Faulding, folding
Faut, want, lack
Fawsont, decent, seemly
Feal, a field, smooth, loyal
Fearfu', frightful
Feart, frighted

Feat, neat, spruce
Fecht, to fight
Fechtin, fighting
Feck, quantity, plenty
Fecket, an under waistcoat with sleeves
Feckfu', large, brawny, stout
Feckless, puny, weak, silly
Feckly, nearly
Feg, a fig
Feide, feud, enmity
Feire, stout, vigorous, healthy
Fell, keen, biting
Fen, successful struggle, fight
Fend, to provide for
Ferlie, to wonder, a wonder, a term of contempt
Fetch, to pull by fits
Fetch't, pulled intermittently
Fidge, to fidget
Fiel, soft, smooth
Fient, fiend, a petty oath
Fier, sound, healthy, a brother, friend
Fissle, to make a rustling noise, to fidget, a bustle
Fit, a foot
Fittie-lan, the nearer horse of the hindmost pair in the plough
Fizz, to make a hissing noise, like fermentation
Flannin, flannel
Fleech, to supplicate in a flattering manner
Fleech'd, supplicated
Fleeching, supplicating
Fleesh, a fleece
Fleg, a random stroke, a fright
Flether, to decoy by fair words
Fletherin, flattering
Fley, to scare, to frighten
Flichter, to flutter, as young nestlings when their dam approaches
Flinders, shreds, broken pieces, splinters
Flinging-tree, a piece of timber hung by way of partition between two horses in a stable, a flail
Flisk, to fret at the yoke
Flisket, fretted
Flitter, to vibrate like the wings of small birds
Fodgel, squat and plump
Foord, a ford
Forbears, forefathers
Forbye, besides
Forfairn, distressed, worn out, jaded
Forfoughten, fatigued
Forgather, to meet, to encounter with
Forgie, to forgive
Forjesket, jaded with fatigue
Fother, fodder
Fou, full, drunk
Foughten, troubled, harassed
Fouth, plenty, enough, or more than enough
Fow, a bushel, etc., also a pitch-fork
Frammit, strange, estranged from, at enmity with
Freath, froth
Fud, the scut, or tail of the hare, cony, etc.
Fuff, to blow intermittently

Fur, a furrow
Fyk, trifling cares
Fyle, to soil, to dirty

Gab, the mouth, to speak boldly or pertly
Gaberlunzie, an old man
Gadsman, a ploughboy, the boy that drives the horses in the plough
Gae, to go; gaed, went; gaen, or gane, gone; gaun, going
Gaet or gate, way, manner, road
Gairs, triangular pieces of cloth sewed on the bottom of a gown etc.
Gang, to go, to walk
Gar, to make, to force to
Gar't, forced to
Garten, a garter
Gash, wise, sagacious, talkative, to converse
Gashin, conversing
Gaucy, jolly, large
Gaud, a goad
Gear, riches, goods of any kind
Geck, to toss the head in wantonness or scorn
Ged, a pike, a greedy person
Gentles, great folk, gentry
Genty, elegantly formed, neat
Geordie, a guinea
Get, a child, a young one
Ghaist, a ghost
Gie, to give; gied, gave; gien, given
Giftie, diminutive of gift
Giglets, playful girls
Gillie, diminutive of gill
Gilpey, a half-grown, half-formed boy or girl, a romping lad, a hoyden
Gimmer, a ewe from one to two years old
Gin, if, against
Gipsey, a young girl
Girning, grinning
Gizz, a periwig
Glaiket, inattentive, foolish
Glaive, a sword
Gawky, half-witted, foolish, romping
Glaizie, glittering, smooth like glass
Glaum, to snatch greedily
Glaum'd, aimed, snatched
Gleck, sharp, ready
Gleg, sharp, ready
Glieb, glebe
Glen, a dale, a deep valley
Gley, a squint, to squint; a-gley, off at a side, wrong
Glib-gabbit, smooth and ready in speech
Glint, to peep
Glinted, peeped
Glintin, peeping
Gloamin, the twilight
Glowr, to stare, to look, a stare, a look
Glowred, looked, stared
Glunsh, a frown, a sour look
Goavan, looking round with a strange inquiring gaze, staring stupidly
Gowan, the wild daisy
Gowany, daisies, abounding with daisies

Gowd, gold

Gowff, the game of golf, to strike as the club does the ball at golf

Gowff'd, struck

Gowk, a cuckoo, a term of contempt

Gowl, to howl

Grane or grain, a groan, to groan

Grain'd and grunted, groaned and grunted

Graining, groaning

Graip, a pronged instrument for cleaning cowhouses

Graith, harness, furniture, dress, gear

Grannie, grandmother

Grape, to grope

Grapit, groped

Grat, wept, shed tears

Great, intimate, familiar

Gree, to agree; to bear the gree, to be decidedly victor

Gree't, agreed.

Greet, to shed tears, to weep

Gripit, caught, seized

Groat; to get the whistle of one's groat, to play a losing game

Grousome, repulsively grim

Grozet, a gooseberry

Grumph, a grunt, to grunt

Grumphie, a sow

Grun', ground

Grunstane, a grindstone

Gruntle, the phiz; a grunting noise

Grunzie, mouth

Grushie, thick, of thriving growth

Gude, the Supreme Being, good

Guid, good

Guid-morning, good morrow

Guid-e'en, good-evening

Guidman and guidwife, the master and mistress of the house; young guidman, a man newly married

Guid-willie, liberal, cordial

Guid-father, Guid-mother, father-in-law and mother-in-law

Gully, or Gullie, a large knife

Gumlie, muddy

Gusty, tasteful

HA'-BIBLE, the Family Bible

Haen, had, the participle

Haet, fient haet, a petty oath of negation, nothing

Haffet, the temple, the side of the head

Hafflins, nearly half, partly

Hag, a scar, or gulf in mosses and moors

Haggis, a kind of pudding boiled in the stomach of a cow or sheep

Hain, to spare, to save

Hairst, harvest

Haith, a petty oath

Haivers, nonsense, speaking without thought

Hal' or Hald, an abiding place

Hallan, a particular partition-wall in a cottage, or more properly a seat of turf at the outside

Hallowmas, Hallow-eve, the 31st of October

Hap, an outer garment, mantle, plaid, etc.; to wrap, to cover, to hop

Hap step an' loup, hop skip and leap

Harkit, hearkened

Harn, very coarse linen

Hastit, hastened

Haughs, low lying rich lands, valleys

Haurl, to drag, to peel

Haurlin, peeling

Haverel, a half-witted person, half-witted

Havins, good manners, decorum, good sense

Hawkie, a cow, properly one with a white face

Heapit, heaped

Healsom, healthful, wholesome

Hearse, hoarse

Hear't, hear it

Heather, heath

Hech! oh! strange!

Hecht, promised, to foretell something that is to be got or given, foretold, the thing foretold, offered

Heckle, a board. in which are fixed a number of sharp pins, used in dressing hemp and flax

Heeze, to elevate, to raise

Herry, to plunder, most properly to plunder birds' nests

Herryment, plundering, devastation

Hessel, so many cattle as one person can attend

Heugh, a crag, a coalpit

Hilch, a hobble, to halt

Hilchin, halting

Hiney, honey

Hirple, to walk lamely, to creep

Hitch, a loop, a knot

Hizzie, a hussy, a young girl

Hog-score, a kind of distance line in curling, drawn across the rink

Hog-shouther, a kind of horse play, by jostling with the shoulders, to jostle

Hool, outer skin or case, a nut-shell, a pea-husk

Hoolie, slowly, leisurely

Hoolie! take leisure, stop

Hoord, a hoard, to hoard

Hoordit, hoarded

Horn, a spoon made of horn

Hornie, one of the many names of the devil

Host or Hoast, to cough, a cough

Hostin', coughing

Hosts, coughs

Hotch'd, turned topsyturvy, blended, mixed

Houlet, an owl

Housie, diminutive of house

Hove, to heave, to swell

Hoved, heaved, swelled

Howdie, a midwife

Howe, hollow, a hollow or dell

Howe-backit, sunk in the back, spoken of a horse

Howff, a tippling house, a house of resort

Howk, to dig

Howkit, digged

Howlet, an owl

Hoy, to urge

Hoy't, urged

Hoyse, to pull upwards

Hoyte, to amble crazily

Hurcheon, a hedgehog

Hurdies, the loins, the crupper

Hushion, a cushion

IER-OE, a great-grandchild

Ilk or Ilka, each, every

Ill-willie, ill-natured, malicious, niggardly

Ingine, genius, ingenuity

Ingle, fire, fireplace

Ise, I shall or will

Ither, other, one another

JAD, jade, also a familiar term among country folks for a giddy young girl

Jauk, to dally, to trifle

Jaukin, trifling, dallying

Jaup, a jerk of water, to jerk as agitating water

Jaw, coarse raillery, to pour out, to throw out water

Jerkinet, a jerkin or short gown

Jillet, a jilt, or giddy girl

Jimp, to jump, slender in the waist, handsome

Jimps, easy stays

Jink, to dodge, to turn a corner, a sudden turning a corner

Jinker, that turns quickly, a gay sprightly girl, a wag

Jinkin, dodging

Jirk, a jerk

Jocteleg, a kind of knife

Jouk, to stoop, to bow the head

Jow, to jow, a verb which includes both the swinging motion and pealing sound of a large bell

Jundie, to jostle

KAE, a daw

Kail, colewort, broth

Kain, fowls, etc., paid as rent by farmer

Kebbuck, a cheese

Keckle, to giggle, to cackle as a hen

Keek, a peep, to peep

Kelpies, mischievous spirits, said to haunt fords and ferries at night

Ken, to know; Kend or Kenn'd, known

Kennin, a small matter

Kenspeckle, well known, easily known

Ket, matted, hairy, a fleece of woo

Kilt, to truss up the clothes

Kimmer, a young girl, a gossip

Kin, kindred

Kin', kind (adj.)

King's-hood, a certain part of the entrails of an ox, etc.

Kintra, country

Kirn, the harvest supper, a churn

Kirsen, to christen, to baptize

Kist, a chest, a shop counter

Kitchen, anything that eats with bread, to serve for soup, gravy, etc.

Kith, kindred

Kittle, to tickle, ticklish, lively, apt

Kittlin, a kitten

Kiuttle, to cuddle

Kiuttling, cuddling

Knaggie, like knags, or points of rocks

Knap, to strike smartly, a smart blow

Knappin-hammer, a hammer for breaking stones

Knowe, a small round hillock

Knurl, a dwarf

Kye, cows
Kyte, the belly
Kythe, to discover, to show one's self

Laddie, diminutive of lad
Laigh, low
Lairing, wading and sinking in snow or mud.
Laith, loath
Laithfu', bashful, sheepish
Lambie, diminutive of lamb
Lampit, a kind of shell-fish, a limpit
Lane, lone; my lane, thy lane, etc., myself alone, etc.
Lap, did leap
Lave, the rest, the remainder, the others
Laverock, the lark
Lawin, shot, reckoning, bill
Lawlan, lowland
Lea'e, to leave
Leal, loyal, true, faithful
Lea-rig, grassy ridge
Lear, learning
Lee-lang, livelong
Leesome, pleasant
Leeze-me, a phrase of endearment
Leister, a three-pronged spear for striking fish
Leugh, did laugh
Leuk, a look, to look
Libbet, gelded
Lift, the sky
Lightly, sneeringly, to sneer at
Lilt, a ballad, a tune, to sing
Limmer, a kept mistress, a strumpet
Limp't, limped, hobbled
Link, to trip along
Linkin, tripping
Linn, a waterfall, a precipice
Lint, flax; Lint i' the bell, flax in the flower
Lintie, Lintwhite, a linnet
Lintwhite, white as flax, flaxen
Loan, or loanin, the place of milking
Loof, the palm of the hand
Loot, did let
Loon, a fellow, a ragamuffin
Loup, jump, leap
Lowe, a flame
Lowin, flaming
Lowse, to loose
Lows'd, loosed
Lug, the ear, a handle
Lugget, having a handle
Luggie, a small wooden dish with a handle
Lum, the chimney
Lunch, a large piece of cheese, flesh, etc.
Lunt, a column of smoke, to smoke
Luntin, smoking
Lyart, of a mixed colour, grey

Mae, more
Mailen, a farm
Mang, among
Marled, variegated, spotted
Mar's year, the year 1715
Mashlum, Meslin, mixed corn
Mask, to mash, as malt; to infuse, etc.
Maskin-pat, a tea-pot
Maud, Maad, a plaid worn by shepherds, etc.

Maukin, a hare
Maun, must
Mavis, the thrush
Maw, to mow
Mawin, mowing
Meere, a mare
Meikle, Meickle, much
Melder, corn, or grain of any kind, sent to the mill to be ground
Mell, to meddle; also a mallet for pounding barley in a stone trough
Melvie, to soil with meal
Mense, good manners, decorum
Menseless, ill-bred, rude, impudent
Messan, a mongrel dog
Midden, a dunghill
Midden-hole, a hole to contain dung
Mim, prim, affectedly meek
Min', mind, remembrance
Mind't, mind it, resolved, intending
Minnie, mother, dam
Mirk, Mirkest, dark, darkest
Misca', to abuse, to call names
Misca'd, abused
Misleared, mischievous, unmannerly
Mixtie-maxty, confusedly mixed
Moistify, to moisten
Mony or Monie, many
Mools, dust, earth, the earth of the grave; To rake i' the mools, To lay in the dust
Moop, to nibble as a sheep
Moorlan', of or belonging to moors
Morn, the next day, to-morrow
Mou, the mouth
Moudiwort, a mole
Mousie, diminutive of mouse
Muckle or mickle, great, big, much
Musie, diminutive of muse
Muslin-kail, broth, composed simply of water, shelled barley, and greens
Mutchkin, an English pint
Mysel, myself

Naig, a horse
Nane, none
Nappy, ale, to be tipsy
Neuk, a nook
Neist, next
Nieve, the fist
Nievefu', handful
Niffer, an exchange, to exchange, to barter
Nine-tailed-cat, a hangman's whip
Nit, a nut
Norland, of or belonging to the north
Nowte, black cattle

O haith, O faith! an oath
Ony or Onie, any
Or is often used for ere, before
Ora or Orra, supernumerary, that can be spared
O't, of it
Ourie, shivering, drooping
Outlers, cattle not housed
Owre, over, too
Owre-hip, a way of striking a blow with the hammer over the arm

Pack, intimate, familiar, twelve stone of wool
Painch, paunch

Paitrick, a partridge
Pang, to cram
Parle, speech
Parritch, oatmeal pudding, a well-known Scottish dish
Pat, did put, a pot
Pattle or Pettle, a plough-staff
Paughty, proud, haughty
Pauky or Pawkie, cunning, sly
Pay't, paid, beat
Pech, to fetch the breath short, as in an asthma
Pechan, the crop, the stomach
Peelin, peeling, the rind of fruit
Pettle, to cherish, a plough-staff
Philabeg, the Highland kilt
Phraise, fair speeches, flattery, to flatter
Phraisin', flattering
Pibroch, Highland war music adapted to the bagpipe
Pickle, a small quantity
Pine, pain, uneasiness
Pit, to put
Placad, public proclamation
Plack, an old Scottish coin, the third part of a Scottish penny, twelve of which make an English penny
Plackless, penniless, without money
Plaitie, diminutive of plate
Plew or Pleugh, a plough
Pliskie, a trick
Poind, to seize cattle or goods for rent, as the laws of Scotland allow
Poortith, poverty
Pou, to pull
Pouk, to pluck
Poussie, a hare, a cat
Pout, a poult, a chick
Pou't, did pull
Pow, the head, the skull
Powther or Pouther, powder
Powthery, like powder
Preen, a pin
Prent, to print, print
Prie, to taste
Prie'd, tasted
Prief, proof
Prig, to cheapen, to dispute
Priggin, cheapening
Primsie, demure, precise
Propone, to lay down, to propose
Provoses, provosts
Puddock-stool, a mushroom, fungus
Pund, pound, pounds
Pyle,—a pyle o' caff, a single grain of chaff

Quat, to quit
Quak, to quake
Quey, a cow from one to two years old

Ragweed, the herb ragwort
Raible, to rattle nonsense
Rair, to roar
Raize, to madden, to inflame
Ramfeez'led, fatigued, overspread
Ramstam, thoughtless, forward
Raploch, properly a coarse cloth, but used as an adnoun for coarse
Rarely, excellently, very well
Rash, a rush; rash-buss, a bush of rushes
Ratton, a rat

Raucle, rash, stout, fearless
Raught, reached
Raw, a row
Rax, to stretch
Ream, cream, to cream
Reaming, brimful, frothing
Reave, rove
Reck, to heed
Rede, counsel, to counsel
Red-wat-shod, walking in blood over the shoe-tops
Red-wud, stark mad
Ree, half drunk, fuddled
Reek, smoke
Reekin', smoking
Reekit, smoked, smoky
Reestit, stood restive, stunted, withered
Remead, remedy
Rest, to stand restive
Restricked, restricted
Rief, Reef, plenty
Rief randies, sturdy beggars
Rig, a ridge
Rigwiddie, rigwoodie, the rope or chain that crosses the saddle of a horse to support the shafts of a cart; spare, withered, sapless
Rink, a term in curling on ice
Rip, a handful of unthreshed corn
Riskit, make a noise like the tearing of roots
Rockin', spinning on the rock, or distaff
Rood, stands likewise for the plural roods
Roon, a shred, a border or selvedge
Roose, to praise, to comment
Roosty, rusty
Roun', round, in the circle of neighbourhood
Roupet, hoarse, as with a cold
Routhie, plentiful
Row, to roll, to wrap
Row't, rolled, wrapped
Rowte, to low, to bellow
Rowth or Routh, plenty
Rowtin', lowing
Rozet, rosin
Rung, a cudgel
Runkled, wrinkled
Runt, the stem of colewort or cabbage
Ryke, to reach

SAIR, to serve, a sore
Sairly or Sairlie, sorely
Sair't, served
Sark, a shirt, a shift
Sarkit, provided in shirts
Saugh, the willow
Saumont, salmon
Saunt, a saint
Saw, to sow
Scaith, to damage, to injure, injury
Scar, a cliff
Scaud, to scald
Scauld, to scold
Scaur, apt to be scared
Scawl, a scold, a termagant
Scone, a cake of bread
Sconner, a loathing, to loathe
Scraich, to scream as a hen, partridge, etc.
Screed, to tear, a rent
Scrieve, to glide swiftly along
Scrievin, gleesomely, swiftly

Scrimp, to scant
Scrimpet, did scant, scanty
Seed, did see
Seizin', seizing
Sel, self; a body's sel, one's self alone
Sell't, did sell
Sen', to send
Sen't, I, etc., sent, or did send it
Servan', servant
Settlin', settling; to get a settlin', to be frightened into quietness
Sets, sets off, goes away
Shachled, distorted, shapeless
Shaird, a shred, a shard
Shangan, a stick cleft at one end for putting the tail of a dog, etc., into, by way of mischief, or to frighten him away
Shaver, a humorous wag, a barber
Shaw, to show, a small wood in a hollow
Sheen, bright, shining
Sheep-shank; to think one's self nae sheep-shank, to be conceited
Sheugh, a ditch, a trench, a sluice
Shiel, a shed
Shill, shrill
Shog, a shock, a push off at one side
Shool, a shovel
Shoon, shoes
Shore, to offer, to threaten
Shor'd, offered
Shouther, the shoulder
Shure, did shear, shore
Sic, such
Sicker, sure, steady, exacting
Sidelins, sidelong, slanting
Sin', since
Skellum, a worthless fellow
Skelp, to strike, to slap, to walk with a smart tripping step, a smart stroke
Skelpie-limmer, a reproachful term in female scolding
Skiegh, proud, nice, high-mettled
Skinklin, a small portion
Skirl, to shriek, to cry shrilly
Sklent, slant; to run aslant, to deviate from truth
Sklented, ran, or, hit, in an oblique direction
Skouth, freedom to converse without restraint, range, scope
Skriegh, a scream, to scream
Skyrin, shining, making a great show
Skyte, force, very forcible motion
Slae, a sloe
Slade, did slide
Slap, a gate, a breach in a fence
Slaver, saliva, to emit saliva
Slee, sly; sleest, sliest
Sleekit, sleek, sly
Sliddery, slippery
Slype, to fall over, as a wet furrow from the plough
Slypet, fell
Sma', small
Smeddum, dust, powder, mettle, sense, smartness
Smiddy, a smithy
Smoor, to smother
Smoor'd, smothered
Smoutie, Smuttie, obscene, ugly
Smytrie, a numerous collection of small individuals

Snapper, to stumble, a stumble
Snash, abuse, bad language
Snaw-broo, melted snow
Snawie, snowie
Sneck, the latch of a door
Sned, to lop, to cut off
Sneeshin, snuff
Sneeshin-mull, a snuff-box
Sneck-drawing, trick-contriving, crafty
Snell, bitter, biting
Snirtle, to laugh restrainedly
Snood, a ribbon for binding the hair
Snool, one whose spirit is broken with oppressive slavery, to submit tamely, to sneak
Snoove, to go smoothly and constantly, to sneak
Snowk, to scent or snuff, as a dog, etc.
Snowkit, scented, snuffed
Sonsie, having sweet, engaging looks, lucky, jolly
Soom, to swim
Sooth, truth, a petty oath
Sough, a heavy sigh, a sound dying on the ear
Souple, flexible, swift
Souter, a shoemaker
Sowens, a dish made of oatmeal, the seeds of oatmeal soured, etc., flummery
Sowp, a spoonful, a small quantity of anything liquid
Sowth, to try over a tune with a low whistle
Sowther, solder, to solder, to cement
Spae, to prophesy, to divine
Spaul, a limb
Spairge, to dash, to soil, as with mire
Spaviet, having the spavin
Spean, Spane, to wean
Speat or Spate, a sweeping torrent after rain or thaw
Speel, to climb
Spence, the country parlour
Spier, to ask, to inquire
Spier't, inquired
Splatter, a splutter, to splutter
Spleughan, a tobacco-pouch
Splore, a frolic, a noise, riot
Sprackle, sprachle, to clamber
Sprattle, to scramble
Spreckled, spotted, speckled
Spring, a quick air in music, a Scottish reel
Sprit, a tough-rooted plant, something like rushes
Sprittie, full of spirits
Spunk, fire, mettle, wit
Spunkie, mettlesome, fiery, will-o'-wisp, or ignis fatuus
Spurtle, a stick used in making porridge
Squatter, to flutter in water, as a wild duck
Squattle, to sprawl
Squeel, a scream, a screech, to scream
Stacher, to stagger
Stack, a rick of corn, hay, etc.
Staggie, the diminutive of stag
Stalwart, strong, stout
Stan, to stand; stan't, did stand
Stang, an acute pain, a twinge, to sting

Stank, did stink, a pool of standing water
Stap, stop
Stark, stout
Staumrel, a blockhead, half-witted
Staw, did steal, to surfeit
Stech, to cram the belly
Stechin, cramming
Steek, to shut, a stitch
Steer, to molest, to stir
Steeve, firm, compacted
Stell, a still
Sten, to rear as a horse
Sten't, reared
Stents, tribute, dues of any kind
Stey, steep; steyest, steepest
Stibble, stubble
Stibble-rig, the reaper in harvest who takes the lead
Stick an' stow, totally, altogether
Stilt, a crutch, to halt, to limp
Stimpart, the eighth part of a bushel
Stirk, a cow or bullock a year old
Stock, a plant or root of colewort, cabbage, etc.
Stoiter, to stagger, to stammer
Stooked, made up in shocks as corn
Stoor, sounding hollow, strong, and hoarse
Stot, an ox
Stoup or Stowp, a kind of jug or dish with a handle
Stoure, dust, more particularly dust in motion
Stowlins, by stealth
Stown, stolen
Stoyte, to stumble
Strack, did strike
Strae, straw; to die a fair strae death, to die a natural death
Strnik, did strike
Straikit, stroked
Strappin, tall and handsome
Straught, straight, to straighten
Streek, stretched, tight; to stretch
Striddle, to straddle
Studdie, a stithy
Strunt, spirituous liquor of any kind, to walk sturdily, huff, sullenness
Sturt, trouble, to molest
Sturtin, frighted
Sucker, sugar
Sud, should
Sugh, the continued rushing noise of wind or water
Swaird, sward
Swall'd, swelled
Swank, stately, jolly
Swankie or Swanker, a tight strapping young fellow or girl
Swap, an exchange, to barter
Swarf, to swoon, a swoon
Swat, did sweat
Swatch, a sample
Swats, drink, good ale
Sweatin', sweating
Sweer, lazy, averse; dead-sweer, extremely averse
Swoor, swore, did swear
Swinge, to beat, to whip
Swirl, a curve, an eddying blast or pool, a knot in wood
Swirlie, knaggie, full of knots
Swith, get away

Swither, to hesitate in choice; an irresolute wavering in choice
Syne, since, ago, then

Tackets, nails for boots and shoes
Tae, a toe; three-tae'd, having three prongs
Tairge, a target
Tak, to take; takin', taking
Tangle, a sea-weed
Tap, the top
Tapetless, heedless, foolish
Tarrow, to murmur at one's allowance
Tarrow't, murmured
Tarry-breeks, a sailor
Tauld or Tald, told
Taupie, a foolish, thoughtless, young woman
Tauted or Tautie, matted together, spoken of hair or wool
Tawie, that allows itself peaceably to be handled, spoken of a horse, cow, etc.
Teat, a small quantity
Teen, to provoke, provocation
Tedding, spreading after the mower
Ten-hours' bite, a slight feed to the horse while in the yoke, in the forenoon
Tent, a field-pulpit, heed, caution, to heed, to tend or herd cattle
Tentie, heedful, cautious
Tentless, heedless
Teugh, tough
Thack, thatch; thack an' rape, clothing, necessaries
Thae, these
Thairms, small guts, fiddle-strings
Theekit, thatched
Thick, intimate, familiar
Thieveless, cold, dry, spited, spoken of a person's demeanour
Thir, these
Thirl, thrill
Thirled, thrilled, vibrated
Thole, to suffer, to endure
Thowe, a thaw, to thaw
Thowless, slack, lazy
Thrang, throng, a crowd
Thrapple, throat, windpipe
Thrave, twenty-four sheaves or two shocks of corn, a considerable number
Thraw, to sprain, to twist, to contradict
Threap, to maintain by dint of assertion
Threshin', thrashing
Threteen, thirteen
Thristle, thistle
Through, to go on with, to make out
Throu'ther, pell-mell, confusedly
Thud, to make a loud intermittent noise
Thumpit, thumped
Till't, to it
Timmer, timber
Tine, to lose; tint, lost
Tinkler, a tinker
Tint the gate, lost the way
Tip, a ram
Tirl, to make a slight noise; to uncover

Tirlin, uncovering
Tither, the other
Tittle, to whisper
Tittlin, whispering
Tocher, marriage portion
Tod, a fox
Toddle, to totter, like the walk of a child
Toddlin', tottering
Toom, empty, to empty
Toop, a ram
Toun, a hamlet, a farm-house
Tout, the blast of a horn or trumpet, to blow a horn, etc.
Tow, a rope
Towmond, a twelvemonth
Towzie, rough, shaggy
Toy, a very old fashion of female head-dress
Toyte, to totter like old age
Trashtrie, trash, rubbish
Trews, trowsers
Trickie, full of tricks
Trig, spruce, neat
Trimly, neatly, tidily
Trow, to believe
Trowth, truth, a petty oath
Tryste, an appointment, a fair
Trysted, appointed; to tryste, to make an appointment
Try't, tried
Tug, raw hide, of which in olden times plough-traces were frequently made
Tulzie, a quarrel, to quarrel, to fight
Twa-three, a few
'Twad, it would
Twal, twelve; twal-pennie worth, a small quantity, a pennyworth. *N.B.*—One penny English is 12d. Scotch
Twin, to part
Tyke, a dog

Unco, strange, uncouth, very, very great, prodigious
Uncos, news
Unkenn'd, unknown
Unsicker, unsure, unsteady
Unskaith'd, undamaged, unhurt
Unweeting, unwittingly, unknowingly
Urchin, a hedgehog

Vap'rin, vapouring
Vera, very
Virl, a ring round a walking-stick, etc.
Vittle, corn of all kinds, food

Wa', wall; wa's, walls
Wabster, a weaver
Wad, would, to bet, a bet, a pledge
Wadna, would not
Wae, wo, sorrowful
Waefu', woful, sorrowful, wailing
Waesucks! or Waes me! alas! O the pity!
Waft, the cross thread that goes from the shuttle through the web, woof
Wair, to lay out, to expend
Wale, choice, to choose
Waled, chose, chosen
Walie, ample, large, jolly, also an interjection of distress
Wame, the belly

Wamefu', a belly-full
Wanchancie, unlucky
Wanrestfu', restless
Wark-lume, a tool to work with
Warl or Warld, world
Warlock, a wizard
Warly, worldly, eager on amassing wealth
Warran, a warrant, to warrant
Warstl'd or Warsl'd, wrestled
Wastrie, prodigality
Wat, wet; I wat, I wot. I know
Water-brose, brose made of meal and water
Wattle, a twig, a wand
Wauble, to swing, to reel
Waught, a draught
Waukit, thickened as fullers do cloth
Waukrife, not apt to sleep
Waur, worse, to worst
Waur't, worsted
Wean or Weanie, a child
Wearie or Weary, feeble, causing trouble
Weason, windpipe
Wee, little; wee thing, little one; wee bit, a small matter
Weel, well
Weelfare, welfare
Weet, rain, wetness
Weir'd, fate
We'se, we shall
Wha, who
Whaizle, to wheeze
Whalpit, whelped
Whang, a leathern string
Whare, where
Whare'er, wherever
Wheep, to fly nimbly, jerk; penny-wheep, small beer
Whase, whose
What reck, nevertheless
Whid, the motion of a hare, running but not frighted, a lie

Whiddin', running as a hare or cony
Whigmeleeries, whims, fancies, crotchets
Whingin', crying, complaining, fretting
Whirligigums, useless ornaments, trifling appendages
Whissle, a whistle, to whistle
Whisht, silence; to hold one's whisht, to be silent
Whisk, to sleep, to lash
Whiskit, lashed
Whitter, a hearty draught of liquor
Whun-stane, a whinstone
Whyles, whiles, sometimes
Wicht, wight, powerful, strong, inventive, of a superior genius
Wick, to strike a stone in an oblique direction, a term in curling
Wicker, willow (the smaller sort)
Wiel, a small whirlpool
Willyart, bashful and reserved, avoiding society or appearing awkward in it, wild, strange, timid
Wimple, to meander
Wimpl't, meandered
Wimplin', waving, meandering
Win, to win, to winnow
Win't, winded as a bottom of yarn
Winna, will not
Winnock, a window
Winsome, hearty, vaunted, gay
Wintle, a staggering motion; to stagger, to reel
Winze, an oath
Wiss, to wish
Withouten, without
Wizen'd, hide-bound, dried, shrunk
Wonner, a wonder; a contemptuous appellation
Wons, dwells
Woo', wool
Woo, to court, to make love to

Woodie, a rope, more properly one made of withes or willows
Wooer-bab, the garter-knot below the knee with a couple of loops
Wordy, worthy
Worset, worsted
Wow, an exclamation of pleasure or wonder
Wrack, to teaze, to vex
Wraith, a spirit, or ghost, an apparition exactly like a living person, whose appearance is said to forebode the person's approaching death
Wrang, wrong, to wrong
Wreath, a drifted heap of snow
Wud, mad, distracted
Wyle, to beguile
Wyliecoat, a flannel vest
Wyte, blame, to blame

Yad, an old mare, a worn-out horse
Ye, this pronoun is frequently used for thou
Yearns, longs much
Yearlings, born in the same year, coevals
Yearn, earn, an eagle, an osprey
Yell, barren, that gives no milk
Yerk, to lash, to jerk
Yerkit, jerked, lashed
Yestreen, yesternight
Yett, a gate, such as is usually at the entrance into a farm-yard or field
Yill, ale
Yird, earth
Yokin', yoking, quarrelling or disputing
Yont, beyond
Yowe, a ewe
Yowie, diminutive of ewe
Yule, Christmas

Printed by R. & R. CLARK, *Edinburgh.*